Journeys

Journeys

Modern Australian Short Stories

Edited by **Barry Oakley**

The Five Mile Press

The Five Mile Press Pty Ltd
950 Stud Road, Rowville
Victoria 3178 Australia
Email: publishing@fivemile.com.au
Website: www.fivemile.com.au

Introduction © Barry Oakley
Short stories © individual authors
This anthology © The Five Mile Press Pty Ltd, 2007

All rights reserved. No part of this book may be reproduced,
stored in a retrieval system, or transmitted by any form or by any means,
electronic, mechanical, photocopying, recording or otherwise,
without the prior written permission of the publisher.

First published 2007

Cover design: Aimee Zumis
Internal design: Zoë Murphy

The National Library of Australia Cataloguing-in-Publication data
Journeys: modern Australian short stories

Ist ed.
ISBN 978 1 74178 457 2.

1. Short stories, Australian. I. Oakley, Barry.

A823.0108

CONTENTS

INTRODUCTION 7

DISCOVERIES
On the Trail of *Ptilorus magnificus* — Robert Adamson 13
Big World — Tim Winton 33

UNFAMILIAR TERRITORY
Serious Swimmers — Michel Faber 49
Elsewhere — David Malouf 61
Dark Roots — Cate Kennedy 79
Night Growing Longer Now — Anthony Lynch 93
In Shadows — Bill Collopy 105

HOMELANDS
The Romance of Steam — Ian Callinan 115
Driving the Inland Road — Julie Gittus 129

FOREIGN PARTS
In Barcelona — Laurie Clancy 139
The Fellow Passenger — Elizabeth Jolley 149
Travelling — Joan London 166
September 11, 2001 — Ken Haley 185

CLOSE-UPS

The Last Visit — Paddy O'Reilly   197

The Worst Thing — Philip Canon   208

Fear of Flying — Danielle Wood   221

Matrimonial Home — Beverley Farmer   229

MYTHICALITIES

Ithaca — Luke Slattery   247

Stone — Liam Davison   267

Rite of Spring — Margo Lanagan   277

GETTING TO THE END

What Do I 'Do' with Cancer? — Steve J. Spears   289

A Perfect Circle — Peter Symons   298

At the Morgue — Helen Garner   303

NOTES ON CONTRIBUTORS   315

ACKNOWLEDGEMENTS   318

INTRODUCTION

This country was built on journeys. First the Aboriginal people, far back in time, came down from the north. Then came the whites, thousands of years later. The phrase is 'white settlement', but this is only part of the truth. Many never stopped journeying, striking out from the safety of the coast to the hazards of the interior.

Journeying, then, is in our blood – which made the selection of these stories such a challenge. This is the fifth themed collection I have put together for The Five Mile Press, and because there were so many, published and unpublished, to choose from, the criterion had to be strict.

In a travel story, the writer tells us what he or she sees. The person doing the seeing tends to keep to the background. In a journey story, these positions are reversed. The landscape takes second place to the drama of the self: psychology rather than topology.

Which is why, in some of these pieces, there's little physical movement. The teller takes us on a journey into his or her self. And because this emotional movement doesn't always categorise easily, some of the sections into which they are divided overlap. The divisions are there for ease of reading only, with fact freely mixed with fiction. Sometimes, teasingly, we're not sure which is which.

In this emotional sense there's no such thing as an armchair traveller. We all have to make the journey – day to night, week to week, birth to death. Whether sitting or sleeping, we never stop moving. That's the underlying message of these stories, richly varied though they are.

The opening piece is from Robert Adamson's memorable memoir *Inside Out*. It describes, with a poet's eye, young Robert's descent into delinquency, and the Dickensian horrors of the boys' shelter he was sent to as a result. Equally vivid, though fictional, is Tim Winton's account of another young man, who leaves his dead-end job at the meatworks and heads off with his mate in an ancient Kombi van to the freedom of the 'Big World'.

Moving into even more UNFAMILIAR TERRITORY, we meet, in Michel Faber's 'Serious Swimmers', a recovering junkie called Gail, whom life has left worn and withered, as she moves uncertainly towards a reconciliation with her estranged son. In 'Elsewhere', David Malouf's Andy, a rough and ready miner, is similarly out of his depth when he travels to Sydney for his bohemian sister-in-law's funeral. Her friends are so free and easy, and he's so uptight. How much in life has he missed?

In 'Dark Roots' Mel is having an affair, which seems familiar enough, except that he's a mere boy of 26 and she's close to 40. Is this reinvigorating love, or is she just kidding herself? Fran has no such problem in Anthony Lynch's story. She wants a divorce, but there are forms and formalities to negotiate, plus an aggrieved husband, until she hears the blessed word 'Dissolved'. And Bill Collopy's 'In Shadows' graphically depicts the ultimate unfamiliarity: Ali, caged for ten months in an Australia he's unable to understand. An asylum seeker, he's left one form of intolerance only to land in another.

In HOMELANDS 'The Romance of Steam' brings us back to wartime Australia, where a military trip from Sydney to Brisbane take 33 hours, with no food or drink provided. Desperate measures are called for (and taken). 'Driving the Inland Road' describes another long journey, a bumpy pilgrimage to a bush block that a couple hope will provide a setting for their relationship, but the reality proves to be different.

FOREIGN PARTS begins with Laurie Clancy's story about Barcelona, where John and Magdalene Prescott hope to enjoy a long-delayed honeymoon. But there's a frightening underside to the vibrancy of the famous thoroughfare of La Rambla. 'The Fellow Passenger', by the late Elizabeth Jolley, concerns a sea voyage, from the old world to the new. The games and drinks and general jollity fail to disguise the fact that Dr Abrahams, the protagonist, is embarking on a disturbing emotional journey of his own.

The four characters in Joan London's 'Travelling' stay close, because they're in 'quietly dangerous' Laos, but the more they're pressed together, the more they get on one another's nerves. Ken Haley ('September 11, 2001') on the other hand, is a loner. A wheelchair traveller, he has a fierce independence, and in the places he's going through he needs it – especially after he sees the attack on the Twin Towers on an old black-and-white TV in the Georgian capital, Tbilisi.

CLOSE-UPS tightens the focus. For Paddy O'Reilly's Amanda, it's downhill all the way, but her innocent sister Georgie thinks her wasted condition could only be anorexia. The fact that it might be something addictive and worse never enters her head. We meet another damaged narrator in Philip Canon's 'The Worst Thing' – he's a separated father, fearful that he might also suffer separation from his son.

Danielle Wood's 'Fear of Flying' also explores the possibility of loss. After ten years of marriage, Leif still isn't sure whether his wife, a biologist, prefers the remote island that irresistibly draws her, to himself.

If the above three pieces dramatise the possibility of departure, Beverley Farmer's story is about coming home. A husband who had left his wife now wants to come back, and the moves and counter-moves of two damaged people are subtly calibrated.

HOMECOMING is also the theme of the opening story in the next section, which explores the resonances of myth. Luke Slattery investigates whether Ithaca was indeed the home of Homer's wandering Odysseus, and in the process finds his own spiritual anchorage there. Questions are also at the heart of Liam Davison's tale. Were the patterns of stones found by explorers in Victoria's Western District natural, or were they man-made? From this puzzle, in the imagination of the settlers, a legend grew of a great wall stretching across the land.

Then Margo Lanagan takes us into myth's very heart: a boy in a golden robe, on a mountain, in a blizzard, who must say the ritual words in exactly the right order for spring to come.

Steve J. Spears brings us almost to the end of the journey in his autobiographical 'What Do I "Do" With Cancer?' What he does is face it with a bracing mix of bewilderment and humour. With 'A Perfect Circle' we've reached the terminus: a dying father, a dutifully visiting son. How does he behave in such a situation? What words can he offer? He needn't have worried. As his father's breath fails, he manages to sing.

There's only one stop past the terminus and that's the morgue. Helen Garner ventures where few of the living willingly go. She watches autopsies without fainting, and discovers that a body has its own mysterious authority and presence, even though the person has gone. It has a paradoxical existence of its own.

And that, inevitably, is where our journey finishes. These gifted writers offer drama, humour and pathos all along the way – from the promise of childhood to what's waiting at the end of the line. Enjoy your trip.

Barry Oakley
2007

DISCOVERIES

On the Trail of *Ptilorus magnificus*

ROBERT ADAMSON

Robert learns that there's nothing petty about petty crime – and learns it the hard way.

Towards the end of primary school, I spent a lot of time with a neighbour of mine – leading him astray, my mother would later insist. Dexter and I both loved contraptions and inventions. We'd often take simple projects and transform them into something more serious and elaborate: our first telecommunications device consisted of a length of cotton stretched between a couple of matchboxes, but we'd soon graduated to fishing line strung between our bedroom windows from the telegraph poles along our street. Tin cans at either end kept us in constant contact.

Sometimes I'd come up with imaginary inventions that would somehow, miraculously, turn into real ones. I once put together a crystal radio set out of bits and pieces of wiring and circuitry I didn't understand – I just bunged them together with glue, put them inside an old bakelite shell and told Dexter it was a radio transmitter. I insisted I'd rewired the whole thing so that it would broadcast, if only we had a huge transmitting tower – but I was saving, I told him, and then we'd be on the air. Dexter soon realised that this wasn't true, but became so interested in crystal radio sets that he soon learned how to make one. You could simultaneously send and receive on the set he built.

I also constructed a model plane I passed off as a Tiger Moth…

Between primary school and high school – it must have been the summer of 1954–55 – Dexter and I started a newspaper, the *Byrnes Avenue Times*. It was a single-sided sheet for its first three issues; its last two were double-sided. We used a crude monotype press with letterblocks made from hard rubber; a single page took days to set. The first issue was mainly headlines and an announcement of intent: 'To tell the Truth no matter how painful the Truth might be.'

We went to all the local shops and asked if they'd be interested in advertising with us. None of them were. We thought about alternative approaches – bribery, barter, a protection racket – and decided on a combination. We made thorough nuisances of ourselves at the fruit shop, then the fish-and-chip shop and the grocer, and nailed a deal with the fruit shop: they'd give us their 'specks' in exchange for an endorsement saying 'Joe's Fruit is Fresher'...

It wasn't until the fifth issue of the *Byrnes Avenue Times* – which came out early in the year I started high school – that Dexter and I got our big scoop. Mr Breen, Dexter's next-door neighbour, fell from the top of a ladder whilst cutting his hedge in the front garden. Dexter was an eyewitness. He raced around to my place immediately and we set about preparing the headline: MR BREEN CRASHES TO EARTH. Then Beverly burst into the house and into my bedroom, crying. Mr Breen, she told us, had been taken away in an ambulance. He'd had a heart attack and they couldn't revive him. Mr Breen was dead.

We were solemn for a moment. We knew we had to print the news, but in 1950s Neutral Bay, nobody spoke about death. Once, I'd done a school project on the Royal Flying Doctor Service that had involved surveying my friends and classmates. Had any of them seen a dead body?

None of them had. I was fascinated. Hundreds of people all around Neutral Bay had never once seen a corpse, never confronted death.

The next day we composed the headline for our fifth issue: MR BREEN DROPS DEAD IN FRONT YARD. It took up so much space that the story itself was only two sentences long. We doubled our normal print run, since we expected a lot of interest. The pages were hung up to dry on a fishing line strung across my bedroom. When the first run dried, Dexter dropped them into letterboxes along Byrnes Avenue, as well as onto shop counters and under the front doors of our advertisers, while I waited for the next run to dry so I could fold them. We printed the entire edition of thirty copies over a single weekend and by early Sunday evening had distributed every one.

When Dexter and I arrived home the following afternoon, all hell broke loose. It was an outrage, my mother told me; we were cruel, heartless, ill-mannered and had probably broken the law. I was stunned to see how deeply upset she was. Dexter and I were told to apologise to Mrs Breen. We went to see her, standing there with our mothers watching as she sobbed and accepted our apology. Our newspaper days were over, we were told. The other kids in the street were all warned to keep away from us and we weren't allowed out for a fortnight.

. . .

Another associate of mine at the time was someone I'll call Rick the Trick, an apprentice jockey who'd already, at the age of seventeen, been disbarred for fixing a race. He also lived in Byrnes Avenue. We had birds in common: Rick had racing pigeons and was a paid-up member of a pigeon-racing club at Mosman. He knew a few boys who'd been in reform school and was very proud of the fact that one of his older mates had been acquainted with the famous fence Tilly Divine.

Rick was interested in breeding birds such as canaries and African lovebirds and selling them to pet shops. He taught me how to trap wild finches. He knew how to make intricate traps; when a double-bar or zebra finch landed on a little platform, weight-measuring scales would ensure the bird was slowly lowered into a part of the trap it couldn't escape from. Rick would place a male finch in the cage and some millet seeds on the trapdoor, then set the cage in a clearing where he knew finches lived. We'd pedal out to Epping Forest on our bikes to set these traps, catching a dozen or more finches on each trip, then sell them to the pet shop in Crows Nest.

We didn't just go after the wild birds. 'How can anyone own a bird?' Rick would ask. 'They're part of nature. If anyone owns them, it's God, if He exists.' I was impressed. He made the kind of sense I wanted to hear. Soon we were stealing breeding canaries from aviaries around the North Shore – roller canaries and African lovebirds were worth quite a lot of money and the pet shops would pay cash, no questions asked.

I was still drawing birds and had started keeping notebooks about them. I'd keep records of the birds I spotted wherever I went. I had long lists of the species I'd seen; every time I saw one that wasn't on my list, I'd enter it into my log and note the time and place.

One night I went with Rick while he raided a breeder's aviary in Mosman. I was supposed to keep watch while he stole the African lovebirds, but there was a shed in the backyard that warranted further investigation, and when I broke into it I discovered a pair of binoculars and a Zeiss camera: birdwatching equipment. I stuffed them into one of the sugarbags we used for carrying the birds. These bags let the bird breathe because of the loose weave, but quietened them down because they were dark inside. When we arrived back at Rick's and he opened my bag and found the camera and binoculars, he seemed angry I'd stolen them. He said they could bring us undone.

. . .

My marks weren't good enough to get me into North Sydney Boys' High, where most of my primary school friends went, so I was sent to Crows Nest Technical High School instead. I found it confusing and disheartening, being surrounded by strangers and having a different teacher for every subject, and slid behind, especially in maths.

I somehow survived a year and a half of high school, but don't ask me how, or what happened – I don't remember. Because of the large class sizes, nobody noticed how little I was learning. I'd lie in bed in the early hours of the morning imagining how my mother would react when she saw my school reports, and began experiencing the headaches that have plagued me ever since.

I'd daydream about burning down the school. I'd picture myself climbing in under the foundations and sitting there in the clammy dark, calculating details: how much kerosene it would take, how many loads of half-empty drums I'd have to carry there on my bike. I decided I'd strike the day I finished my exams, before they had a chance to mark them.

I must admit I found the idea of committing a criminal act appealing. But didn't, in the end, commit arson.

From the time of my eleventh birthday, I'd grown increasingly obsessed by *Ptilorus magnificus*, which I'd read about in What Bird Is That? No matter how many fascinating pages I found in this book I kept coming back to this bird, also known as the magnificent riflebird. My primary school drawings of falcons and eagles all began turning into drawings of this extraordinary creature.

My book's coloured illustration showed a plump-bodied bird that looked as though it was dressed for a palace costume party: it had a little cap of iridescent green feathers and an elegant chocolate-coloured mask running from its long, curved beak, over its eyes and down over its shoulder. Its neck feathers were shimmering turquoise edged by what looked like a rope of pearls, and its breastplate might have been beaten copper, glinting in the painter's spotlight. It wore a skirt of shaggy feathers, like strands of hanging silk, and looked, compared to its relatives, huge. I wanted to find out more.

At some point during my last year at primary school, I summoned the courage to cross the Bridge and went into the Mitchell Library. I found anything to do with officialdom or authority terrifying and was shy anyway, so I suppose you might say I slunk through the doors. I sidled over to the shelves and flicked furtively through some pages. Town planning. I looked around. There were thousands of books, every one of them possibly about town planning. I realised I'd need help.

The first librarian I approached rebuffed me, but the second – his kindlier, more maternal-looking colleague – invited me to sit at a desk and brought me a feast of first editions. I no longer remember what they were, but some contained illustrations by John Gould. I sat there for hours, mesmerised, taking notes, and went back several times over the next few weeks. On a hunch, I also went to the Australian Museum and sure enough, they had a stuffed riflebird. It was much smaller than I'd imagined from my book, but it was magnificent. I sketched it, not from life perhaps, but the nearest I could get to at the time.

During my first year at high school, I discovered that Taronga Park Zoo had a riflebird in a specially designed enclosure, tucked away in a part of the zoo I seldom went to. I knew that if I failed my exams, as I surely would, I'd have next to no chance of ever getting my leaving certificate and becoming an ornithologist – and no chance of ever getting closer than the general public to this incredible bird. Riflebirds were rare, not like road-peckers. I couldn't just go out and get one. Unless, it suddenly dawned on me, I stole the one they had at the zoo.

It would be like a bank robbery, I thought. It might make national news – certainly it would make local headlines – so I'd have to cover my tracks. I'd also have to be well-prepared. I'd learned that riflebirds wouldn't survive in captivity without a humid atmosphere; I'd have to provide one. I'd have to make it a nest too, of a 'shallow bowl of vine-tendrils and dead leaves, lined with fine stems and twigs and ornamented around the rim with portions of snakeskins.'

I bought some snakeskins from Tony Montage and used them to line the nest I made with stuff scavenged from Primrose and Tunks parks. As for the humidity – well, that year, Sunbeam had introduced a wonderful new frypan with a thermostat, the first of its kind, and I'd seen one through the kitchen window of one of the flats whose drainpipes I scaled in search of squeakers. I calculated that six of them under a false floor, and a drip arrangement made from a hose, should do the trick.

This particular block of flats – a fairly new one – turned out to be harbouring three of them, a bonanza! No one seemed to be at home in any of these flats during the day.

It was easy to climb up and help myself.

In the end I made do with just three. I made tiny holes with a nail in a length of hose and rigged it so that it dripped into the frypans, which were laid out under a cage inside my pigeon coop – a cage within a cage, invisible from outside – which had a false floor. It worked, though not straight away. It took more than a fortnight of trial and error before I'd finally created just the steamy, sub-tropical atmosphere I wanted, the kind a riflebird might survive in.

The last touches were the mangoes and white mice. Riflebirds eat mainly insects, native fruits and berries (hence the mangoes) but, my bird book told me, sometimes, in captivity, they go off these, preferring instead 'to kill mice and small birds and eat only the brains.'

. . .

The riflebird's cage was more strongly fortified than most at Taronga. It was made from glass, to retain the humidity, reinforced with wire mesh. I needed tools: a hammer to smash the glass and some wire-cutters and tin-snips to deal with the mesh. I also took a small crowbar. I put the tools in my fishing basket, tied it to my bike and strapped a fishing rod alongside. This was camouflage: if you were out late at night and the cops asked you what you were doing, fishing was okay – it was a normal, healthy pursuit for a boy. The afternoon before, I'd stashed a cockatoo cage wrapped in hessian in some bushes near the zoo so I wouldn't have to haul it through the streets at night. If all went according to plan, I'd be leaving the zoo just on dawn and be going home in broad daylight.

I arrived at Taronga about 2 am and went down the back towards the quarantine area, where I knew I could climb the fence. I threw the tools and cage over first, then followed.

I knew there was a night watchman who patrolled every two hours, so I waited by the cages where the riflebird was kept until he'd passed by, then set to work. I didn't want to traumatise the bird or draw attention to myself by making a lot of noise, so I used the hessian to muffle the hefty whack I delivered to the glass with the hammer.

When the glass barely registered the assault – it cracked a little and buckled slightly – I panicked. I threw the hessian away and began hurling blow after blow at the glass. After half an hour or so, I did finally make enough of a hole to get at the mesh, but as soon as I felt the resistance if offered, I knew that my tin-snips were useless. Nothing short of bolt cutters would be likely to have an effect. There was nothing to do but bail out.

I went back over the fence and wiped my fingerprints off the tools with my T-shirt, then hid them under some bushes. But I hadn't given up. A couple of days later, I returned in daylight to see what they'd done about the cage. It was surrounded by a kind of barrier, like the crime scene it was. It was empty. I was devastated, thinking they'd moved the bird to protect it from theft. It was probably in far north Queensland by now.

But as I was leaving via my access point near the quarantine section, I heard the unmistakable call of *Ptilorus magnificus* – the 'harsh rasping notes' described by Neville W. Cayley – coming from one of the sheds. They'd moved it to protect it, not from theft, but from louts and vandals. The quarantine area wasn't well known or readily accessible to the public and was therefore low security. I was thrilled: my plan was back in action.

The following night I made my way back to the zoo with the cockatoo cage. I'd seen where they kept the keys to the quarantine sheds on previous expeditions, though I'd never before had a reason to use them, and collected a bunch. I couldn't believe my luck. I found the riflebird without much trouble in a hospital section in one of the sheds, where it was probably recovering from shock. It was in a special cage, designed for easy veterinary access, that slid out on a little tray and fitted snugly inside my cockatoo cage. As the sun came up, I was lugging it home. The riflebird was mine.

. . .

I didn't tell Dexter or Rick. Dexter wasn't all that interested in birds, and Rick would have seen it only in terms of its cash value. Besides, he'd probably go off his brain if I told him I'd stolen it from the zoo. The fewer who knew the better, I decided.

The house at Neutral Bay was behind a shopfront that had been used as a factory of some kind – I remember copper coils and valves – until the owner died suddenly and the factory shut down. Nobody was using it, but the power was still connected. The electric frying pans were plugged into a long extension cord that ran from my pigeon coop, down the side of the house and in through the factory door to a socket in a brick storeroom. It all worked beautifully, though at first the riflebird wouldn't eat. I had to feed it with syringes I'd salvaged from the local doctor's rubbish. I gave it mixtures of fruit and crushed insects and after about a week it started eating mangoes on its own.

By now I had lots of birds: homing pigeons, racing pigeons and various kinds of finch (double-bar, zebra, firetail and Gouldian painted finches) – some of which I'd stolen with Rick – as well as my quails, turtle doves, cockatiels, budgerigars and a kookaburra called Jack. I'd raised Jack from when he was a chick and he seemed to think I was his mother. I loved the idea of having the largest kingfisher in the world as a pet. Jack would sit on my shoulder and follow me round the yard as I released my pigeons and watered Dad's vegetable garden.

About two weeks after I'd brought the riflebird home, Jack flew into the yard next door. The lady there didn't like us, and when I jumped the fence and started calling Jack, who was perched in a frangipani tree, she was outside in an instant, screaming at me to get off her garden. She looked completely baffled when he flew straight from the tree onto my shoulder.

The next day when I came home, there was a grim committee waiting for me. Our neighbour had called the RSPCA and told them I had a kookaburra with clipped wings. The RSPCA had come to investigate while I was out. My mother had told them they were free to look around, and when they searched through the cages and found the magnificent riflebird, they rang the police, who also turned up to investigate. They called in a keeper from Taronga Park Zoo, but were more interested in the canaries and African lovebirds Rick and I had stolen – from, it turned out, a Mosman councillor. He'd been pressuring local detectives to find his birds.

My mother told them what she assumed to be true – that I'd caught these birds at Primrose Park – but by the time I got home, the keeper had identified the stolen *Ptilorus magnificus* and the police were confident they'd found the councillor's missing lovebirds. They took me to North Sydney police station, where some detectives asked me questions. I told them I wanted to make a full confession – and did, too. I gave them all the details, as one of them typed it up, about how

I'd stolen the riflebird, as well as all the others, and spilled the beans on Rick.

This was the first of a series of confessions I made to various detectives over the course of the following decade. I remember signing the finished document with some pride, not because of the facts it related, but because – with the assistance of the police, who added their own jargon – I'd produced an official-looking document that would be read and taken seriously in court.

It was two weeks before my case was heard. I spent them in the Yasma shelter for delinquent boys under the age of twelve. I remember only neat lawns and concrete yards and a stretch of utter darkness.

My mother and father came with me to court, where I was charged with break, enter and steal – not just for the birds, but also for the camera and binoculars they'd found at Rick's place. He and I agreed they'd been taken by me. I was also charged with stealing a number of items I knew nothing about but nonetheless took the blame for.

Because of Rick's age, he was cast as the ringleader. Maybe he was. When the magistrate at my hearing asked me whether I had anything to say, I parroted Rick: 'How can anyone steal a bird, Your Honour? They belong to God.'

His Honour stared at me stony-faced before giving me a six-month sentence to Mittagong Boys' Home. It was through a kind of haze that I heard him suspend my sentence provided I accepted a bond to be of good behaviour for eighteen months and not to consort with Rick again. I never did.

. . .

I went back to school, but my heart wasn't in it. I couldn't even think about homework. I started hanging out at my former school, Neutral Bay Primary, at night and on weekends, looking for squeakers. I knew the buildings well. I climbed the drainpipes and walked across the slate roof, stuffing the squeakers into my jumper and taking them home to my coop.

On one of these raids, I climbed onto a ledge and got into the school through a window with a broken latch, then walked down a corridor, idly exploring. I came to the staffroom, where there was a Gestetner copier sitting on a bench. I'd helped print the school newsletter and one of the teachers had shown me how it worked. This was exactly what was needed, I thought, for relaunching the *Byrnes Avenue* Times in a bigger, more serious format.

I was inspired. We could rename the paper and expand our print run with a machine like this. We could strike back at the prudery of parents. We could do a big expose on the hypocrisy of Byrnes Avenue – an in-depth story on Death that spelled out in gruesome detail just what happened to the bodies of your neighbours after they were buried.

I raced straight over to Dexter's house. We had to have the Gestetner, I told him. We had to go back there and get it. He seemed a bit doubtful. He muttered stuff about its weight, the problem of getting it home, and the killer – where would we put it? I let these objections wash over me while I continued talking up the idea, listing the names of businesses that might be prepared to advertise if the newspaper looked professional enough and we could offer the large print runs Gestetners could produce.

Dexter and I both had paper runs for the local community newspaper, which was given away free. We knew it worked on advertising and that what attracted advertisers was distribution. We were already being paid to do the rounds of local letterboxes, so that was the first step taken care of. Then I hit on a solution to the problem of where to put the Gestetner. There was a locked shed in our backyard that belonged to the empty shop. Dexter and I both had access to it – we'd found a way in through the skylight – but the windows had been painted over and it was impossible even for mothers to see through them. Once you were inside, you could open the back door, which had an internal lock.

It was a mysterious, alluring place. I decided it would be the perfect headquarters for our publishing venture – and even called it that out loud, enjoying the sound of the word: 'Headquarters'. We'd take the Gestetner there at night. We could bring it from the school to the shed by billycart – we still had our racing billycarts, with their low-slung hardwood frames, wooden axles and wheels made from big ball-bearing bushes we'd found in this very shed.

It took me a week to talk Dexter into helping. We went to the school late the following Sunday afternoon so we could check things out whilst pretending to race our billycarts up and down the street outside. Then, after dark, I scaled the drainpipe, got into the staffroom through the broken-latched window, went down the stairs and let Dexter in through the front door. He was waiting with our billycarts behind the toilets. It was weird being inside those dark school corridors, passing our old classrooms and climbing the still-familiar stairs. The place felt haunted. I'd brought along a small torch that we were careful not to shine above window level.

It took both of us to slide the Gestetner from its table, carry it into the hallway and put it on the floor. I suggested that, since we were here, we should look for other stuff we might need – reams of paper, a typewriter, ink. This is how my plans always work: I focus on the main feature and fill in the details as I go. But I could see by the look of Dexter's face that I'd lost him. 'Let's leave it,' he said, 'let's just go before we get caught.' I was furious. I told him he should have the guts to help me finish what we'd started – that I was going to drag the Gestetner out of there no matter what and was determined to get it to Headquarters.

We wrestled the machine downstairs and onto my billy-cart, then went clattering out through the school gates and rattling down the road. We both noticed a woman staring at us from a balcony over the sandwich shop opposite, but she didn't seem worried and went back inside and pulled her blinds. We, too, were preoccupied. We had to stop at every kerb and take the contraption off, then put it back on again, as we trundled the few blocks home.

When we got to my place, Dexter refused to come inside. He decided he'd had enough. I must have made a bit of a racket trying to wrestle the Gestetner into place myself, because my mother called out to ask what I was doing – I told her I was looking after squeakers. Finally I got it into the shed and mounted it on its bench.

The next day Dexter wouldn't talk to me at school. Telling myself it made no difference, I ran home after classes and got my hosing duties out of the way, then climbed into Headquarters through the skylight. It was a dramatic moment as I raised the hessian bags to reveal a machine I knew could change the world. It also dawned on me at that moment that the Gestetner wouldn't do this by itself. I'd need a typewriter, stencils, ink, paper; I'd need to be able to write like a journalist, sell advertising space like a salesman and manage the distribution. In other words, I'd need help. Maybe I could co-opt Rick, I thought. Maybe we could create some kind of pigeon club newsletter for the pigeon-fancying residents of Neutral Bay – I remember seeing a copy of something called *Racing Pigeon News* on his kitchen bench once. Lots of possibilities raced through my mind, but they all evaporated quickly. I sat there in the semi-darkness feeling flustered, thinking that maybe Dexter had been right, maybe this hadn't been a great idea. I thought of my good behaviour bond and worried about possible charges.

I didn't have to worry long. A few days later the police came to my school and I was called to the headmaster's office. I already knew the detective I was introduced to and he knew me as the kid who'd stolen the riflebird. He was the hard man in charge of cleaning up juvenile delinquency around the Northern Beaches. We called him Rockhopper because he was a rock fisherman on his days off. He didn't seem to like me.

The headmaster said an eyewitness had seen me and another boy carrying something away from the school last Sunday – they knew who the other boy was too, their witness could identify us both – so I took them by surprise and confessed. The headmaster became cross when I corrected the detective, explaining that I didn't actually 'break and enter', I just climbed in through an available window, and accused me of 'impudence and outright rudeness'.

It was all over. I'd broken my bond. I'd be expelled, of course, and probably sent to a boys' home. I put these consequences out of my mind and focused instead on my narrative abilities, delivering a detailed confession to Rockhopper and his partner down at North Sydney police station. My mother seemed more upset about my influence on Dexter than about the crime I'd committed, and wasn't at all sympathetic to my 'desperate need' for a Gestetner. Because he'd never been in trouble before and his father could afford a solicitor, and because I was happy to take the blame, Dexter was let off with a caution. I was charged and locked up.

. . .

I remember my second period of remand much more vividly than the first. I was held at Albion Street Boys' Shelter – probably the most Dickensian of all the institutions I've experienced. The building was over a hundred years old and had never been renovated except by the innumerable coats of paint applied and continually reapplied by inmates. I was given the job of scraping mouldy paint from the malodorous walls of the dormitory with a blunt scraper. Due to the rising damp, the paint began peeling off almost as soon as it was applied. It was then scraped back and repainted, and so on. This meant there was always something to keep the inmates busy. The task was made more difficult by the dimness of the place. No sunlight ever entered: the only light came from weak light bulbs encased in cages of thick wire mesh.

The toilets were appalling: no matter how much ammonia got splashed around, the coarse concrete floors and the turpentine beams, scarred with years of obscene graffiti, still gave off the stink of stressed boys' urine.

You'd bruise your knees or shins every morning when the bell rang, because the beds in the dormitory were so close. You had to jump up and stand by the foot of your bed. Any boy who was slow getting up got a clip around the ears. I don't know why we were rushing. There was no educational activity of any kind and our exercise consisted of marching back and forth in the small cobbled yard. The cells used for solitary confinement were below street level and were frequently occupied. The Child Welfare officers were brutish and strict and many of the boys were psychotic, with a twisted hatred of everyone and everything. Some were wards of the state and had no family, others were abused children who had become so institutionalised they'd hack at their wrists if they heard so much as a rumour that they might be released.

A few days after arriving I was involved in a fight; when it looked as though I might be a match for the boy who'd punched me first, his friend stepped in and I ended up being bashed and kicked in a corner by the two of them. The officers took ten minutes before breaking it up and throwing us all into solitary for twenty-four hours on bread and water. On this occasion, I didn't appreciate the subtle cruelty of solitary confinement. In fact, I liked it. The worst thing about Albion Street Shelter was that there was no place to hide; at least when I was in solitary I had privacy.

I didn't understand why the others didn't like me until towards the end of the month I spent there, when a boy I befriended told me that it was because of the way I spoke. 'You talk like a queer,' he said. I was stunned. Maybe, I thought later, it was the sibilance of my voice, or the way I flapped about like a bird and perched rather than sat or stood.

When I appeared before the magistrate he invoked the terms of my bond and gave me the maximum sentence: eighteen months. Two days later, my mother came to visit and told me I was going to be sent to Mount Penang Training School for Boys. 'You're going to find out the hard way,' she said, 'the meaning of your crimes.' I was ashamed to have her see me in there and couldn't wait for her to leave.

The next morning I was on my way to Gosford, but not before I was paraded through Central Station with my right wrist handcuffed – like I was some sort of crim – to the left wrist of a Child Welfare officer. He was a broken sort of man who wasn't as hard as the ones at Albion Street. He took the handcuffs off once we were on the train and I promised not to attempt an escape. He told me I seemed different from the boys he usually escorted. We were travelling on a steam train and as we headed down the line from Mount Ku-ring-gai I stuck my head out the window to take a look at the Hawkesbury River. A piece of cinder got lodged in my eye.

I pulled back quickly, but had tears streaming down my cheek for the rest of the trip as the cinder scratched at the surface of my eyeball. The Welfare officer tried to comfort me by offering me one of his cheese sandwiches. He kept on saying, in his broken way, 'It's for the best son, it's for the best'.

— From *Inside Out: An Autobiography*

. . . . . .

Big World

TIM WINTON

Hitting the road in a Kombi that's like a garden shed on wheels.

After five years of high school the final November arrives and leaves as suddenly as a spring storm. Exams. Graduation. Huge beach parties. Biggie and me, we're feverish with anticipation; we steel ourselves for a season of pandemonium. But after the initial celebrations, nothing really happens, not even summer itself. Week after week an endless misting drizzle wafts in from the sea. It beads in our hair and hangs from the tips of our noses while we trudge around town in the vain hope of scaring up some action. The southern sky presses down and the beaches and bays turn the colour of dirty tin. Somehow our crappy Saturday job at the meatworks becomes full-time and then Christmas comes and so do the dreaded exam results. The news is not good. A few of our classmates pack their bags for university and shoot through. Cheryl Button gets into Medicine. Vic Lang, the copper's kid, is dux of the school and doesn't even stay for graduation. And suddenly there we are, Biggie and me, heading to work every morning in a frigid wind in the January of our new lives, still in jeans and boots and flannel shirts, with beanies on our heads and the horizon around our ears.

The job mostly consists of hosing blood off the floors. Plumes of the stuff go into the harbour and old men sit in dinghies offshore to catch herring in the slick. Some days

I can see me and Biggie out there as old codgers, anchored to the friggin' place, stuck forever. Our time at the meatworks is supposed to be temporary. We're saving for a car, the V-8 Sandman we've been promising ourselves since we were fourteen. Mag wheels, a lurid spray job like something off a Yes album and a filthy great mattress in the back. A chick magnet, that's what we want. Until now we've had a biscuit tin full of twos and fivers but now we're making real money.

Trouble is, I can't stand it. I just know I won't last long enough to get that car. There's something I've never told Biggie in all our years of being mates. That I dream of escaping, of pissing off north to find some blue sky. Unlike him I'm not really *from* here. It's not hosing blood that shits me off – it's Angelus itself; I'm going nuts here. Until now, out of loyalty, I've kept it to myself, but by the beginning of February I'm chipping away at our old fantasy, talking instead about sitting under a mango tree with a cold beer, walking in a shady banana plantation with a girl in a cheesecloth dress. On our long walks home I bang on about cutting our own pineapples and climbing for coconuts. Mate, I say, can't you see yourself rubbing baby oil into a girl's strapless back on Cable Beach? Up north, mate, think north! I know Biggie loves this town and he's committed to the shared vision of the panel van, but I white-ant him day after day until it starts to pay off.

By the last weeks of February Biggie's starting to come around. He's talking wide open spaces now, trails to adventure, and I'm like this little urger in his ear. Then one grey day he crosses the line. We've been deputised to help pack skins. For eight hours we stand on the line fighting slippery chunks of cow hide into boxes so they can be sold as craybait. Our arms are slick with gore and pasted with orange and black beef-hairs. The smell isn't good but that's nothing compared with the feel of all those severed nostrils and lips and ears between your fingers. I don't make a sound, don't even stop for lunch, can't think about it. I'm just glad all those chunks are fresh because at least my hands are warm. Beside me Biggie's face gets darker and darker, and when the shift horn sounds he lurches away, his last carton half-empty. Fuck it, he says. We're outta here. That afternoon we ditch the Sandman idea and buy a Kombi from a hippy on the wharf. Two hundred bucks each.

We put in two last weeks at the meatworks and collect our pay. We fill the ancient VW with tinned food and all our camping junk and rack off without telling a soul. Monday morning everyone thinks we're off to work as usual, but in ten minutes we're out past the town limits going like hell. Well, going the way a 1967 Kombi will go. Our getaway vehicle is a garden shed on wheels.

It's a mad feeling, sitting up so high like that with the road flashing under your feet. For a couple of hours we're laughing and pointing and shoving and farting and then we settle down a bit. We go quiet and just listen to the Volkswagen's engine threshing away behind us. I can't believe we've done it. If either of us had let on to anybody these past couple of weeks we'd never have gone through with it; we'd have piked for sure. We'd be like all the other poor stranded failures who stayed in Angelus. But now we're on the road, it's time for second thoughts. Nothing said, but I can feel it.

The plan is to call from somewhere the other side of Perth when we're out of reach. I want to be safe from the guilts – the old girl will crack a sad on me – but Biggie has bigger things to fear. His old man will beat the shit out of him when he finds out. We can't change our minds now.

The longer we drive the more the sky and the bush open up. Now and then Biggie looks at me and leers. He's got a face only a mother could love. One eye's looking at you and the other eye's looking *for* you. He's kind of pear-shaped, but you'd be a brave bugger calling him a barge-arse. The fists on him. To be honest he's not really my sort of bloke at all, but somehow he's my best mate.

We buzz north through hours of good farm country. The big, neat paddocks get browner and drier all the while and the air feels thick and warm. Biggie drives. He has the habit of punctuating his sentences with jabs on the accelerator and although the gutless old Volksie doesn't exactly give you whiplash at every flourish, it's enough to give a bloke a headache. We wind through the remnant jarrah forest, and the sickly-looking regrowth is so rain-parched it almost crackles when you look at it.

When Perth comes into view, its dun plain shimmering with heat and distant towers ablaze with midday sun, we get all nervous and giggly, like a pair of tipsy netballers. The big city. We give each other the full Groucho Marx eyebrow routine but we're not stopping. Biggie's a country boy through and through. Cities confound him, he can't see the point of them. He honestly wonders how people can live in each other's pockets like that. He's revolted and a little frightened at the thought. Me, I love the city, I'm from there originally. I really thought I'd be moving back this month. But I won't, of course. Not after blowing my exams. I'm glad we're not stopping. It'd be like having your nose rubbed in it. Failure, that is. I can't tell Biggie this but missing out on uni really stings. When the results came I cried my eyes out. I thought about killing myself.

To get past Perth we navigate the blowsy strips of caryards

and showrooms and crappy subdivisions on the outskirts. Soon we're out the other side into vineyards and horse paddocks with the sky blue as mouthwash ahead. Then finally, open road. We've reached a world where it isn't bloody raining all the time, where nobody knows us and nobody cares. There's just us and the Love Machine. We get the giggles. We go off; we blat the horn and hoot and chuck maps and burger wrappers around the cabin. Two mad southern boys still wearing beanies in March.

I'm laughing. I'm kicking the dash. That ache is still there inside me but this is the best I've felt since the news about the exams. For once I'm not faking it. I look across at Biggie. His huge, unlovely face is creased with merriment. I just know I'll never be able to tell him about the hopes I had for myself and for a little while I don't care about any of it; I'm almost as happy as him. Biggie's results were even worse than mine – he really fried – but he didn't have his heart set on doing well; he couldn't give a rat's ring. For him, our bombing out is a huge joke. In his head he's always seen himself at the meatworks or the cannery until he inherits the salmon-netting licence from his old man. He's content, he belongs. His outlook drives my mother wild with frustration but in a way I envy him. My mother calls us Lenny and George. She teaches English; she thinks that's funny. She's trying to wean me off Biggie Botson. In fact she's got a program all mapped out to get me back on track, to take the year again and re-sit the exams. But I've blown all that off now. Biggie's not the brightest crayon in the box but he's the most loyal person I know. He's the real deal and you can't say that about many people.

My mother won't chase me up; she's kind of preoccupied. She's in love with the deputy principal. He's married. He uses the school office to sell Amway. Both of them believe that Civics should be reintroduced as a compulsory course.

We get out into rolling pasture and granite country and then wheat-lands where the ground is freshly torn up in the hope of rain. The VW shakes like a boiling billy and we've finally woken up to ourselves and sheepishly dragged our beanies off. The windows are down and the hot wind rips through our hair.

Biggie must have secrets. Everyone dreams of things in private. There must be stuff he doesn't tell me. I know about the floggings he and his mum get, but I don't know what he wants deep down. He won't say. But then I don't say either. I never tell him about the Skeleton Coast in Africa where ships come aground on surf beaches and lie there broken-bellied until the dunes bury them. And the picture I have of myself in a café on the Piazza San Marco leaving a tip so big that the waiter inhales his moustache. Dreams of the big world beyond. Manila. Monterey. Places in books. In all these years I never let on. But then Biggie's never there in the picture with me. In those daydreams he doesn't figure, and maybe I'm guilty about that.

After a while we pull over for a leak. The sunlight is creamy up here. Standing at the roadside with it roasting my back and arms through the heavy shirt, I don't care that picking guavas and papaya doesn't pay much more than hosing the floor of an abattoir. If it's outside in the sun, that's fine by me. We'll be growing things, not killing them. We'll move with the seasons. We'll be free.

Mum thinks Biggie's an oaf, that he's holding me back. She doesn't know that without Biggie there'd be nothing left of me to hold back. It sounds weak, but he saved my life.

We didn't meet until the second week of high school.

I was new in town and right from the start a kid called Tony Macoli became fixated on me. He was very short with a rodent's big eyes and narrow teeth. He sat behind me every class he could and whispered weird threats under the uncomprehending gaze of the teachers, especially my mother. He liked to jab me in the back with the point of his compass and lob spitballs into my hair. He trod on my feet in passing and gleefully broke my pencils. I'd never been a brawler but I was confident that I could knock him down. Trouble was, my parents were new to the school – this was before the old man pissed off – and I didn't want to make trouble. I already sensed their mutual misery and I felt responsible somehow. So I put up with it. I hadn't even spoken to Tony Macoli. I was shocked by the hatred in his wan little face. I couldn't imagine how I'd put him out so thoroughly. It seemed that my very existence offended him.

The little bastard kept at me but I didn't touch him. After a week I didn't even react. I wasn't scared. It wasn't passive resistance or anything. I just got all weird and listless. I reckon I was depressed. But the less I responded the more Tony Macoli paid out on me.

On the second Monday of term I was shoved into a hedge, tripped in the corridor so that my books sprayed across the linoleum, and had my fingers slammed in a desk – all this before morning recess. Each little coup brought out Macoli's wheezy little laugh. It rocked his body and tilted his head back on his neck so that the whites of his eyes showed. At morning recess I was wiping mud from my pants while he gave in to the convulsive laugh. The wind blew his tie over his left shoulder and my pulse felt shallow, as though I was only barely alive. As I got wearily back to my feet, a shambling figure passed me and I saw the flash of a fist. One second

Tony Macoli was laughing himself sick, and the next his nose was pointed over his shoulder in the same direction as his wind-blown tie. Blood spurted, Macoli went down and I can still hear the sweet melon sound of his head hitting the path. Macoli went to the district hospital and Biggie Botson began two weeks' suspension.

That's how it started. A single decisive act of violence that joined me to Biggie forever. If you believe him on the subject he acted more out of animal irritation that charity. But I felt like somebody ransomed and set free. Until that moment I was disappearing. School, home, the new town, they were all misery. If Biggie hadn't come along I don't know what would have become of me. Exam week, five years later, wasn't the first time I thought of necking myself. Biggie become my mate, my constant companion, and Tony Macoli was suddenly landscape.

For a while my mother thought Biggie and me were gay. She did the big *tolerance* routine that dried up when she realized we weren't poofs.

Back on the road again I'm thinking boab trees and red dirt, girls in sarongs, cold beer, parking the Vee Dub on some endless beach to sleep. And mangoes. Is there anything sexier than a mango?

I suppose we're all wrong for each other, Biggie and me. He's not a very introspective bloke. Sometimes he makes me restless. But we get along pretty well most of the time. We go camping a lot, hike out to all sorts of places and set up on our own. Biggie loves all the practical stuff, reading maps, trying survival techniques, learning bushcraft. I'm more into the birds and plants and stars and things. Some mornings out in the misty ranges the world looks like it means something, some simple thing just out of my reach, but there anyway.

That's why I go. And both of us dig the fact that nobody else is out there pursing their lips at us or taking a swing.

Biggie truly is a funny bugger. He can do Elvis with his belly-button – *thank you very much* – a toothless King sprouting manky black hairs in a face made of fat. He can fart whole sentences, a skill St Augustine admired in others. He's not much for hygiene. His hair's always greasy and that navel smells like toejam. He doesn't swim. He couldn't carry a tune in a bucket but he can find true north by instinct. On his day he's a frightening fast bowler but most days he can't hit the pitch for love or money. He once surfed a school bus thirty miles. He caught nineteen herring with the same single green pea and an unweighted hook. And he was the only one in the class brave enough to hold the bin for the student teacher while she puked so hard it came out her nose. His sole academic success was his essay on the demise of Led Zeppelin, but then I wrote that for him.

Friendship, I suppose, comes at a price. There have been girls I've disqualified myself from because of Biggie. Not everyone wants to have him tagging along everywhere, though in the days before we get our licences there are those who don't mind walking out with us to the drive-ins. I figure we're not glamorous but we're entertaining in our way. Right through high school I have occasional moments, evenings, encounters with girls but no real girlfriend and mostly I don't regret it. Except for Briony Nevis. For two years we're sort of watching each other from a distance. Sidelong glances. She's flat-out beautiful, long black hair like some kind of Indian. Glossy skin, dark eyes. She's funny in a wry, hurt kind of way, and smart. In class she goads me, says I'm not as stupid as I make out. I kiss her once at a party. Well, maybe she kisses me. Hair like a satin pillowslip. Body all sprung as though she's ready to bolt. A long, long kiss, deep and playful as a conversation. But there at the corner of my eye is Biggie along on the smoky verandah, waiting to go home. I don't go to him straight up. I do make him wait a fair old while but I don't go on with Briony Nevis the way I badly want to because I know Biggie will be left behind for good. Not that I don't think about her. Hell, I write poems to her, draw pictures of her, construct filthy elaborate fantasies she'll never know about. But I never touch her again. Out of loyalty. Briony isn't exactly crushed. If anything she seems amused. She sees how things are.

And she's right, you know, I'm not as stupid as I make out. It's a survival thing, making yourself a small target. But even now, feeling kind of euphoric, buzzing up the highway, I know I'm stuck in something that I can't figure my way out of.

You see, back in first year, right at the beginning when Biggie was my saviour and still doing his two weeks' suspension for busting Tony Macoli's nose, I kept notes for the full fortnight and more or less wrote Biggie's essays for him when he got back. He didn't care if he passed or failed but I wanted to do it for him, and so what began as a gesture of gratitude became a pattern for the rest of our schooling. I made him look brighter than he was and me a little dimmer. His old man preferred him to be a dolt. My mother expected me to be an academic suckhole. Most of the time Biggie couldn't give a damn but sometimes I think he really got his hopes up. I feel responsible, like my ghost work stopped him from learning. In a way I ruined his chances. For five years I worked my arse off. I really did all our work. Out of loyalty, yeah, but also from sheer vanity. And the fact is, I blew it. I got us both to the finish line but ensured that neither of us got across it. Biggie hadn't learnt anything that he could display in an exam and I was too worn out and cocky to make sense. We fried. We're idiots of a different species but we are both bloody idiots.

At New Norcia we pull in to fuel up and use the phone. Biggie decides that he's not calling home so he sits in the VW while I reverse the charges and get an earful. My mother wails and cries. I'm vague about my whereabouts and look out at the monastery and church spires and whitewashed walls of the town while she tells me I'm throwing my future away. I hang up and find Biggie talking to a chick with a backpack the size of an elephant saddle. She's tall and not very beautiful with long, shiny brown hair and big knees. She thinks she's on the coast road north and she's mortified to discover otherwise. Biggie explains that this is the inland route, shows her on the map. She wants to get to Exmouth, she says. I can see Biggie falling in love with her moment by moment. My heart sinks.

There isn't really even much consultation. We just pull out with this chick in the back. Meg is her name. I know it's hot and she's had a tough day but she's on the nose. She's got a purple tanktop on and every time she lifts an arm there's a blast of BO that could kill a wildebeest. Biggie doesn't seem to notice. He's twisted around in his seat laughing and chatting and pointing and listening while I drive in something close to a sullen silence.

Meg is as thick as a box of hammers. It's alarming to see how enthralled Biggie is. He goes ahead and tells her about life in the salmon camp every season when all the huts are full and the tractors are hauling nets up the beach and trucks pull down to the water's edge to load up for the cannery. All the drinking and fighting, the sharks and the jetboats, the great green masses of fish pressed inside the headlands. He doesn't tell Meg that it's all for petfood, that his mother cries every night, that he's given up defending her, not even urging her to leave now, but nobody could hold that against him. Meg, this mouth-breathing moron, is staring at Biggie like he's a guru, and I just drive and try to avoid the rearview mirror.

I get to thinking about the last night of school and the bonfire at Massacre Point, the beginning of that short period of grace when my very limbs tingled with relief and the dread of failure had yet to set in. Someone had a kite in the air and its tail was on fire, looping and spiralling orange and pink against the night sky, so beautiful I almost cried. I was smashed and exhausted; I suppose any little thing would have seemed poignant and beautiful. But I really felt that I'd reached the edge of something. I had a power and a promise I'd never sensed before. The fact that the burning kite consumed its own tail and fluttered down into the sea didn't really register. I didn't see it as an omen. Biggie and I drank Bacardi and Coke and watched some lunatic fishing for sharks with a Land Rover. Briony Nevis was there, teeth flashing in the firelight. I was too pissed to go over to her. I fell asleep trying to work up the nerve.

We woke by a huge lake of glowing embers, our sleeping bags damp, the tide out and our heads pounding, but it was the smiling that hurt the most. Biggie wanted to stay a while in that tangle of blankets and swags but I convinced him to get up with me and swim bare-arsed in the cold clear water inside the rocky promontory before we stole back through the sleeping crowd towards my mother's car. That was a great feeling, tingling, awake, up first, seeing everybody sprawled in hilarious and unlikely pairings and postures. The air was soupy, salty, and as we padded up the sand track with birds in the mint-scented scrub all round, I just couldn't imagine disappointment. The world felt new, specially made for us. It was only on the drive back to town that our hangovers caught up.

While I'm thinking about all of this Biggie's gone and climbed over into the back and Meg's lit up a number and they're toking away on it with their feet up like I'm some kind of chauffeur. The country is all low and spare now and the further we go the redder it gets. Biggie's never had much luck with girls. I should be glad for him. But I'm totally pissed off.

In the mirror Biggie has this big wonky grin going. He sits back with his legs stretched out and crossed at the ankles, his Blundstones poking through the gap in the seats at my elbow. Meg murmurs and exclaims at the beauty of the country and Biggie just nods slit-eyed with smoke and anticipation while I boil.

Late in the day, when Biggie and Meg are quizzing each other on the theme tunes to TV sitcoms, we come upon a maze of salt lakes that blaze silver and pearly in the sun and stretch to the horizon in every direction. I begin to have the panicky feeling that the land and this very afternoon might go on forever. Biggie's really enjoying himself back there and I slowly understand why. There's the obvious thing of course, the fact that he's in with a big chance with Meg come nightfall. But something else, the thing that eats at me, is the way he's enjoying being brighter than her, being a step ahead, feeling somehow senior and secure in himself. It's me all over. It's how I am with him and it's not pretty.

The Kombi fills with smoke again but this time it's bitter and metallic and I'm halfway to asking them to leave off and open a bloody window when I see the plume trailing us down the highway and I understand that we're on fire. I pull over into a tottery skid in the gravel at the roadside and jump out to see just how much grey smoke is pouring out of the rear grille. When Biggie and Meg join me we stand there a few moments before it dawns on us that the whole thing could blow at any moment and everything we own is inside. So we fall over each other digging our stuff free, tossing it as far into the samphire edges of the saltpan as we can. Without an extinguisher there's not much else we can do once we're standing back out there in the litter of our belongings waiting for the VW to explode. But it just smoulders and hisses a while as the sun sinks behind us. In the end, with the smoke almost gone and the wiring cooked, it's obvious we're not going anywhere. We turn our attention to the sunset. Meg rolls another spliff and we share it standing there taking in the vast shimmering pink lake that suddenly looks full of rippling water. We don't say anything. The sun flattens itself against the saltpan and disappears. The sky goes all acid blue and there's just this huge silence. It's like the world's stopped.

Right then I can't imagine an end to the quiet. The horizon fades. Everything looks impossibly far off. In two hours I'll hear Biggie and Meg in his sleeping bag and she'll cry out like a bird and become so beautiful, so desirable in the total dark that I'll begin to cry. In a week Biggie and Meg will blow me off in Broome and I'll be on the bus south for a second chance at the exams. In a year Biggie will be dead in a mining accident in the Pilbara and I'll be reading Robert Louis Stevenson at his funeral while his relatives shuffle and mutter with contempt. Meg won't show. I'll grow up and have a family of my own and see Briony Nevis, tired and lined in a supermarket queue, and wonder what all the fuss was about. And one night I'll turn on the TV to discover the fact that Tony Macoli, the little man with the nose that could sniff around corners, is Australia's richest merchant banker. All of the unimaginable. Right now, standing with Biggie on the salt lake at sunset, each of us still in our southern-boy uniform of boots, jeans and flannel shirt, I don't care what happens beyond this moment. In the hot northern dusk, the world suddenly gets big around us, so big we just give in and watch.

. . . . . .

UNFAMILIAR TERRITORY

Serious Swimmers

MICHEL FABER

Gail's little son is in foster care on account of her drug habit. Can she cope with having him back?

There were a couple of hiccups between Gail and Ant before they even got to the swimming pool.

For a start, 'My name's not Ant,' the child said. 'It's Anthony.' Now why did he have to say that, with the social worker right there in the car with them, listening to everything? For a few moments (none of Gail's emotions lasted very long) she hated her little boy so much she couldn't breathe, and she hated the social worker even more, for being there to hear Ant's complaint. She wished the social worker could die somehow and take the knowledge of Gail's humiliation with him; he deserved to die anyway, the parasite. But the social worker remained alive and at the wheel, noting Gail's come-uppance in his little black book of a brain, and then – Jesus Christ! – Ant went and did it again when they were almost there, by asking Gail, 'What was that little drink you had back there?'

'What little drink?'

'The little drink you had at the chemist. In the little plastic cup.'

'Medicine, cutie.'

'My name's not cutie,' stated the child. 'It's Anthony.'

Then, as the car was drawing to a halt in front of the Melbourne public baths, this kid, this Anthony who had grown out of being the Ant she'd lost to the State five years ago, said to her, 'Are you still sick?'

'I used to be really sick,' was Gail's answer. 'Now I'm a lot better.'

The boy looked unimpressed.

'Moira says people shouldn't take medicine if they're not sick.'

Moira was Anthony's foster-carer. He didn't call her Mum. But then he didn't call Gail Mum either. He was careful not to call her anything.

'Your Mum is only a little bit sick now,' the social worker chipped in, his head twisted away as he parked the car. 'The last bit.'

Gail hadn't expected this from him. She was glad the social worker was alive now, grateful. She was willing to do anything for him, anything he wanted, like for free. Although she'd better be careful who she slept with these days, if she wanted to get Ant back.

'Two,' she told the swimming cashier. 'One child and one ... ah ... grown-up.' She flinched at the stumble: years of addiction had half-dissolved lots of words she'd once had no problem coming out with. They were like things you leave in a box in the garage and then when you look for them years later you find the water's got to them.

. . .

This visit to the swimming pool wasn't Ant's idea, as far as Gail knew. She didn't know very far, though. The social worker would suggest an outing with Anthony, like going to the movies, and Gail would go to the movies with Anthony. Everything was arranged: which movie, which cinema, which session time. Who decided? Gail wasn't sure, except that it wasn't her. Maybe Anthony had told Moira he really liked swimming and Moira had told the social worker, and the social worker had taken it from there. Maybe it was the other way around.

Gail had never been to this swimming pool before, had never been to any swimming pool since she'd been a schoolgirl, slouching in the audience at the water sports finals, distracted by nicotine craving. Those trials had been held in the open air, in a giant complex of pools. This place she and Ant were entering now was different altogether, an indoor place, like a railway-station-sized bathroom built around a railway-platform-sized bath. A combination of electric light and sunshine from the many windows and skylights made it a kind of in-between world, neither inside nor out.

The water was warm, something Gail didn't really believe until she dangled her naked foot off the edge. She'd imagined that 'heated' meant the water sort of had the chill taken off it, but it was as warm as a bath: body temperature maybe. She couldn't be sure. Her own body thermostat had been well and truly fucked for years.

Gail and Ant didn't need to go to the changing rooms; they both had their swimgear on underneath their street clothes – another detail overseen by the social worker, this man who brought them together and, just by existing, kept them officially apart.

There were only about ten or eleven people in the pool, half of them adults swimming or hanging off the sides near the deep end. One length of the pool had been roped off by a floating divider of coloured plastic, to give serious swimmers one narrow lane to do their laps in. A well-muscled Japanese man prepared to enter this strip: a well-fleshed Australian woman was doing the backstroke. Everyone else was in the unrestricted part of the pool. Teenagers, children and their parents played at the shallow end, taking no notice of Gail and

Anthony climbing in. Anthony was six and the water was up to his chest; Gail was twenty-three and the water was up to her navel. She squatted to come down to his level, and because it was warmer underwater.

'Can you swim?' she asked, noticing how awkwardly Ant was looking down at the water around his chest and his faraway feet on the bottom of the pool.

'Yeah, I swim all the time,' he said. 'I swim real good,' and immediately he gave a succession of startling demonstrations which consisted of throwing himself forward in the water, sinking, thrashing his arms and legs as rapidly as he could, and surfacing in a blind sputter. He couldn't even tell which direction he was facing when he surfaced, and he would swivel his head, blinking and burping, trying to orient himself to where he had started.

'I can swim too,' said Gail. 'But not very well.'

She'd learned to swim in a backyard swimming pool, one of those round, blue, free-standing things from the Clark Rubber store in Ferntree Gully, and she had been Anthony's age. The boy whose family owned the pool had shown her how to float and how to move forward. He also tried to show her how to synchronise the arm and leg movements and turn her head from side to side to get the breaths in, but she hadn't mastered that part. Then he had shown her his penis, and she had shown him her chubby little vulva: the pre-agreed reason for the game.

She wasn't chubby now. She was thin and grown-up. It had cost her $2.80 to get into the pool, twice as much as Ant. That was where growing up got you: ADULTS, $2.80.

A grotesquely overweight man climbed in at the children's end and waded out towards the deep, rolls of fat on his back humping in and out of the water as he began to swim.

'How come that man's swimming when he's so fat?' Anthony whispered to her, his awe overwhelming his reserve. Anxious to have the answer, Gail had to think hard. Other people's motivations, or even her own, were not her strong point.

'His doctor probably told him to,' she said at last.

She didn't perceive the man as being particularly grotesque. He was a member of the straight world, and members of the straight world were normal, they had their place. The fat man belonged here with the mothers and their paddling children, the idle athletes and goggled teenagers. He could claim the right to displace as much water as he wished, whereas Gail, pale from night-living and wasted by narcotics, was an alien object which might at any moment be fished out of the pool by an angry official. She looked down at herself in the water, at the spindly white legs coming out of the oversized red shorts, and then looked at Ant. His shorts were oversized too, yet they were very cute on him: he looked as if he was about to grow into them, whereas she seemed to be shrinking out of hers.

Anthony continued to demonstrate his mastery of swimming for her, throwing himself, thrashing furiously underwater, and surfacing: Gail tried to look as if she were looking on approvingly, but really she was staring at the well-fleshed woman swimming backstroke in the roped-off lane. This woman was so powerful and steady, completing length after length, from the deep end to the shallow and back to the deep, a serious swimmer, her breasts sticking up out of the water. She was another species, as different from Gail as a seal or a porpoise. Gail laid one hand across her own breast. Her tube top had almost nothing inside it: her wrist rested against bone. Heroin had wasted her. The first time the social workers had taken Ant away from her, they had given her a milk expresser, but there had been nothing to express.

On impulse she started swimming, in her own way. All she could do was lie face-down in the water until her body started to float up to the top, and then with slow, sweeping strokes she moved forward. Once again, for the first time since learning to swim in that backyard pool, she tried the breathing part, but as soon as she lifted her head out of the water the rest of her started to sink. She was disappointed; she had hoped that somehow during the long and horrible lifetime she'd lived since first trying, she might have gained the knack sort of automatically.

She lay face down in the water again, waiting to be buoyed up, and then she swan and swam, back and forth across the shallow end of the pool. At first she swan with her eyes closed, anticipating the touch of her fingers against the pool's side or the floating rope, but after she'd hit her head on the tiles twice, and been kicked by one of the serious swimmers, she swam with her eyes open, surprised to find it didn't hurt. She couldn't see much except luminous chlorine blue, disturbed every now and then by a psychedelic glimpse of an approaching body. Sometimes it was Anthony's body trying to swim beside her, a blue of flailing little arms and legs distorted by motion and diffusion.

Eventually she worked up the courage to touch him, to signal him up.

'It's better if you float first,' she said. 'Watch me.'

She demonstrated, and he watched, and then, when she'd surfaced and was waiting for him to imitate her, he said,

'I've been watching you. I've been doing the same as you for ages.'

'You don't wait long enough. You start trying to move

around before you're floating.'

His answer to that was to throw himself forward in the water next to her, to demonstrate that no matter how many long, long microseconds he could bear to wait, his body wasn't borne up the way hers was. Gail thought of telling him to keep still longer, but suddenly she was sickened by an image, rammed into her mind like a slide into a slide-viewer, of Ant floating on top of the water, dead.

'How about you hold on to me while I swim?' she suggested, so shaken by the dead son still floating in her head that she forgot to be afraid of rejection.

Anthony looked away from her, ignoring her suggestion it seemed, towards a part of the pool where a burly Italian man was playing a game with his daughter. Over and over the man would lift the child out of the water, arrange her weight carefully in his arms, and toss her as far and as high as he could. The girl shrieked with delight every time she made her splash.

'Can you do that to me?' Anthony asked.

No, Gail thought automatically, the way she'd always done when asked to attempt anything not related to heroin. Everything else was too hard.

'I'm only little,' she tried to explain.

Anthony looked at her as if she was crazy: couldn't she see the difference between them? To make him happy was so easy: a simple physical act. He was a child, she was a grown-up, therefore she could do it: the pleasure was hers to give or withhold.

Gail looked down at him, trying to assess how big or small he really was. Excitement shone on his face, like a sheen of chemical which could contort his features into joy or distress depending on what happened next.

What happened next was that she picked him up and

threw him as far as she could. He shrieked with delight, just like the Italian man's little girl. It was as simple as that.

'Again! Again!' he squealed, wading back to her, and they did it again. He had forgotten to be wary of her, and Gail felt secure enough to cope with the possibility of his remembering. It wouldn't last, but she was happy, incredibly happy, treating herself to dose after dose of infectious excitement.

Eventually, when she was too exhausted to toss him any more she did some more swimming, and this time he held on to her, pulled through the water at first by his hand on her ankle, then by his arms around her neck. His weight was the most satisfying physical sensation she could ever remember having.

She couldn't get over how easy physical intimacy was in the water. They were more buoyant; if they moved towards each other they were together so suddenly that there was nothing to do about it but accept. Also the water was a reassuring medium between them – she could even embrace him, his legs wrapped around her waist, and the water would keep their bodies discrete and a little unreal, just enough to make it possible. An embrace in the empty air out there in the real world would be so much more difficult. How could you start it out there, with nothing helping you towards the other person, and how could you end it, with no medium to ease you apart, only the awkward unclenching of decision? She remembered their previous outings together, which had been visits to the movies mostly. Gail had sat there in the dark next to Anthony, wondering if she could get away with laying her arm along the top of his seat so that when he sat back he might feel it there around his shoulders. She remembered the mingled taste of Methadone and choc-top ice cream, and the gigantic images of robots, monsters and explosions whose reflected light flickered on the face of her son.

Never again, she thought. *It's the pool from now on.*

But already there was a problem.

The familiar pain in her guts had come.

'We have to get out soon,' she said to Anthony, but he played on as if he had water in his ears.

'We have to get out now,' she said a few moments later, as the pain screwed deeper.

'Oh, please, not yet Mum!'

Hearing it, she realised she would do anything, anything for that last word.

'OK, you stay for a while,' she said. 'But I have to get out now. I'll come back and watch you from the edge.'

He seemed happy with that, so she climbed up the little steel ladder out of the pool. The unheated air felt freezing. Her shorts stuck heavily to her goose-pimpled flesh, and underneath her sodden tank top her nipples tightened painfully. She hobbled to where she had left her clothes, scooped them up and rushed to the changing rooms.

Her body temperature seemed to be dropping at the rate of one degree per second, and she undressed in a clumsy frenzy. The vision of Anthony floating face down in the water slotted into her mind again; he looked dead, as only a dead child can look.

The well-fleshed woman, the serious swimmer, was in the changing room too, observing Gail's anxiousness with mild curiosity as she stepped backwards into a steaming shower. Her pubic hair was thick and black; she was probably wondering why Gail had none. *Really*, thought Gail, *now that I'm off the game I should stop shaving it, let it grow...*

Every twenty seconds or so Gail hurried to the door of the changing room, towel wrapped around her, to make sure her boy was still alive, then she would hurry back inside and dry herself some more. Her skinny limbs seemed to slip through the fabric of the towel untouched, remaining cold and wet no matter how much she rubbed. There was water in the hollows of her collarbones, water running down the hardened lines of her arms and legs. The pain in her guts grew and grew as she dressed, and finally she couldn't contain it any longer. After checking on Anthony one more time, she shut herself into the toilet and stayed there, doubled up, for many minutes.

The diarrhoea took its sweet time as usual, and all the while her son was in the pool gasping blue water into his lungs, thrashing around under the surface in such a way that the others would think he was just playing, no different from when his mother had been in there with him. She was dizzy with pain and panic, considered staggering out there with her jeans around her ankles. Then suddenly the pain subsided. Something had rearranged itself inside her.

Back at the poolside moments later, she determined at a glance that none of the heads above water was Anthony's, and she peered anxiously at the indistinct bodies underneath. In the outside world the sun was setting, so that the indoor light was all electric now, cold and brutal. Running sideways along the edge of the pool, Gail become aware of the social worker standing on the other side, looking in also, but she didn't really care. She understood that if he was blaming her for Anthony's death, this was less important than Anthony's death itself.

'Anthony!' she called.

A hand on her arm sent a shock through her, like a stray electric spark. Anthony had emerged from the other changing room, dressed and dry, his hair nearly combed. Of course she'd imagined that when the time came for him to come out of the pool she would have to take him into the changing room with her, the way she's always taken him into toilets when he was a baby, but she could see now that that was half a lifetime ago.

With an inarticulate noise of relief and effort, she swept him up into her arms, swaying a little, surprised at his weight out of the water.

Simultaneously she wished never to let him go, and yet longed to put him down; his intrusion into her was so shocking, deeper and more merciless than anything she had ever suffered from men or needles. How could they compare, those thousand shallow, anaesthetic penetrations, when here she was fully clothed at a suburban swimming pool, blasted open and infused by this little alien she herself had made?

She'd had enough for one day, she was ready to call it quits, to sleep alone in her empty flat for fourteen hours and hand this heavy, heavy child of hers over to the social worker, and on to Moira Whatsername, until she'd recovered and was ready to cope with this feeling again.

But as the social worker walked towards them, Anthony leaned close to her face and whispered in her ear,

'That was fun, Mum. What's next?'

. . . . . .

Elsewhere

DAVID MALOUF

When Andy, a down-to-earth miner, drives to Sydney for his bohemian sister-in-law's funeral, a new world opens up to him.

When Debbie Larcombe died she had not been home to her family for nearly three years. Her father decided at once that he would go down to Sydney for the funeral, which was already arranged. There was no suggestion of her being brought back to Lithgow. Her sister Helen couldn't go. She had the children. So Harry's son-in-law, Andy Mayo, would go with him. The two men worked together down the mine and were mates.

Andy was a steady fellow of thirty-three. He'd been to Sydney once, with a rugby team, when he was nineteen. The prospect of driving down and seeing something of the Big Smoke excited him, but he felt he should disguise the fact. After all it was a funeral. 'Are you sure?' he asked Helen, who was kneeling at the bathtub bathing their youngest.

'It's only for the day,' she told him. 'And Dad would like it. I'd be worried about him going down all on his own.'

She paused at her work and said for the third or fourth time, 'It's so sudden! I can hardly believe it.'

Andy, stirred by a rush of tenderness, but also of tender sensuality, brought his fingertips to a strand of hair, damp with steam, that had stuck to the soft white of her neck. Responding, she leaned back for a moment into the firmness, against her nape, of his extended forefinger and thumb, which lightly stroked.

He'd barely known Debbie; in fact he'd met her only twice. She had already left home when he arrived on the scene. After training college at Bathurst she had taught in country towns all up and down the state and had ended up at Balmain, in Sydney. She was four years older than Helen.

The one occasion they'd spent any time together – he had sat up late with her on the night of her mother Dorothy's funeral – Andy had been impressed but had also felt uneasy. She was nothing like Helen, except a little in looks – same nose, same big hands. Keen that she should see him as more than the usual run of small-town fatheads and mug lairs she had known before she left, but unpractised, he was soon out of his depth. They'd gotten drunk together – she was quite a drinker – and he was the one, being unused to spirits, who had ended up fuzzy-headed.

She sat with her legs crossed and smoked non-stop. Her legs were rather plump, but the shoes she wore, which had thin straps across the instep, were very fashionable-looking. Expensive, Any thought. Though in no way glamorous, she was a woman who took trouble with herself.

The impression he'd got was that she moved in a pretty fast crowd down there, and some of what he caught on to of what Balmain was, and the people she knew – poets and that – and the fact that she lived now with one poet, and had been the girlfriend earlier of another, excited him. He had had very little of that sort of excitement in his own life.

He'd been a football player, good but not good enough. At sixteen he'd gone down the mine. Married at twenty. That there was another life somewhere he had picked up from the magazines he saw and the talk, some of it rough, of fellows who got down to the city pretty regularly and had much to tell. In Debbie, he had, for an hour or so, felt the breath of something he had missed out on. Something extra, something more. Now she was dead.

At thirty-six, some woman's problem. An abortion he guessed, though Helen had done no more than raise a suspicion and the old man of course knew nothing at all. So far as Harry knew, all Debbie had been was a high-school science teacher.

It hadn't struck Andy till now, but everything he'd heard of Debbie's doings had come from Helen and he wondered how much more she knew than she let on. Out of loyalty to Debbie no doubt – but also, he thought, to protect him from a side of herself that might be less surprised by Debbie's way of life, and less disapproving of it, than she pretended.

He felt, vaguely, that here too he had missed out. There was something more he hungered for, and occasionally pushed towards, that Helen would not admit. Because for all the twelve years they had passed in the closest intimacy, she did not want him to see in her the sort of woman who might recognise or allow it.

. . .

The drive down was uneventful. Harry was silent, but that wasn't unusual. They were often silent together.

All this, Andy thought, must be hard on him. He'd never asked himself how Harry felt about Debbie's being away. Proud of her, certainly, as the only one of them who had got enough of an education to make a new life for herself. Sad to see so little of her. Worried on occasion. Now this.

Andy followed these thoughts on Harry's behalf – he was fond of Harry – then followed his own.

Which sprang from the lightness he felt at having a day off like this in the middle of the week. The sunlight. The high white clouds set above open country. The freedom of being behind the wheel. The freedom too – he felt guilty to be thinking this way – of being off the hook, away from home and its constructions. And along with all that, the exhilaration, the allure, of a faster and more crowded world 'down there' that he would finally get to see and feel the proximity of.

He was surprised at himself. Here he was, a grown man, twelve years married, two kids, seated side by side with his father-in-law, both of them in suits on the way to a funeral, and he might have been seventeen, a kid again, he was so full of expectation at what the day might offer. In some secret place where the life in him was most immediately physical, he still clung to a vision of himself that for a time back there had seemed golden and inextinguishable. He thought he had dealt with it, outgrown it, let it go, and without too much disappointment replaced its bouts of extravagant yearning with the reality of small prospects, work, the life he and Helen had made together. And now this.

He was surprised, ashamed even. What would Harry think? But not enough, it seemed, to subdue the flutter he had felt in his belly the moment the idea of the trip came up, or the heat his body was giving off inside the suit.

. . .

They arrived early: To kill the time they drove out to Bondi and sat in the car eating egg hamburgers in greasy paper and watching the surf.

Boardriders miraculously rose up and for long moments kept their balance on running sunlight, then went down in a flurry of foam.

Mothers, their skirts round their thighs, tempted little kiddies too far past the waterline for them to run back when the sea, in a rush, came sparkling round their feet. Surprised beyond tears, they considered a moment, then squealed with delight.

Andy thought of his girls. He should bring them down here, show them the ocean. They hadn't seen it yet. He had only seen it one other time himself.

On their rugby trip they had come down here in the dark, half a dozen of them, seriously pissed, and had chased about naked on the soft sand after midnight, skylarking, taking flying tackles at each other, wrestling, kicking up light in gritty showers, then stood awestruck down at the edge, watching a huge surf rise up like a wall, and roar and crash against the stars.

He glanced sideways now to see what Harry was making of it, this immense wonder that at every moment surrounded them.

'That's South America out there,' Harry informed him. 'Peru.'

As if, by narrowing your eyes and getting the focus right, you might actually see it.

Andy narrowed his eyes. What his quickened senses caught out there was the outstretched figure of a long-bodied woman under a sheet, thin as a veil, slowly turning in her sleep.

. . .

The funeral was a quiet affair, with everyone more respectable-looking than Andy had expected, though the fellow who gave the service, which wasn't really a service – no prayers or hymns – was jollier than is normal on such occasions. He talked of Debbie's life and how full it had been. How full of life *she* had been, and how they all liked her and what a good time they'd had together.

He did not refer to the fact that she was actually here, screwed down now inside the coffin they'd carried in.

Andy himself was actually aware of that. It made him uncomfortably hot. He pushed a finger into his collar and eased it a bit, but felt the blood swelling in the veins of his neck.

It was the bulk of his own body he felt crammed into a coffin. How close the lid would be over his head. And how dark it must be in there when the chapel all around was so full of sunlight and the pleasantness of women in short-sleeved frocks, and a humming from the garden walks outside, of bees. The big-boned woman he'd spent a night drinking vodka with seemed very close: the heaviness of her crossed legs in the expensive-looking shoes, and her determination, which he had missed at the time but saw clearly now, to outdrink him. He wondered what shoes she was wearing in there. Then wondered, again, what Harry was thinking.

Harry looked very dignified in his suit and tie. Andy had last seen him in it at Dorothy's funeral, a very different affair from this. It was hard to tell from the straightness of him, and the line of his jaw, what he might be feeling. Andy looked more than once and could not tell.

It's his daughter, he thought. He's the father. Someone ought to have mentioned that.

But there was no talk of Debbie's family at all. Didn't they have families, these people? Or was it that they thought of *themselves* as a family? He couldn't work it out, their ties to one another – wives and husbands, mothers and fathers.

Still, it went well. People listened quietly. One or two of the women cried. People laughed, a bit too heartily he thought, at the speaker's jokes. They were private jokes that Andy did not catch, and he wondered what Harry thought of *that*. A couple of poems were read, by an older fellow with a ponytail who seemed to be drunk and swallowed all his words. When the curtains parted and the coffin tilted and began to slide away, there was music.

At least that part was like a funeral. Except that the music was another fellow singing to a guitar: Dylan's 'Sad-eyed Lady of the Lowlands'. Andy cast a glance at Harry and laid his hand for a moment on the soft pad of his father-in-law's shoulder, but Harry gave no sign.

. . .

They drove for nearly half an hour to the wake, through heavy traffic, the city dim with smoke but the various bits of water they crossed or saw in the distance – the Harbour – brightly glinting. They stopped at a phone box and he called Helen, who was full of questions he found it hard to answer. He had really called – the idea occurred to him towards the end of the service – so that Harry could speak to her.

When Harry took the phone he walked away from the box and stood on the pavement in the sun, and only once looked back to see how things were going.

It was hot in the sun. Too hot for a suit. He was sweating under the arms and in the small of his back. Most of the passers-by wore jeans and T-shirts. It was a run-down neighbourhood of old factory buildings, with a view of wharves stacked with containers, and on the dirty waters of the bay a busy movement of ships.

He took his jacket off, hooking his finger into the collar and letting it trail over his shoulder.

He felt easier back in his own loose body, though he continued to sweat. He rolled his shirtsleeves, but only halfway.

At last Harry appeared. He pursed his lips and nodded, which Andy took as an indication that the talk with Helen had gone well. Well, that was something. When they got back into the car he remained silent, but his silence, Andy thought, was of a different kind. More relaxed. Something had broken.

When they got to the house and found a parking place, Harry, who had not removed his jacket, stood waiting for Andy to resume his. Which he did, out of respect. For Harry. For the fact that Harry thought it was the right thing to do.

The front door of the house was open and a crush of people, all with drinks in hand, spilled out on to the narrow verandah that ran right across the one-storeyed cottage and down on to the footpath. They pushed through, conspicuous, Andy thought, in their suits. People looked and raised an eyebrow. Maybe they think we're cops, Andy thought. It made him smile.

The hallway, which ran right through to the back door, was crowded. It was noisy in the small rooms with their tongue-and-groove walls, so noisy you could barely hear yourself speak. Music. Voices.

'Debbie's brother-in-law,' he shouted to a fellow who gave him a beer, and offered the man his hand. The man took it but looked surprised.

'Debbie's father,' he explained when, with just a glance, the fellow looked to where Harry was standing, towering in fact, in his pinstriped double-breasted suit, against the wall.

The fellow was fifty or so, in a black skivvy, and bearded, with a chain and a big clanking medal around his neck.

'Well, cheers,' he said, looking uncertain.

'Cheers,' Andy replied, raising the can.

He took a good long swig of the beer, which was very cold and immediately did something to restore him – his confidence, his interest. He looked around, still feeling that he stuck out here like a sore thumb; so did Harry. But that was to be expected.

This was *it*. Elsewhere. He was in the middle of it.

But he wished Harry would relax a bit. Trouble was, he didn't know what to do or say that would help. He had to tell himself again that Harry was a man standing in the hallway of a house full of people shouting at one another over a continuous din of party music, at his daughter's wake. He felt protective of Harry, most of all of Harry's feelings, but he also wanted to range out. All this represented a set of possibilities that might not come his way again. His own impatience, the itch he felt to move away, be on his own, see for himself what was going on here, seemed like a betrayal.

'Listen,' he said to a woman who was pushing past with two cans of beer in her hand and a fag hanging from the corner of her mouth. 'Where can I get a drink for my mate?' He jerked his head in Harry's direction. 'He's Debbie's father,' he told her, lowering his voice.

The woman looked. 'Agh!' she said. 'Here, take one a'these.' Then, with lowered voice and a stricken glance in Harry's direction, 'I didn't know that was Debbie's father.

'It is,' he told her. 'I'm her brother-in-law.'

He took the beer, thanked her, then carried it over to Harry. They stood together, side by side in the hallway, and drank.

'Thanks, mate,' Harry told him.

. . .

Andy stood, taking in the changing scene. People pushing past to the front door and the verandah. Pausing to greet others. Joking, laughing. More guests kept arriving, some with crates of beer. He still hadn't said more than a word or two to anyone else, but felt a rising excitement. He would move out and get into it in a minute. He was very willing to be sociable. It was just a matter, among these people, of how to make a start.

He was curious, considering the mixture, about who they were, how they were related to Debbie and came to be here, and increasingly confident, looking around, of what he himself might have to offer. He caught that from the eye of some of the girls – the women – who went by. Things were developing.

He had another beer, then another, lost track of Harry, got involved with one group, then a second – but only at the edge. Just listening.

He drifted out to the kitchen, where people were seated around a scrubbed-pine table stacked with empties and strewn with scraps. Others leaned against the fridge and the old-fashioned porcelain sink. He leaned too.

No one paid any attention to him, though they weren't hostile. They just went on arguing.

Politics. Though it wasn't really an argument either, since they all agreed.

He stepped past them to a little back porch with three steps down to a sloping yard, grassy, the edges of it, near the fence, thick with sword fern in healthy clumps. It was getting dark.

There was a big camphor laurel tree, huge really, and a Hills Hoist turning slowly in the breeze that he felt, just faintly, on his brow, and clothes pegged out to dry that no one had bothered to bring in. They were hung out just anyhow. Not the way a woman would do it.

He watched them for a while: the shirts white in the

growing darkness, filling with air a moment, then collapsing; the tree, also stirring, filling with air and all its crowded gathering of leaves responding, shivering. He too felt something. Something familiar and near.

He thought of Helen. Of the girls. He did not want the feeling of sadness that came to him, which had been there all day, he felt, under the throb of expectation, and which declared itself now in the way these clothes had been hung out, the tea towels all crooked, the shirts pegged awkwardly at the shoulder so that the sleeves hung empty and slack.

Back in the hallway he got talking to a very young woman in a miniskirt, hot pink, with a tight-fitting hot-pink top and a glossy bag over her shoulder, and glossy cork-heeled sandals, her toenails painted the same hot pink as her lips and clothes. He hadn't seen her at the funeral. She had just arrived. He introduced himself. 'I'm Debbie's brother-in-law,' he told her, but without making it sound, he hoped, like a claim.

The girl took a sip from her glass and looked up at him, all eyelashes. 'Who's Debbie?' she asked, genuinely stumped.

He opened his mouth but felt it would be foolish to explain. Still, he was shocked.

A little later he found himself engaged with another woman, older and very drunk, who in just minutes began pushing herself against him. He was a bit drunk himself at this stage. Not very drunk, but enough to go where his senses took him. He stood with his back against a wall of the crowded hallway and the woman pushed her knee between his thighs in the thick woollen suit and her tongue into his mouth. Her fingers were in his hair. He was sweating.

She undid a button on his shirt, put her nose in. 'Ummm,' she murmured, '*au naturel*. I like it. Where have they been keeping you?' When they broke briefly to catch their breath he glanced around in case Harry was close by.

All this now was what he had expected or hoped for, but he was surprised how little of the initiative was his. Somewhere in the back of his head, as the woman urged her tongue into it and her hand went exploring below, he was repeating to himself: 'I'm Debbie's brother-in-law. She's dead, this is her wake.' Since he had arrived in this house he was the only one, so far as he knew, who'd volunteered her name.

Things were going fast down in his pants, the woman luxuriously leading. He liked it that for once someone else was making the moves. A small noise struggled in his throat. No one around seemed to care, or even to have noticed. He wondered how far all this was to go, and saw that he could simply go with it. He was pleased, in a quiet, self-congratulatory way, that this was how he was taking it.

The woman drew her head back, looked at him quizzically, and smiled. 'Ummm,' she said, 'nice. I'll be back.' Then, fixing her hair with a deft hand, she disengaged; gently, as he thought of it, set him down. He was left red-faced and bothered, fiercely sweating.

He dealt with his own hair, a few flat-handed slaps, discreetly adjusted things below. He felt like a kid. What was he supposed to do now? Wait for her to come back? Follow? He leaned against the wall and stared at the plaster ceiling. His head was reeling. He decided to stumble after her, but she was gone in the crowd and instead he found Harry, squatting on a low three-legged stool that was too small for him, his thumb in a book.

'Harry?'

Harry glanced up over the big horn-rimmed glasses he used for reading. He looked like a professor, Andy thought with amusement, but could not fathom his expression. Harry handed him the book.

It was a poetry book. There were more, exactly like the one he was holding, on the shelf at Harry's elbow, with the gap between them where he had pulled this one out. Andy shifted his shoulders, rubbed the end of his nose, consulted Harry. Who nodded.

Andy rubbed his nose again and opened the book, turning one page, then the next. *To Debbie*, he read on a page all to itself. All through, he could see, her name was scattered. Debbie. Sometimes Deb.

He was puzzled. Impressed. The book looked substantial but he had no way of judging how important or serious such a thing might be, or whether Harry, in showing it to him, had meant him to see in it a justification or an affront. It was about things that were private, that's what he saw. But here they were in a book that just anyone could pick up.

He turned more pages, mostly so as not to face Harry. Odd words jumped out at him. 'Witchery' was one – he hoped Harry hadn't seen that one. In another place, 'cunt'. Right there on the page. So unexpected it made his stomach jump. In a book of poetry! He didn't understand that. Or any of this. He snapped the book shut, and moved to restore it to the shelf, but Harry reached out and took it from him.

Andy frowned, uncertain where Harry's mind was moving.

Using both hands, Harry eased himself upright, slipped his glasses into one pocket of his jacket, forced the book into another, and turned down the hallway towards the front door.

Andy followed.

So it was over, they were leaving. It struck Andy that he had never discovered whose house this was.

'You need to say goodbye to anyone?' he asked Harry.

'Never bloody met anyone,' Harry told him.

Outside it was night-time, blue and cool. Some people on the steps got up to let them through. One of them said, 'Oh, you're leaving,' and another, 'Goodbye', - strangers, incurious about who they might be but with that much in them of politeness or affability.

They found the car, and Andy took his jacket off and tossed it into the back seat. Harry retained his.

They drove across bridges, through night traffic now. Past water riddled with red and green neon, and high tower blocks where all the fluorescent panels in the ceilings of empty offices were brightly pulsing.

After a bit, Harry asked out of nowhere, 'What's a muse? Do you know what it means? A muse?'

'Amuse?' Andy asked in turn. 'Like when you're amused?' He didn't get it.

'No. A – muse. M-U-S-E.'

Andy shook his head.

'Don't worry,' Harry told him. 'I'll ask Macca. He'll know.'

Andy felt slighted, but Harry was right, Macca would know. Macca was a workmate of theirs, a reader. If anyone knew, Macca would. But the book in Harry's pocket was a worry to Andy. He hoped Macca wouldn't uncover *too* much of what was in it. He'd seen enough, himself, to be disturbed by how much that was personal, and which you might want to keep that way, was set down bold as brass for any Tom, Dick or Harry – ah, Harry – to butt in on. He didn't understand that, and doubted Harry would either.

Suddenly Harry spoke again.

'She was such a bright little thing,' he said. 'You wouldn't credit.'

Andy swallowed. This was it. A single bald statement breaking surface out of the stream of thought Harry was adrift in – which was all, Andy thought, he might ever hear. He kept his eyes dead ahead.

What Harry was thinking of, he knew, was how far that bright little thing he had been so fond of, all that time ago, had moved away from him, how far he had lost track of her.

He had his own bright little girl, Janine. She was ten. He felt sweetly bound to her – painfully bound, he felt now, in the prospect of inevitable loss. She too would go off, go elsewhere.

At the time Harry was recalling, Andy thought, he would have been a young man, the same age I am now. He had never thought of Harry as young. There was a lot he had not thought of.

He glanced at Harry. Nothing more would be said. Those last few words had risen up out of a swell of feeling, unbearable perhaps, that Harry was still caught up in, but when Andy looked again – the look could only be brief – he got no clue.

A wave of sadness struck him. Not only for Harry's isolation but for his own. He was fond of Harry, but they might as well have been on different planets.

'Have a bit of a nap if you like,' he told Harry gently. 'You must be buggered. I'll be right.' What he meant, though Harry would not take it that way, was that he wanted to be alone.

In just minutes Harry had sunk down in the seat, letting the seat belt take his weight, and had followed his thoughts deeper, then deeper again, into sleep. Andy focused on the road ahead, his hands resting lightly on the wheel. Free now to follow his own thoughts. Not thinking exactly. Letting the thoughts rise up and flow into him. Flow through him.

Something had come to him back there and changed things. When? he wondered. In the noisy hallway? Where in a world that was so far outside his experience, and among people whose lives were so different from his own, he'd given himself over to what might come? No, he'd been fooling himself, and he blushed now, though no one but himself would ever know about it. Earlier than that.

His body, which knew better than his slow mind, set him back in the bluish dusk of that back porch.

For a moment there he had been out of things, looking down from high up into a quiet backyard. A camphor laurel tree, its swarming leaves lifted by a quickening of the air. The same breeze touching skirts pegged awkwardly on a line, filling them with breath. Then like fingers in his hair. It was something in those particular objects that had struck him. Something he felt, almost grasped, that was near and familiar.

Or it was a way of looking at things that was in himself. That was himself. A lonely thought, this – the beginning, perhaps, of another kind of loss, though his own healthy resilience told him it need not be.

He drove. The road was straight now, a double highway running fast through blue night scrub. Under banks of smoky cloud a rounded moon bounced along treetops. He put on speed and felt released. Not from his body – he was more aware than ever of that, of its blockiness and persistence – but from the earth's pull upon it. As if, seated here in this metal capsule knees flexed, spine propped against tilted leather, it was the far high universe they were sailing through, and those lights off to the side of the ribboning highway – small townships settled down to the night's TV, roadside service stations all lit up in the dark, with their aisles of chocolate biscuits and potato crisps – were far-flung constellations, and Harry, afloat now in the vast realm of sleep, and he, in a lapse of consciousness of a different kind, had taken off, and weightless as in space or in flying dreams, were flying.

. . . . . .

Dark Roots

CATE KENNEDY

If he were almost 40 and she 26, there'd be no problem.
But it's much harder when it's the other way round.

You'll be fitting your key in the lock when you hear the phone start ringing, and straight away your hand will be fumbling with haste. The answering machine will kick in and when your heart squirms up around your throat somewhere, you'll know. Call it what you like, we think it's love, but it's chemical. It's endorphins, that high-octane fuel, revving the engine and drowning out the faint carburettor warning sound in the back of the head, the out-of-tune chug that says *wait, wait*, in its prim, irritating little voice.

At the doctor's, you'll keep your eyes on the package of contraceptive pills made into a desk paperweight. Your doctor will look over your card, tapping a pen, then reach for the prescription pad, and ask you if you've been on these before.

'Oh, many years ago now,' you say.

'Any side-effects?'

You remember being twenty-two, going on the pill for the first time, and lock onto the memory of your own body in a swooping rush. You remember your long thighs in those slimline jeans, and your flat stomach which effortlessly stayed that way, hard with muscles you'd done nothing to deserve. You remember – and what woman over thirty-five doesn't? – pulling your long hair up over a sun visor and sitting on beaches with boyfriends for hours, squinting into the glaring, ruinous sun, glorifying in being tanned.

'No side-effects that I can remember,' you say. 'Maybe an increased appetite.'

The doctor smiles briefly. 'Yeah, they'll give you the munchies all right, you'll have to watch that. You're not a smoker, are you?'

'No.'

'Only because if you were, at your age, I'd never be prescribing this brand.'

And you feel that little swoop again, hear the *at your age* like stepping on a sharp piece of gravel, a wince of ludicrous defensiveness.

It's the same when you break the news to your friends.

'Come on then,' they say. 'No one *cares*, Mel. Just tell us how much younger the guy is.'

'Thirteen years,' you answer. You want – no, you *need* – one of them to come in on cue now, with something sisterly about nobody even *commenting* on the difference if it was the other way round. Instead there is a surprised silence. Come on, somebody.

'Well,' says Helen abruptly, 'I mean, for godsakes. If he was thirty-nine and you were thirteen years younger nobody would turn a hair. I say go for it.'

You will crush the lemon slice in your drink with the edge of your straw. You need more.

'I mean, look at you, you're gorgeous. No wonder,' says Sandy. 'I bet the guy can't believe his luck. What is it you said he did?'

You wonder, later, why you lie here. Why you say Paul is an academic, even though he's actually just finishing his PhD and tutoring. Why you have to add: 'And he writes movie reviews.'

Then later, standing in your bathroom, about to perforate

the foil package and take that first pill of the cycle, you will glance up into the mirror and notice what people at work have been stopping to comment on: how good you're looking lately. You can see it yourself. That fuel pumping through the body, firing up the colour in your face. It's lust that'll do that to you, every time. Being the object of desire. Three weeks into it, and just look at the difference.

. . .

Once upon a time you would have said, confidently: show me someone who says they've never had a fantasy of being the Older Woman, and I'll show you a liar. It's like one of those dreams where you're walking through your ordinary familiar house feeling its confines and thinking nothing's going to change now, might as well accept it, when you notice a door you've never seen before. And you open it and on the other side is another whole possible living space, another alternative route through each day.

Before you get up, now, you think about what you're going to wear. You find lipstick, and put it on. You keep eye contact for longer than you need to.

Here's a dead giveaway: in the supermarket, in that third week, your hand will reach out and take a box of hair colour and it's the easiest thing in the world to appear the next day with red highlights. Who can blame you? This will induce recklessness: a 26 year old guy ringing you up every night and saying he misses you when you're not together. Telling you you're beautiful and you shiver, feeling his hand move under your linen shirt (ironing clothes again!) and across your stomach. Sure, a little more effort's needed at thirty-nine. Of course you want that stomach to be as concave as it had been on the beach at twenty-two, back when you were busy prematurely ageing your face, carefree and oblivious and immortal. You have to suck in your breath, under that hand. You have to stay on your guard.

. . .

You tell your friends where you met, at a film screening. You can't wait to talk about him.

It had been an industry preview with complimentary tickets, you say, and people seem to chat more when nobody's paid for their tickets. 'He asked me if his backpack bag thing was annoying me next to my feet, and I said no.'

'They're not called backpacks now,' Sandy interrupts. 'They're called *crumplers*.'

'Well, whatever. When the film ended he was taking a few notes and I asked him about it, we got chatting and went out for a drink.

'Out for a drink where?'

'Mario's. and just talked for an hour about the film.'

'Aha,' said Helen. 'Mario's. Over-thirties lighting.' But you see she's listening as avidly as anyone, to learn how to chance it, getting something started gracefully.

. . .

For a while now, you've avoided looking at yourself in the full-length mirror in the bathroom by neglecting to put the ventilation fan on. You hurry to dry yourself and get out of there before the mirror unsteams. Life, if we hold it up to the light, contains many of these foolish rituals. Like the one you notice lately where you always turn off the bedside lamp before you slide into bed with him, and the way you don't wear your glasses at the movies.

You want his appreciation newly minted, you want to

believe he actually can hardly believe his luck. The endorphins must bathe your brain with these possibilities. With every phone call, every new plan he proposes for the two of you, you start to believe you could maybe leave the bathroom fan on sometime soon, and deal with that scrutiny. You start thinking you actually have those rich chestnut highlights in your hair naturally. Well. You know the rest. You know how it all goes.

. . .

Then, a week into the contraceptives, you're ravenous. Standing there in the kitchen eating spoonfuls of rice out of the saucepan, chewing and staring at the notices under the fridge magnets. Walking through the house gnawing on chicken legs, buying croissants at morning tea. Back at home you take the packet of contraceptives out of the bathroom cupboard and read the side-effects again – *increased appetite, tendency to hirsuteness, loss of libido, double vision, nausea* – and resolve to eat less, use sunscreen more, avoid alcohol except in moderation. This demands vigilance. Six weeks now, and soon you will be going down the coast for the weekend, like a proper couple on a romantic getaway, and all you can think about is how your thighs will look in a swimsuit.

Six weeks, and in two more months you will be forty, and the friends are making jokes about a party to run this new guy through his paces – this thinking woman's toy boy, as they call him – an event it is impossible to comfortably imagine. Forty, and Sandy knows what a crumpler is because she has a thirteen-year-old son, whereas you, you have to keep smothering a rising panic that you've missed the bus. Thirteen years ago you were living in London, fervently avoiding any chance of children. Now you're one of those nuisance women obstetricians must hate, waking up to the alarm on your biological clock just before it runs itself down.

So you find yourself at the chemist buying the sunscreen for mature skin, the moisturiser with concealer that guarantees a visible difference. Forty, and your fertile years are waning away in a dwindling flush of denial and negation, each lost month rushing closer like concrete pylons on the female superhighway, a marker of defeat, and if you were honest, you would admit that every pill sticks in your throat like a sugar-coated lie. Instead you swallow it with eyes closed, the better to avoid seeing details in that mirror. All those permutations, all those possible side-effects.

. . .

While you're at the chemist, you buy another box of hair dye promising those living colour highlights. Your hair needs a wash – you glance at it in one of the make-up mirrors. Dark roots are showing through, an abrupt line drawn against the scalp like a growth ring on a tree, exposing a weak moment where you succumbed to vanity. Since you dyed it the chemicals have lightened it; the auburn highlights have disappeared. It looks kind of yellowish. Brassy, your mother would call it. Time to go to a salon and have a cut and colour, she would say, with that complacent little sigh acknowledging the mysterious burden of female duty.

You should leave it there, to grow out. But there is grey amongst the dark hair, a nasty cigarette-ash colour you tell yourself you haven't noticed before. In the privacy of your own bathroom you shake together the contents of two ammonia-smelling bottles of chemicals and cover up those roots. Even as you sit waiting the allotted time, feeling vain and foolish but wanting lustrous highlighted hair for the weekend, you happen to glance in the afternoon light at your neck and see the downy hairs on your chin and throat are silhouetted, and they are dark.

In strong light you can see them perfectly clearly. Another side-effect, just as the contraceptive packet predicted. So, naturally, you grab the tweezers and pull them out. But when you tilt your head into that hard light you see dark hairs coming through on your upper lip, too. Jesus, no. If you start yanking these you'll never be able to stop, you'll be like one of those bristly old women with moustaches, stiff hairs you can feel when you kiss.

So. More vigilance, you think, grimacing. Pluck and cover. Smirking into the mirror, then deciding it's one joke you'll never be able to tell him.

. . .

It's a slippery slope, once you start on it, once you've ignored that knock in the engine for long enough and it starts to miss occasionally as you careen down some hill dazedly gripping the wheel.

At the beach the sun comes out and the sea glitters to the horizon, and Paul is content to sit and watch the surfers for a while. When you're twenty-six, obviously that's what you do, because it's still within the radar range of things you might conceivably try yourself. Then he goes and buys fish and chips and you eat them at a picnic table, everything dazzling and warm. But once that poison has started, once you're committed to giving yourself a measured dose of it every day, nothing's going to be enough. You have traded in your unselfconsciousness for this double-visioned state of standing outside yourself, watchful and tensed for exposure. You will despise yourself for every mouthful and for your insatiable hunger, and you will despise yourself more for breaking away from him as you walk out of the surf to hurry back to your towel to get your sarong and cover up. So that even as he grins at you sitting on the sand and says, 'Isn't this great?', a small, snarling bitter voice will be sounding in the back of your head saying *Yeah. I'm sitting squinting into the sun getting crow's-feet and eating saturated fats. Great.*

Waiting for him to unlock the car to leave, don't, whatever you do, look at your silhouette in the reflection of the car window. It will show you nothing but hard contrast. In the solarised shadow and light, you will see lines on your forehead, and those ones etched between your nose and mouth, the awful twist of discontent. Old harridan lines.

Just get in the car. Put your sunglasses on, and get in the car.

. . .

And later, when he's not watching, feel disgusted scorn for yourself as you try to covertly open your bag and get out the factor-fifteen moisturiser, and put it on. Neck as well as face. Think of all the mornings when you get up and your neck and chest are creased like an old sheet. Jowls. Crepey skin. Turkey neck. Spinster aunt skin. Wonder if he wakes before you, and looks at those creases as you're asleep, exposed, in the bright morning light.

The ever-relentless sun, inescapable, beats down on you through the windscreen.

All those hours you mindlessly lay on your towel in your twenties, and tilted your face up into it, heedless. You look across at his face, and of course he doesn't care, he doesn't need to. He's got years.

Inexorable, this spiral down. Tell him later than no, really you want the light off. Don't say a word about turning forty. When he says he loves you, some reflex from those side-effects will mean you won't let yourself believe it. Censor everything. Swallow the pill. Remember this: let the smallest reference to babies slip, and you can kiss this guy goodbye.

. . .

Funny how the dye seems to have missed the odd grey hairs, which seem stronger and wirier than the others. And the way you only notice them when you can't really lean forward and do anything about them – when you're looking in the mirror of a change room, for example, in a fairly expensive department store on your afternoon off, and the sight of your own cellulite (all those chips!) so disgusts you and saps your energy that you doubt whether you can actually get dressed again and drag yourself out of there, away from that ridiculous lingerie or the jeans you've chosen. Why are you even wasting your time with this guy? Why don't you find someone your own age who might actually be interested in a late bid for last-minute parenthood, someone who might be in for the long haul? You're too pathetic to believe yourself. And just as you grab your hairbrush after changing back into your stupid frump clothes, just as you think for a minute you'll at least brush your hair, you notice in these unforgiving overhead lights those dark roots coming through again already – any fool could see your colour's not natural. Your hair sits lank and dried-out against your head.

You've got to stop this. But you can't help yourself. While you're in the hair salon buying shampoo for colour-treated hair, you find yourself making an appointment for a leg wax. You will be hairless. Forty is the new thirty. You will be smooth, controlled, gym-toned, with the body of a woman in her late twenties, lushly in her prime and way ahead of the game.

And the voice you hear now as you sit in the salon leafing through the magazines before your appointment will be a whiny, accusing one, nitpicking and obsessive, poking you on the shoulder say: *Look, Goldie Hawn, nearly sixty. Look, Sharon Stone, slim and elegant, had a baby at forty-four.*

The receptionist says, 'This your first visit?' Her fingernails are curved like talons, alternately purple and yellow, and you see they are fake and stuck on with superglue. They are so long she can hardly write – but she can hardly write anyway, breathing laboriously as she prints your details in big Grade Five letters. Then into the back room and up onto the crackling paper sheet. Butcher's paper for a slab of meat. You make nervous small talk.

'Do you wax guys?' you blurt.

'All the time.' The girl stirs wax implacably, arranges things on the counter like a dental nurse. 'You'd be surprised.' You lie back. She chats on.

'Guys come in here, want their backs waxed, their arses.'

'You're kidding.'

'Nope. I do everything. You wouldn't believe it. A week before Mardi Gras, or when there's a bike race or the City to Surf, I'm booked out.'

Suddenly there is a hot stroke of wax on your shin, a pause, then blinding pain.

'*Ow.* Jesus.

'Haven't had them done for a while, that's why it hurts more.'

'Actually this is my first time ever.'

'Really? Oh well, it won't take long.'

Another rip that brings tears to your eyes.

'Brazilians are all the go now,' she says. 'You want pain, boy …'

'Don't tell me.'

She tilts your leg, ices on some more wax, rips it away.

'Yep, everything. Completely hairless. Like a Barbie doll.'

You shudder and lie back, willing it to be over. Like having a cavity drilled, you try to take your thoughts away. Paul, and what he would say if he could see you now. Think then about your first argument, the other night. 'Don't tell me what I'm going to do next,' he'd finally fumed. 'And Jesus, will you just relax and stop worrying about your weight? How much reassurance do you need?'

'I don't need reassurance.'

'Yes, you do. It's so bloody tiring. It's like you've already decided to end it and you're just waiting for me to slip up so you can blame me.'

You'd opened and closed your mouth like a stunned fish. A wave of nausea. You'd clenched your jaw, saying nothing. *Don't cry,* you'd ordered yourself, *don't you dare. Mascara running. Haggard. Lines. Ugly. Old.*

'Let's just light a candle then, if you don't want the lamp on,' he'd said later in bed, at his place. And you'd shaken your head, taken the matches from him.

'No,' you'd answered. 'Let's not. Really. I like the dark.'

She's up to your groin and you feel the wax getting daubed around your undies line. She holds the skin taut and pulls. It's excruciating.

'Bloody hell!' you gasp.

'Yeah, the pubic hairs always hurt more – deeper roots.'

'And people have the whole lot ripped out?'

'All the time.'

You look down at the reddened patch and see tiny prick

marks of blood appearing where the hairs have been yanked out. It feels like you've had a layer of skin torn off. Like you've been peeled.

'God, how could they stand it?'

She considers, moving her chewing gum around her mouth. 'They reckon it looks clean.'

'Clean?'

'Sexy. Their boyfriends ask 'em to do it, they say.'

Rip. She's on the other ankle. *Clean*, you think. Prepubescent, more like it. Like pink latex, like a blow-up fantasy doll, that sickly plastic smell of Barbie. The rip across the knee works like a quick, stinging, sobering slap to the face, finally waking you up.

'That'll do,' you hear yourself say.

'But we're only halfway through.' She stops, staring, rotating a glob of slipping yellow wax slowly on the hovering spatula.

'That's okay, I'll pay for the whole thing. I just … that's it.'

'It's not hurting that much, is it?'

You swing your tingling legs off the table and reach for your jeans.

She's looking at you, moving the chewy around in her lip-glossed mouth.

'Okay, then,' she says with a shrug. And, half-finished, like someone released from custody, you're out of there.

. . .

Later that night, there'll be tiny dark patches on your bare legs when you take your jeans off, where wax has stuck spots of lint to the skin, but you will pull a sheet over your legs instead of jumping up instantly and washing it off in the shower. Your energy for subterfuge seems spent now;

like the tank's empty. In the dark, all other senses are more acute; the brush of skin on skin, the scent of hair, a whisper blooming next to you on the pillow; risky secrets that cannot be taken back. You will feel things coast to a stop, sharpened into wakefulness, and steady yourself. You open your mouth and set whatever's coming next in motion.

'I'll be forty in a fortnight,' you say.

Impossible to gauge his real, unadorned reaction to that news. You'll have to turn the light on for that.

. . . . . .

Night Growing Longer Now

ANTHONY LYNCH

*Seven steps towards a divorce –
and none of them easy.*

A. BEFORE FILLING IN THIS FORM

She once heard a theory. Women give their all to a marriage, and when it fails they move on quickly without turning back because they know they did everything they could to make it work. Men don't give their all to marriage, and when it fails they're always looking back. They know they could have done more.

Therefore, after breakup, women are hard and men are soft.

Fran didn't feel hard now. She felt tense rather than hard. She had imagined a crumbling mausoleum with high ceilings, dark panels and a few white wigs, but the building was new and the waiting room a soundproof box. The people, mostly standing for insufficient seats, were depressingly plain. She stood and shuffled her feet on the grey carpet. Closed interview rooms lined one wall, and a small sign on the door before her said *Court*.

She counted eighteen women and two men. The women pursed their lips and occasionally raised their eyebrows briefly at each other. Some dabbed handkerchiefs at their nostrils and smeared their lipstick. A few like her had dressed for business, others wore faded jeans or tracksuit pants that made soup bowls at their knees.

Except for one man and woman who went in together, one by one they entered the court and came out two minutes later. Most looked dazed and unsure whether to be happy or sad, as if they'd had a tooth removed or donated blood.

B. STEP-BY-STEP GUIDE

Three months earlier, Connie had visited Fran's house when the form came in the mail. The house had once been Matt and Fran's, now it was Fran's. They sat in the living area that looked out on the courtyard and the small olive trees becoming inky with night, skimmed the paperwork and read the section on common mistakes when completing the form.

'I've already made a common mistake, that's why I've got the form,' Fran said.

Connie helped her fill it out. 'It costs $574 all up, which you pay when you file. You normally split the cost.' She cleared cups off the table and pushed her hair back behind her ear, read out questions and ticked boxes as Fran answered. When had they last lived as husband and wife? Were they likely to reconcile and live as husband and wife? Fran said the questions were stupid.

They completed the form but Fran needed a witness. 'A JP or solicitor, someone from the old guard.'

Connie drove them to an all-night chemist. A pharmacist with wild, silver eyebrows and who reminded Fran of a priest, read aloud a statement about truth and identity. He looked over his glasses at her while she nodded. He handed her a thick pen with a drug company's name on the side. After they'd signed, Fran bought a packet of antiseptic lozenges.

'You give the form to Matt and provided he agrees, he signs too,' Connie told Fran on the way home. 'Don't just throw it in front of him.'

'I'll post it with a Sign Here tag on the dotted line,' Fran said. 'Okay, I'll have it delivered in person. *You'd* be the right kind of person. You made a good bridesmaid.'

Connie smiled but looked at Fran when they stopped at traffic lights. The red light made the form glow on Fran's lap.

'I don't want a scene, and you'd do it with care,' Fran added. 'Besides, I found a trophy of Matt's I've been meaning to return. A football trophy he won in a tipping competition, his biggest sporting triumph. It won't fit in the postbox.'

The lights changed and they drove another three blocks. At the next red light Connie said she'd deliver it any night except Wednesday, when she had her Italian class. But it was up to Fran to make a time.

'Matt knows you've gone ahead with this?' Connie asked. 'You *have* told him?'

'Thanks Connie, I owe you,' Fran said. 'Matt could really use that trophy.'

C. HOW TO PROCEED

When Fran rang Matt she said she knew it was difficult, but she thought she'd get the ball rolling. She'd got the form and filled out her bit, and he had to check that he agreed and sign too. Connie could drop the form over any night that week.

'I think ... tomorrow.' His voice was small and tight. 'Yes, tomorrow.'

'Tomorrow, that's Wednesday. Connie's busy Wednesdays with a class.'

'So, not *any* night?

'Any night except Wednesday. What about Thursday?' She used the reasonable, pressing voice adults have with children.

Matt said he couldn't wait. Fran told him not to be like that. She knew it was no fun; it was no fun for her either. Matt said she hadn't wasted time.

'Wasting time won't help. Matt, I think for both our sakes it's better to move on.'

He said nothing. Fran sat back on the couch, cradled the cordless between her chin and shoulder and picked at a rough band of skin on her foot. She asked if he was still there, and he made a noise she used to hear when he slept beside her.

'This form, much to it?'

'You put in your details and tick some boxes. Then you sign.'

'That's it?'

'Essentially,' she said, unless he wanted to appear in court in a few months' time, but it wasn't necessary for both of them to go.

There was of course a cost, though it would be free if she were a single parent and filing. He said they'd missed their chance, and she took a breath and said, 'Don't let up, do you?' He asked what the damage was, and she bit her lip for a moment before replying.

'It'll cost $1148 with the Family Court. I thought we could split the cost and that makes your share five hundred and seventy-four.'

'Five seventy-four,' he repeated, as if to jot the figure in his head. He was probably jotting it in a debit column. He had always been particular with figures – a quality she once found endearing, and later infuriating.

'Five seventy-four, if that's all right with you,' she said. She heard him again make the small murmur he used to make when they each turned over in the night.

. . .

D. MARK-THE-BOX OPTIONS

Matt's flat was on the ground floor of a small brown-brick block. Everyone who lived in the block was renting. The light above his door was an inverted dome that looked like a flying saucer, 1950s style.

He offered Connie cask wine. She put the form on the breakfast bar beside the trophy, which had a football player leaping into space with one knee raised to mark the ball. She tried to drop the form beside it lightly, face up but pointing elsewhere. It pointed towards the bathroom.

'You don't have to fill it out now, just when you're ready. Give me a call and I'll collect it. Or just post it to Fran.'

Matt picked up the form and looked at its boxy green face. He flicked through the pages. The ticks were not Fran's but at the end was her signature, leaning forward into the future. He said he might as well do it now. There were enough instructions.

'To confuse you,' she said. 'Most you can ignore. I helped Fran with her bit so I can help with yours if you want. That's what friends are for.'

He reached for a pen. 'And that trophy?'

'That's what I use if you refuse to sign.'

He leant on a magazine and jotted answers. Connie gave advice when he flicked to the instructions. He nodded and ticked boxes. His ticks fell in the same boxes as Fran's except for the question about whether he wanted to attend court, where Fran had answered for him already.

He was fine without her help, so Connie took her drink and strolled around the living room, which was tidy but bare. There was not enough furniture and silverfish had fed on the curtains. She leant against the breakfast bar while he worked on the form as if sitting an exam. He reached the affidavit.

'I need a witness,' he said, and lifted his eyes toward her. 'Have you become a JP by chance?'

'I'm just the messenger,' she said, and drained her glass. 'But I have my contacts.'

The pharmacist raised his wild eyebrows at Connie when they entered.

'Making a business of this?' he asked.

'Commission basis,' she said.

He read out his statement. Matt said yes and signed while a woman waiting for a prescription coughed heavily. She had a small boy who gave a red ball an exploratory bounce. The boy's hair was dark and wavy, like Fran's. The pharmacist put his signature above where he'd signed three nights before. He had the same pen. Hair grew on the back of his fingers.

Matt drove home with his seat back, his arms straight and his elbows locked while his large hands guided the wheel.

'Brave face,' Connie said.

Matt said not at all, that things could get you down but often you didn't realise how much until they were gone. 'So it's true you don't know what you've got until it's gone, but sometimes what you had wasn't good.'

She wanted to see Matt's face properly, but he kept his eyes on the road and clenched his teeth as he stared ahead. He drove a little faster, as if he'd quietly decided the best way home. The dashboard before Connie ducked in and out of shadow.

When they got to his flat Matt said he had something for her. He went inside while she waited beneath the flying saucer light, cloudy with insects. He returned and gave her an envelope.

'Don't worry, it's a cheque to go with the form.' He tapped the form with the envelope. 'Paying my share.'

She kissed him on the cheek. As she walked to her car the door behind her closed, and the light from the flying saucer receded.

E. LODGING YOUR APPLICATION

Fran said the best thing about a bust-up was the tingling you got afterwards.

'It's like when you bang your knee on a table and it hurts like hell. But when the pain fades, you get warmth where the pain had been.'

Connie handed her the completed form. She said that maybe it wasn't a bust-up but a relationship reaching natural closure.

'We have options, and sometimes after a number of years – was it eight? – we choose another option. Or the choice in a sense is made for us, we reach our end.' She turned to face the window, as if those years were passing by out there. She saw their reflections in the glass.

'Seven-and-a-half years too many,' Fran said. She'd cut her hair and applied orange lipstick and to Connie, in the glass, it made her face look bigger.

Fran sent the form by registered mail. She sent it from the main post office, as if to ensure its safe arrival, then walked to the waterfront and entered one of the new cafés overlooking the water. She ordered house white. On the bay beyond the fishing boats whose days seemed numbered, wind clipped the tops off short waves. She sat behind a large window and her coat fell open when she crossed her legs.

Her fingertips broke the frost on the wineglass. Her hands were clear now. Three years into their marriage eczema had begun its journey around her hands and wrists, expanding in small patches that threatened her upper arms and torso.

The day Matt left, it began its retreat. Within two months it was gone.

The wine warmed her. Her legs tingled. On the far side of the bay, an empty cargo ship stood with its hull exposed. Kids rode by on bikes but the fishing boats barely nodded. She would drop him a line as the curtain fell.

And the legalities would cost her nothing. She had seen to that. At some level, he owed her. She did not feel guilty.

On the way to the car she passed a shoe shop. She went inside, pointed at a brown leather slip-on in the window and asked for size 7. They were Italian, simple but with style. She put the caress of new leather on her credit card.

The shop assistant placed her old shoes in the box, and Fran wore the new shoes home. She had always wanted to do that.

F. HELP IN OTHER LANGUAGES

Three months later, at work, he got her email. Her address jumped out at him, as it had once done often and happily. There was nothing in the subject box. After one paragraph confirming the inevitable, she signed *Regards*.

He hated regards, or regards from her. When he'd left the house, the home in which they had plotted their future, planted olive trees, upgraded the kitchen, made love, argued and grown silent, she signed correspondence over separation, property, divorce and the power bill with *Regards*. It was part of her hardening. Her *calcification*. He liked that word and the idea of her heart turning to bone while he, the bean counter, grew soft.

When he received her emails he wanted to send back an electronic scream. He would begin a heated reply, then delete the incomplete message. It was business, so he too signed with regards or with nothing. Once he weakened and signed *Yours always*, but she maintained *Regards*, a form he resumed.

This time he closed the email and rose from his desk, walked past the office reception and through two sets of doors, squinted in the sunlight and shoved his hands in his pockets. He walked without breaking stride.

In the evening he opened a beer and surfed TV channels before killing the sound. He finished the beer and the room darkened quickly with night growing longer now. The TV flung lightning on the walls, and mute actors laughed and frowned on screen.

He trudged to the fridge and foraged for food, pulled out more beer and returned to the lounge. He half closed his eyes and blurred the actors' faces on screen. If he closed them enough, he couldn't tell whether the actors were laughing or crying.

He opened his eyes fully and Fran stared back from the screen eating a chocolate bar – a woman just like Fran, stripping the wrapper from the bar. An untidy strand of hair fell across her face, the same as it had always done before she calcified. A man Matt had never seen before came from behind and bit the bar. Fran snatched it away, and together they fell laughing out of vision.

He remembered when she had, finally, tumbled out of sight. He had told her there'd been someone, briefly. She had stared at him a moment before she said she'd had enough, perhaps they'd both had enough. She said it tiredly, as if she'd realised a plate of pasta was too much or the old fridge had to go.

And he had said okay. He hadn't meant okay but the word floated off his tongue, came out on a reflex. He said it again. They stood there as if they both thought they should say more, but they didn't. His lips went numb, and he had turned to his room and closed the door.

He finished the beer, went to the toilet and washed at the basin. He dried his hands and saw himself in the mirror, shadows spreading around his eyes and his mouth hanging open – vacant, stupid, devoid of answers. He kicked the wall before him. He was wearing boots and he kicked again, delivering short, sharp stab kicks until the green plaster in his bathroom gave.

A small hole opened in the wall near the floor. He went to the living room and collected his trophy, returned to the bathroom and got down on his knees. He nudged at the plaster, pushed the footballer's head into the dark space inside.

G. DECLARATION

She did not feel hard now, except in her throat where a small lump made swallowing more difficult than it should be.

She was third last. The registrar was a woman in a black smock who looked up briefly when Fran entered. Behind the registrar hung a silver coat of arms and beneath her, facing Fran, sat a white-haired man in a navy suit. Fran gave her name. The registrar said okay and read Fran's papers. She checked whether Matt had agreed to the proceedings, and if changes had occurred since they'd lodged the form. She asked questions partly of Fran and partly of herself, it seemed, and Fran offered an occasional yes or no.

'Looks to be in order,' the registrar said. She delivered what Fran took to be regulation patter. As with the priest at their wedding, her voice rose and fell in the rhythms of sleep.

The registrar declared something on behalf of the government. Fran heard her and Matt's names. 'Matthew,' the registrar called him, as Fran had sometimes called him in the early days. 'Dissolved,' the registrar said. The cancellation stamp of her gavel echoed in the room.

She thanked the registrar and left. She stood for a moment in the waiting area. The next woman was called. Fran made as if to rummage for her keys and sunglasses. She had, mentally, allowed all morning for the court, and she wished now that Connie and all her tact were waiting for her on one of the grey chairs.

Fran made her way out but went the wrong way. So she turned right and followed the daylight calling from the hallway, walked through the foyer and out glass doors. The sea air was nudging autumn leaves from trees on the street.

She walked down the street and waited at the lights where new apartments were rising on the opposite corner. She knew the streets backwards but today, entered from the court, they looked different. Even the traffic was quieter. Then a man on a motorbike unzipped the silence, racing through the lights as they changed to red.

. . . . . .

In Shadows

BILL COLLOPY

Ali, a boat person, risks his life for the land of opportunity – and ends up in a cage.

In a mirror of steel the eyes look crazy. He washes his face with water tea-brown. Like a knife Ali holds his anger, telling himself that maybe he only dreams this secret city.

Sunlight stripes his wrists, from bars. Spider webs make nets. Four beds jam together, blankets thin as paper.

Ali grips his knife unseen. They have no right.

. . .

Old Yusuf looks sick yellow. He cannot get out of bed, his pillow a pool of tears. Chewing fingernails, the old man speaks only to say *salat*. Yusuf clutches his *Qur'an* with thumbs flat as a carpenter's pencil, tilting his head as if listening to notes from the page. In the yard sometimes he sings. With him a granddaughter sits, picking lice from his hair.

. . .

Ali must do something besides hate.

On his wall hangs a calendar, one year out of date. He makes the calculation, keeping track of days. He's somewhere in a place of shadows, dying one day at a time, folded into back streets of a city. This country he knows only from pictures. He has not seen a kangaroo.

The room has a radio. Voices in English make jokes and offer to sell things that Ali would not buy even if he needed them. Four nations squeeze into this room. Radio callers cannot know his anger.

. . .

Calculation tells Ali he has been in a cage ten months and, before that, another cage in wilderness where the guards would wave at flies. He gave his mother's money to a man who promised to help, who smuggled him to Pakistan and then a plane to Indonesia. Ali thought the Muslim country would be his new home. Instead he hid from police in shadows. At last the fishing boat sailed, one hundred believers trusting God and the men with guns. He prayed for rescue from waves big as mountains. He saw fishing boat pirates unable to get closer than a man's shout because of current. Rain soaked the boat. He tipped closer to God. A little girl died. Her mother begged to die too. Men dirtied, losing their shame.

. . .

In the hidden city there is a library but Ali has no interest in books of crime or Christian romance in English, though he can read and write the language. Each day other men ask him to translate from a newspaper. They want to know what is happening outside. He turns pages, reading words he knows and puzzling over others he does not. Ali has found no writing about a secret city behind factory streets. He reads letters to the editor. Often these anger the men. People who live in houses and walk to shops write about fairness, using the words *Muslim* and *Arab* as if these are the same. Australians do not understand what separates the prisoners and what unites them. They do not see behind concrete. They speak another country, with free speech and libraries. They treat their animals better than they treat Ali. His shadow thins. He is beginning to forget shapes of home.

. . .

Red in their faces and blue in their eyes, the guards watch Ali and friends seated alone or in pairs. Groups are not allowed. He studies diamond shadows made by wire fence, like a mosaic in cement, and overhears talk from the guards. They work for a company that supplies warders to prisons.

. . .

If his counting is correct, it is two years since he landed. Sailors plucked him from a boat already sinking. He had no papers but he was stronger. He had muscle. Now his brothers would not know him. At home they were arrested and jailed, one by one. His mother knew what would happen to Ali. With two friends from school he ran. They stole bikes and horses. Ali sometimes wonders where his friends finished: in America maybe, or England, where cricket is played.

. . .

He used to dream of leaving home to travel. He studied English and he studied computers. He can use the PC in the common room but it is off-line. He plays solitaire. He listens to guards talk. They fear that the prisoners might communicate with terrorists or learn how to make a bomb out of vegetables and spoons. Fat mouths mutter. Stomachs bulge behind belts.

Ali is beginning to disappear. Some days he forgets boyhood, and the faces of his father and his brothers. It is so wrong. He writes in English, a private shadow. If guards discover it, they will find only thoughts that refuse prison.

In sadness we make, he writes. *That is nature. A woman can not give birth with out sufering. And i pray for freedom but our city is hiden like my words keeping dark in a place under a floor tile the crack invisable. Words look hard and thin like my arms. Words need air too for breathing. So i make this record. May be i hope for a reader even if just a gaurd. They can not lock up words*

. . .

With Iranians and Sunnis he sits at peace in the exercise yard. They pray together, giving worship to God and thanks to the Prophet Mohammed. *Peace be unto him,* writes Ali. At home he would not speak with a Sunni. He might pass robed men beating a woman or bending on prayer mats or punishing children. Here he shares a shadow. Hope beats outside, in the wings of a bird. Men keep hate behind their eyes.

. . .

Not all stay silent. Some burn like a steam kettle, spitting and hissing. Their arms look hard as rifles.

One, a proud spirit called Hamid, tried organising a breakout. He fell tangled in wire, setting off alarms. From hospital the guards brought Hamid back, locking him in the solitary wing. He might still be there, or in a desert jail, or with God. Ali feels the shame of silence.

. . .

He has not yet taken pills but other men do. Doctors give them out, to keep men calm, to help with sleeping. Some collect their pills and hide them away, for a time when they have given up all hope. Anger pulls his soul like a glassmaker, puffing and stretching. He cools but he will smash easily.

If the doors suddenly flew open he could not go home. Where Ali was born, young Hazara are being forced to clear land mines. Those who refuse are shot. That is not a life.

. . .

From mouths of children he hears English words. There is no school, only TV. Some kick a football on the brown lawn but most are too sad. Girls watch TV or pray. Outside the shadow city other girls play on real grass. They sit in classrooms. Ali has seen them on TV. They walk without an uncle or brother at their side. Some even sleep with men that are not their husbands, if TV stories are true. Newspapers forget. Letter writers forget. They talk about Iraq and Olympics.

. . .

One boy cut his wrists. Ali and some others saved him. The boy watches TV at night. He sleeps all day. Another tried to hang himself but the cord was not strong enough. He cannot talk. Dangling from sharp wire hangs a hat stolen from a guard. In the wind it moves, out of reach. Ali watches a shiny band catching sunlight, like laughing.

. . .

His boat would not last another day at sea, up and down. A devil drank and spewed ocean. A metal shell stank of petrol and seasickness. He blinked away flies until he was almost blind. The sun rose, sometimes a colour of blood, sometimes in a sky cracked silver and black. He talked to fish, to stars. He thought the moon was a coin of fire. He thought a boat was following. There were pirates. He screamed. They were coming for him. Another man hit him in the face, saying he talked crazy. Ali could not cry when a baby died. A woman wrapped it to bury the body overboard. They had no Imam. An older man said prayers, calling on the Prophet. They held down the mother, who rocked in madness. Then Ali was blinking at white uniforms of Navy men who arrived as the boat began to sink. Other men, in dark uniforms, took him to a helicopter. Soldiers searched him above the clouds. Ali fainted, too weak to stand. When his eyes opened he was in a bus, driving towards jail.

...

We have no future, he writes. *On the floor is a spill of human heart.*

...

Guards begin the muster. Men shuffle outside, standing washed in the rain of God's tears. Guards search rooms. They do not find his words. A city stays secret.

...

Another day, another search. Old Yusuf collapses. Guards take him to hospital, locked in handcuffs. He has done nothing but to come without permission. From what Ali reads in newspapers, he believes they do not mean to be cruel. But already he hates this land. His friends learn to hate one another.

...

A boy stole a knife from the kitchen then spent weeks in the solitary wing. Where Ali grew up, that boy would have lost his hands. Guards say he is lucky. In the hidden city there is a doctor but no one has told the guards. Aref escaped home because he would not cut off the hands of thieves. His children were bullied. Men spat on his friends. He ran with his wife and daughters. Aref's eyes flutter when he speaks. He worries what might happen to his parents.

Our secret city is a dying man, writes Ali. *Its halls are narrow. we have no trade. The harvest is people. China and Somalia. India and Syria. Palestinian Cambodian Turk. Kept alive by anger. Waiting results of appeal to the minister.*

. . .

Through iron window stripes he's seeing another city: clock towers, spires and green parks. Smoke twists from rooftops behind an empty depot and razor wire. The room sleeps four men. For a time there was a boy but little Abdul had to go back to the desert. His crying kept the men awake. Abdul saw his mother die in a football stadium, executed for letting her hair be seen. His father escaped, only to die beside the boy at sea. Ali prays for Abdul, growing to be a man inside cages.

. . .

Elbows dig a ridge on his window. The building he watches must be apartments. A young man with eyeglasses plays a flute. Another rides a bike to nowhere. A third makes love to women. Ali sees distant shapes leaving to walk the city or ride bicycles to real places. Men drive cars and sit in public libraries. Ali is learning to despise his English.

. . .

Ears trick him. He thought he heard a *muezzin* lifting up the voice for *adhan*, calling the faithful to perform *salat.* Unrolling mats, they bend like reeds in the wind. But it's only a bell for evening meal, an electric sob.

Ali moves his spoon around a plastic plate: boiled meat fit for dogs. The fruit is turning black. The bread has blue spots. He will not eat rice that crawls.

some try to starve, he writes. that is giving in. i eat if it is food. not dog scraps. i tell the men what gaurds say. a company manages us. we keep costs down. i hear gaurds talk how the jails makes a profit but pays men wages. we are the margin for profits. goverment pays a company to keep us hiden.

On the wall someone has flung coffee. Its stain curls like a smile. Ali grins back.

. . .

Some days all he hears are the stories of other men. When he reads the newspaper for them, this is his only true meal. Men assist by holding his paper open.

Ali says they are part of a movement, running from persecution. Men try to convince him that living in fear at home is better than sitting in prison at the bottom of the world.

not easy to bring light in the head of a sad man. some are all ready crazy. one killed himself with a razor. i hear the stories of brothers and freinds hiding in ship containers. lucky ones choke. stories come like words on the pages. i try to write with out tears for women who cling to underneath of jets and children tied to ropes under a floor of trains. i can not stop these stories. but i start to forget who i am. where i come from. rooms of home sink in shadow of other men.

. . .

Smugglers warned that he could not go out. He spent days in Sumatra without fresh air and wept for people he had not loved enough. Police were looking for him and the others. The escape route had to be changed. Ali began to vanish.

. . .

Through window bars his dust is a waterfall. There's a church steeple, a school bell and loudspeakers, but it's too far to make out words. Some nights he hears music. He imagines the dancing and alcohol and fighting. He hears football crowds and ambulance sirens and roadworks. One day there was excitement in the yard when a helicopter began descending to a platform. Cheering turned to panic. What if men were seen in photos? They hid their faces from satellite pictures, which could be used to torment family. Shadows crept from sleeves to shield the beards and eyes.

. . .

From a north wall he hears market day sounds. Breeze dies, trapped in the wire. He wonders what could happen if each prisoner shouted a great word louder than guard noises and the electric bell.

When wind blows he breathes in the cooking smells: fried onion and forbidden meats. Ali has cloud for a garden.

. . . . . .

HOMELANDS

The Romance of Steam

IAN CALLINAN

How do you feed 300 hungry women on a 33-hour wartime train trip from Sydney to Brisbane?

I know that time is fleeting but yet some days I have too much of it. It is then that I read the papers line by line. Today is the day for the lifestyle supplements. How curious it is that each paper has a supplement on the same topic on the same day; education on Monday: IT on Tuesday, motoring on Wednesday; leisure on Thursday; and lifestyle on Friday. The lifestyle supplement is certainly not pitched at my age group. I suppose it does truly reflect the way the fashionable live now even if occasionally I have my doubts: all those acid colours we used in the fifties; stainless steel kitchens, and I see that polished timber floors are making a comeback, although the articles read as if they were recent inventions.

There were two articles in particular that had attracted my attention. The first was about nouvelle cuisine. It was accompanied by pictures of exquisitely arranged tiny portions of meats cooked rare bounded on the plate by arabesques of lime or mango sauce. The other was entitled 'The Romance of Steam'. It was about journeys across continents before the days of diesel and electric locomotives, and the pictures were of streamlined engines with highly polished brass fittings, and uniformed drivers who might have been outfitted by a Saville Row tailor. I could have told their authors some home truths about food and steam trains. Inevitably that thought led to others, ones that hadn't crossed my mind in a long time.

I got up, as always these days, not without difficulty, and went out to the verandah to try to find some privacy. A shortage of it was just another of the deprivations to be endured at my age and in this place. On my Richter scale of complaints it ranks just below the regular assaults on my dignity, not just by poorly trained female nurses, but also by male nurses, who, in my opinion have no place in the bathroom when a woman is showering.

I found a chair at the far end. Perhaps my crusade for solitude was beginning to triumph. There was no one sitting nearby. I looked out on to the small garden, more pavers and pot plants than grass and trees.

I could hardly believe that the events of which the articles reminded me had happened sixty years ago: the month September 1943, early September, and the place Sydney Central Railway Station.

I was twenty-one and a sergeant in the WAAFs. I was the only woman in my muster who had received a tertiary education. That must have been the reason why I had been made an NCO. I had no ambitions for promotion although the extra pay was useful. And for practical matters, mechanics and servicing, the sort of work most of us would be expected to do, I had little aptitude. I had enlisted the day I learned that I had qualified as a teacher.

We had finished our preliminary training and been posted to Queensland. Seventy of us were to travel to Bundaberg where an Empire Air Training Base had been established, and the others were to join a new muster in Brisbane for posting to Townsville, Cairns and Rockhampton.

So there we were, two hundred and ninety-four, not quite pristine young WAAFs full of zeal, lined up on Sydney Central Interstate Platform Number 4. Few of us had ever travelled interstate before. I didn't envy the only commissioned officer, Flying Officer Randall, who was to accompany us on the journey.

She called me over, 'The train's late pulling in'. Of course it was late. I didn't say that though. She should have known far better than I that they always were in those days. 'I can't get any satisfaction out of the station-master' she said. 'Have you spoken to the RTO?' I asked. 'There's no-one in his office' she replied.

Her voice was laboured. For the first time I looked at her closely. She was a heavy woman, and seemed to be in some discomfort. 'Are you all right Ma'am?' I asked.

I just need to sit down for a moment' she said. 'Tell the girls they can stand easy, but don't dismiss them. God only knows where they'll end up if you do that.'

I helped her to a bench and then ordered the squad to stand easy. I went back to FO Randall. She was holding her stomach and was obviously in pain. Unnecessarily I told her not to move and went off to try to find some assistance. I went to the ticket office. That was hopeless. There was a long queue, and only one clerk in attendance. I approached a uniformed ticket inspector. He was unhelpful. He had to board the Broken Hill Express which was due to leave in five minutes.

I stood in the middle of that great cavern of a railway station as soldiers, sailors and airmen milled around. Shunting engines and coupling carriages added to the noise and confusion. Swathes of sooty air condensed above me and clouded the domed ceiling painted with elegant ladies partaking of Schweppes mineral waters spouting from tiered fountains. I particularly remember the condensation. Spring was late that year. It was a cold night but not cold enough I thought, for the dark blue Air Force greatcoat that the officer coming towards me was wearing. I think it was the greatcoat that attracted my attention. Perhaps it was his age. He seemed to be the only old Air Force officer in the precincts.

I dashed up to him. Everything about him was neat and meticulous. His hair, as onyx-black as his gleaming shoes, was carefully parted. He carried himself very erect. His greatcoat had been recently pressed and fitted him perfectly. He was holding a kitbag. It had been packed so that there were no wrinkles in it. Close up I could see that his eyes were dark brown. I could tell from the yellowish tinge of his skin that he must have recently served in the islands and taken the Atebrin that all servicemen were required to take as a prophylactic against malaria. He could have been anything between thirty-five and forty, on any view too old to be a mere Flying Officer. Only later did I come to realise that unless a man was young enough to be in air crew, or so old as to have been in the Citizens Air Force at the outbreak of the war, promotion was slow and limited.

As coherently as I could I told him my problem. In a few words he explained that he was in fact the officer in charge of our train. Mere women, no matter their rank, could NOT possibly command a train in those days. He took charge immediately. 'Go back to the platform. Tell your officer I'll find her a doctor. There must be some Leading Aircraftswomen in your squad. Put each of them in charge of a group. Tell the engine driver when the train comes in – if it does', he added pessimistically. 'The driver may have to wait.'

I saluted and hurried back to the platform. As I did a voice, I think it was his, insistently called over the public address system, upon any doctor at the station, military or civilian, to attend an emergency on Interstate Platform Number 4.

Flying Officer Randall was still doubled up on the seat.

I tried to comfort her but there was nothing I could do. Fortunately, within five minutes a doctor, a civilian, arrived. It took him only a few minutes to diagnose appendicitis. By then, Flying Officer Lincoln, the officer in the greatcoat, had taken charge. He helped the doctor place FO Randall on a trolley and told three of the girls to push it out to the street. In the meantime the doctor arranged for an ambulance.

It was now nine o'clock. The train, which had been due to leave at that hour had still not pulled into the station. None of us had eaten since lunch and I could see girls flitting away to look for food.

'When did you last have something to eat?' Lincoln asked. When I told him he said he would see what he could do. Leaving his kitbag with me he strode off to return empty handed.

'It's always the same. The RTO's out, the station master's too important to be bothered with a detail like food, and the refreshment room is bolted.'

It was then that our train came into the station and the assistant station master appeared. He was, I would have guessed, about the same age as Lincoln, but his uniform wasn't clean and pressed, or his shoes shiny. Even his gait gave an impression of officiousness. When he reached us Lincoln inquired about food.

'Too late for that', the official was pleased to reply. For a moment I thought he might add, 'There's a war on you know'.

'These girls have been a long time without food. It's not their fault the train's late,' Lincoln said.

'Nor mine. Troop trains, goods trains, Yank trains, not enough coal, derailments, schedules changing all the time, shortage of rolling stock, and you say you've got problems.' He moved to turn away.

Lincoln tapped him on the shoulder. The two men were about the same height. They glared at each other for a few moments. Lincoln raised his voice. 'What about some tea? If there's one thing that there ought to be in a railway station it's hot water. Surely you can rake up some tea'. He turned to me then. 'Go and see the driver. Ask him whether he can give us some boiling water, enough for about three hundred people.'

I didn't know how he had done it, but when I came back Lincoln was holding half a dozen packets of Bushell's tea. 'We'll need to ration it, and the girls will have to share the glasses.' By then he had had the girls scavenge some buckets and bring the glasses, which were in each of the compartments, on to a trestle table he had them set up on the platform.

About half the girls had had tea by the time the assistant station master reappeared. 'This train must leave, now,' he said. He stamped his foot for emphasis. 'The rest will just have to forego their tea'.

Lincoln had taken off his greatcoat. He seemed to be shivering but I could see that he was perspiring heavily. There weren't too many of us who by then were not familiar with the symptoms of malaria. 'Is there anything I can do sir?' I asked. I don't think he heard me.

He addressed the railway official. 'You tell them', he said and indicated the WAAFs who were still waiting for some tea.

'Ten minutes then, that's all'. Everyone had finished their tea an hour and a half before the train left at a quarter to midnight. FO Lincoln was allotted a compartment to himself. He told me to take the adjoining one which had been allocated to FO Randall. They were luxurious by comparison with the carriages for the enlisted women. Their seats were bench seats, but there were armrests for each passenger. The walls were panelled in indigenous woods, and were decorated with faded sepia photographs of the wonders of the Jenolan Caves and the beaches of New South Wales.

After the train pulled out I knocked on the door of FO Lincoln's compartment. Having lost one officer I was anxious not to lose another. He beckoned me in. When I saluted he told me not to bother about that. He invited me to sit down. I asked whether there was anything I could get him. He had his greatcoat back on but he seemed to be perspiring less. 'Malaria?' I asked. He nodded. 'Are the girls all settled?' I laughed at that. Two hundred and ninety-four hungry women on the greatest adventure of their lifetimes: how could they be?

'The thing to watch out for is alcohol', he said. 'Even if some of them are used to it, there'll be many who aren't. Otherwise, so long as they don't start wrecking the train or fighting, it doesn't much matter what they do. Now, have you seen any of the railway staff? There should be a porter and an inspector. Refer them to me if you do. It's not worth your while arguing with them.'

I couldn't help asking the question, 'Food Sir, when do you think we might get some?'

'Sergeant?' He asked me my name and then continued, 'Sergeant Hollis, this is the third time I've done this trip. Once the girls were able to share fifty or so meat pies at Newcastle, and the other time we got some soggy bread rolls at Casino before the station master could shut down the refreshment room. I'll do my best, but I can't promise anything. Try to sleep if you can.'

Laboriously the train passed through the outer suburbs of Sydney and entered a dark world fleetingly illuminated by the flames of the old engine. No one thought by then that we would lose the war, but in most places there was still a blackout. The windows of the train had been painted black but I doubted whether the single dull light from my compartment would have been visible from fifteen thousand feet up anyway. Nonetheless I turned it off before I pulled down my window, for the compartment seemed to be heating up. A gust of hot soot with one piece still incandescent flew into the compartment. Even now, I can still feel the grit of it on the seat and in my hair. I pushed the window up as hard as I could. But a gap of about an inch or so remained so that, throughout that night, sprays of coal dust, and cold air swirled around me.

I must have fallen asleep. It was four-thirty by my watch. I was awoken by a tap on my door. I turned on the light. It was FO Lincoln, greatcoated and as neatly groomed as when I had first seen him. 'I should make an inspection,' he said. 'Check whether there are any problems. You'd better come with me.' He must have sensed how untidy I felt. 'I'll come back in ten minutes.'

When I had combed my hair and straightened my uniform I told him I was ready. 'I wouldn't like,' he said, 'to surprise the girls. You go ahead. Tell them I'll be along a few minutes after you.'

As a feminist, a seasoned veteran of the great battles of the sixties, the seventies and the eighties, I understand well the difference between feminism and femininity. It was into a seething mass of the latter that I descended as I made my way down the corridors of that sooty train: girls in various stages of undress, washed underclothing hanging out to dry, dozing girls, angry girls, card-playing girls, singing girls, shrill girls, and long queues for the few rest rooms still functioning. I warned them of the officer's approach. Their preoccupation was the same as mine: food, tea, orange juice, anything edible or drinkable. Some of the girls with clothes unbuttoned made perfunctory efforts to cover up. Some didn't bother at all.

When he entered the first carriage I called out 'Attention!' 'As you were,' he said, cancelling the order. 'Any complaints?' he asked. He was answered by shouts of protest, almost all about the absence of food. 'I can't promise anything,' he said. 'But I'll try. Have you seen a porter or inspector?' Nobody had.

Right at the end of the train there was a small carriage with the entrance door to it locked. Lincoln knocked on the door. There was no reply. He knocked again. Still there was no response. He took his gloves out of his greatcoat pocket, put them on, and hammered hard with his clenched fists. At last the door opened.

The two uniformed railway officials in the small carriage looked unhappy at the intrusion. One was rubbing sleep out of his eyes. Behind him there was a comfortable couch with a blanket on it. There were bread, cheese, butter and a teapot on the small table under the window. 'I would like to know when and where we'll be stopping before breakfast,' Lincoln asked.

The inspector laughed. 'Breakfast! Do you know how far we've travelled?'

'Not very far I assume.'

'About a hundred miles. Soon we'll be pulling into a siding to let a troop train through.'

'This is a troop train,' Lincoln said.

The inspector laughed again. 'Call those women troops? That'll be the day.'

Lincoln looked him up and down. 'These women are volunteers, much more than can be said for people hiding out in reserved occupations. I'm in Compartment J, Carriage 1.'

'I know where you are.'

'Then you'll have no trouble finding me after you've had a chance to get a signal through to the next town where the station has a refreshment room.'

As we returned to our end of the train Lincoln told me of his previous battles with the railways. 'I have never been an emotional person,' he said. 'In fact I am renowned for my patience. But in all the world there is nobody more provocative than a man in a reserved occupation wearing a uniform.'

He asked me to sit with him for a time. To emphasize his innocent intentions he told me had had a son my age. He was not the kind of person to take from his wallet, as most of us did in those days, photographs of his family. 'He's just joined up. He wants to be an air gunner. For God's sake. I saw what happened to them when I was overseas. Air gunners! His mother's distraught. What are you in civilian life Sergeant?' he asked.

When I told him he said, 'That's a good career.' I was not to know then that I would move on after the war to become a professor of Women's Studies, marry, have no children, divorce and become, as the current cliché holds, an icon of the women's movement.

'Yourself, Sir, what were you before the war?'

'An accounts clerk.'

I could see he did not want to talk about it but I couldn't help wondering whether, like so many others, he had been a casualty of the depression forced to work, when work was available, at something beneath his ability. He began to doze off. I returned to my compartment. The cold pre-dawn air was still circulating through it. I took a sweater from my kitbag and put it on.

I started to lose track of time. We were sidelined for three hours as two long troop trains trundled north. The train stopped four other times, for water, for coal, and for other mysterious reasons. Everyone was ravenous. Some of the girls were hysterical. Lincoln seemed to be everywhere: here consoling, there firmly counselling, but always a reassuring presence: 'There's a chance at Casino,' he said. 'It has a big railway refreshment room. It's an important railway junction.'

It took twenty-seven hours to reach Casino. Our spirits rose as the train rolled to a standstill at the platform. There were lights on in both the waiting rooms and the refreshment room. Lincoln instructed us to button our uniforms and line up. He addressed us.

'We are all service-people,' he said. 'We conduct ourselves in an orderly way, unless I indicate otherwise that is. I know you're all exhausted and starving. I'm going to make sure you eat. Now remain in line at ease.'

The RTO's office was closed. Lincoln peered through the windows of the refreshment room. There were waitresses dressed in white still in there. He unsuccessfully tried the door before heading for the stationmaster's office. The stationmaster emerged before Lincoln reached his office. They met, spoke, and turned round to walk towards us. Only when they were halfway along the lines of WAAF's did Lincoln stop. He said in a loud voice, 'You're telling me that the food in the refreshment room is being kept for the Sydney express which is due in two hours?'

'Those are my orders. Just because you're in uniform doesn't mean that civilians have no rights.'

'These girls haven't eaten for more than a day.' Even now I can find nothing offensive in his calling us girls. We had in a sense all become his daughters. His next move did nothing to diminish that.

'I've done a lot of travelling, all of it involuntary, over the last two and a half years. It's possible to tolerate delays, shortages and sheer incompetence, but bloody-minded officiousness, no. I've got about three-hundred starving but still fit young women I've promised a meal. I'll give you sixty seconds to open up the refreshment room. If not, I'm going to turn them loose.' He raised his voice again. 'I'm not going to order them to break down the doors, but I wouldn't be surprised if they do. Squad, attention, about turn.' We were directly facing the refreshment room now. Lincoln pulled back his sleeve and ostentatiously consulted his wristwatch.

The station master was momentarily speechless. 'You can't get away with this.' At last he growled, 'I'll see you court martialled.' Lincoln looked up from his watch. 'Ten seconds to go.' The station master took out a key and opened the refreshment room. Lincoln ordered me to dismiss the squad and turned away.

We streamed into the refreshment room. The waitresses welcomed us. Most of them were middle-aged. Nothing that they could find was denied us. That tea, and those two soggy cheese and tomato bread rolls I had, were the best rea and rolls I've ever had.

After I had eaten I took two sausage rolls and a mug of tea to FO Lincoln. He was seated in the men's waiting room, as usual, in his greatcoat and shivering. He thanked me profusely for the food. 'Have they all eaten? If so, would you get them out on to the platform?' He laughed. 'I'm rather anxious to get out of town.'

We arrived in Brisbane, in daylight, thirty-three hours after we had left Sydney. We were met by WAAF Flight Lieutenant. She and Lincoln saluted each other. He handed her some documents. I heard him say, 'They're all yours now.' He called out to us, 'Goodbye and good luck!'

Spontaneously we clapped and cheered him. Those who could, let out some wolf whistles. We completely ignored the Flight Lieutenant's injunction to be quiet.

Well, there's been a good deal of water under the bridge since then. But as I sit here in my retirement home, retired warrior of the sex wars, or as they say now, the gender wars, I often wonder what happened to Flying Officer Lincoln, just as I wonder what my life would have been like had we been closer in age, and he not the old-fashioned gentleman that he was.

Anyway you can see why an article about food and the romance of steam make me think of the past.

. . . . . .

Driving the Inland Road

JULIE GITTUS

The trip to their bush-block paradise turns sour.

Zac and I are driving the inland road from South to North. Our truck's lights shine on the red reflector triangles, each one springing out from the darkness to guide our way. The vibration of the steering wheel is making my wrists ache. After a thousand kilometres of driving I've learnt there's no comfortable place to grip yet I keep sliding my hands round the thin, slippery surface. I'm tired and I wish Zac could drive but he can't because he lost his licence for speeding on his motorbike. He's playing the harmonica. I can just make him out in the dimness. His bare feet are resting on the dashboard as he sucks and blows. He's practising blues tunes, bending the notes and thumping his heels against the glovebox to beat up a rhythm. Sometimes he sings between riffs and I join in.

Our pace is slow as our truck crawls up the Tablelands. The music stops and so does the heater. My hands aren't cold, just numb. I know in the light they would look pale, almost translucent. I squeeze the steering wheel, trying to bring back the blood. It doesn't help. Up here we are very close to the stars. I tell Zac we are driving under a bowl of stars. He says no, the sky is freckled with them. I say no, no – they're actually millions of pearls that have escaped their string and then he tells me we're driving under a bower of stars and I say never – it's not a bower – we're little chicks under a speckled hen of sky. He laughs and slaps his knee. He tells me I sound like I'm stoned and we haven't even got to Nimbin yet.

It's raining when we arrive. I think it's close to dawn but I can't be sure. Sheets of water slam against the windscreen as I watch Zac in the headlights unhook the wire from the gatepost. The entrance to our block. Five hectares of old dairy country patched with rainforest and bordered by a broad deep creek. A dream that's taken years to pay off.

He climbs back in the cabin, his clothes soaked, his hair plastered flat against his skull. I tell him he looks funny and he says he's been baptised into a new life. Then he leans over and kisses me, a silky kiss soft with rain. Finally I flick off the interior light and put the truck into gear. We drive in.

The track has disappeared under the Crofton weed. As I edge forward, my nose is almost against the windscreen. I play the clutch and guess where our new driveway might be. But I'm wrong. The engine roars and I feel the truck subsiding. He grabs the wheel and yanks it hard. We stall, tilted sideways with my body pressed against the driver door. He hammers the dash with his fist. The windscreen wipers keep slapping. He laughs and shakes his head. It isn't a happy laugh. And then he says welcome to paradise.

The rain stops. We both clamber out and wade through the soaking weeds to the back of the truck. We can only open the door on the low side. In the weak beam of the torch I can see the stuff we've brought with us to set up house tilted on a dangerous angle: the kitchen table, the planks of timber, the boxes, the chairs, the suitcases. Our mattress is perched on the top. We strip off our clothes and climb up. We have to squat down low to fit under the roof. He lies down in the angled hollow and I edge in next to him. The doona is choky with the smell of diesel fumes. Mattress buttons dig into my hip but I don't complain. The only sound is the dollops of water falling from an overhanging tree and then he twists round and clamps his mouth against mine. The sleep that follows is dreamless.

. . .

It takes two weeks to build our kitchen, a tin structure with gaps for windows. We sleep in an old canvas tent with wooden doors for a floor. The view is of rainforest-clad hills and I think they look like rumpled mouldy blankets. I'm homesick for friends and family but I don't let on. I miss our old green bathroom with the pedestal basin, the hot running water. Sometimes I confuse myself by longing for the things I used to complain about like the frosts that gave me chilblains, even the soulless concrete shopping plazas.

We cook over an open fire. We make plans for a garden and an orchard. The weather gets warmer and we start swimming naked every day in the waterhole at the bottom of our property. Our skin turns the colour of caramel. My hair bleaches white.

I see the snake as I search for matches to start a breakfast fire. It's coiled and black and thick as my arm. A ribbon of tongue flickers in my direction as if tasting my scent and then it glides away under our food cupboard. I wake up Zac. He drags a rifle box from under the bed. I wonder out aloud how you can live with someone and never know they own a gun and he tells me now isn't the time to talk about it. He loads the bullets and I hate the snapping click as he prepares to shoot. He crouches and aims. The noise is like a skyrocket going off on cracker night. The snake slithers behind the tea chest we use to store our tools. He leans against the corrugated wall and tries to aim again but he says there isn't enough space. He directs me to pull the tea chest away from the cupboard. I force my legs forward and when I clutch the top of the chest, the metal binding cuts into my skin. Time stretches, expands. There's an explosion of blackness, the scraps of snake swirling through the air. My ears ring. There's blood on my fingers. I'm trembling so hard I can barely stand upright, yet his face looks empty, almost peaceful as he pokes at the pieces of snake with the butt of his rifle.

. . .

Our best friends Phil and Mel are coming to visit. I spend two days slashing the lantana with the brush hook to clear a space for their tent. The work is hot and prickly. The lantana leaves stink of crushed ants. I cook a celebratory fruitcake in the camping pot over the fire. The edges burn but it doesn't matter. I hum as I tidy the food cupboard and set a jug of white Crofton flowers on the table. I drive the truck into town to stock up on supplies. Beer for Phil and cider for Mel. I do our washing at the Laundromat and drink tea in the Rainbow Café while waiting for our clothes to dry. I read the book I borrowed from the mobile library, earmarking the page with the description of a starry sky as 'folds of lace'. I want to read it to Zac, remind him of the journey, remind him of our happiness. I'm late driving home. The sun looks like a flat orange lolly as it slips behind the mountains. Just as the bitumen peters away to dirt, I almost collide with a fast travelling car, a dark blue station wagon, and I have to pull over in the slush of gravel.

I pause in the clearing above the campsite and roll the laundry bag across to my other shoulder, readjust the handles of the shopping bags. Zac is hunched over the fire. Just him alone. I carefully pick my way down the dirt steps we've carved into the slope behind the tin shed. He doesn't look up. I tell him that I'm fairly certain I passed Phil and Mel on the road driving in the wrong direction. He says they've just left. I ask what's going on. He won't look at me when he says they had to go because Phil couldn't put the past behind him. I feel sick. His voice gets louder when he tells me that what went on was no big deal because him and Mel never actually screwed anyway.

I unpack the food with careful attention. I fold our laundered clothes by the light of the kerosene lamp and the fabric crackles and snaps with static electricity. He drinks beer from the bottle. I try and work out the meaning of what I've been told but the words are square and I only have round spaces in my brain.

The next week he gets a letter notifying him that his driver's licence will be reinstated as soon as he fronts to sign the papers. He immediately arranges a lift with a friend heading south the next day. I want to come too but the car is already full. We are lying in the park in town under the shade of a camphor laurel tree when I ask him not to go. He holds my hand and calls me his own precious baby. He tells me to be brave, that I need to keep our new farm going, keep the dream alive. He reminds me how much easier it will be for us to get around when he returns with his motorbike. When I ask if he'll be visiting Mel, he says he wants to sort things out, but he'll have to see if Phil has calmed down. I jam my lips together and study the red dirt caked under his fingernails. He promises to be back within a fortnight.

. . .

I am lonely. Bush rats run across the roof of the tent. I see them in the light of the moon, scampering down the pole close to my face. It rains and I can't get the fire going to cook so I live on bread and peanut butter and muesli with powdered milk. One, two, three times a day I pry the shadows under the cupboards with the torch light looking for snakes, but I don't see any.

I drive the truck to the rainbow dance in town. There's a big crowd and lots of didgeridoos. We dance the Rainbow Serpent Dreaming in a chain, weaving through the hall, our hands resting on the waist of the person in front of us. The man behind me grips me hard. We noticed each other earlier. He asks if I want a drink. We sit outside on the concrete steps sipping lukewarm beer from smudgy glasses. His hair is tied back in a ponytail. I can see the hairs on his chest through the white cheesecloth of his shirt. He says he's from the Buddhist community at the head of the valley, that he's just returned from a three-month meditation retreat. I like the way he laughs – a machine gun of sounds from the base of his throat.

He talks to me about the philosophy of meditation and offers to drop around some books later in the week. I tell him he mightn't find our camp because we have set up deep in the scrub. I know what I'm doing when I ask if he wants to stop by tonight and have a cup of tea. I pretend it's a good plan so that he won't get lost. He says yes and suggests we leave now. I skol my half glass of beer and scrabble in my shoulder bag for the truck keys as I lead the way.

Even though it's close to midnight, it's too hot for tea so we drink water instead. I realise I don't know his name but it seems too late to ask. I can feel salt-water moons of perspiration staining the underarms of my dress. He tightens the guy ropes on the tent and drags the dead branches off the shed roof. I can tell he's unafraid of snakes and rats. He comes up behind me and twists my hair to the side and begins to kiss the nape of my neck. His tongue, his teeth, prickle against my skin. He moves away and adjusts the lamp down low and carries it into the tent. I follow

He leaves for India a week later. I know it would be uncool to make plans for his return so I don't mention it and neither does he. My mouth is left with the subtle, hollow taste of him. I try to count the number of times he visited, but the individual memories have crumbled into a dream. Guilt gnaws at me the way bush rats gnaw at the timber food cupboard. I wash the sheets but the stains won't come out so I bury them down near the creek.

I let things go. Dirty dishes mill about the draining board. The pump packs up which means the end of our water supply. I watch, unmoved as the new seedlings curl and shrivel in the sun. Cauliflower clouds begin to pile high above the hills in massive towers because the wet season is coming.

Zac finds me at the swimming hole around midday when the air is wobbly with heat. His hair is cropped close and I can see the bony prominences of his skull. He squats down beside me on the rock ledge. He smiles and says he missed me. I try to smile like him. He plunges backwards, still in his shorts then swims overarm towards me with his head turning from side to side. Crouched there in the water he massages my toes, the whole time intently watching my face. He asks if I've been screwing someone else. I stare at my leech bites, the red spots peppering my ankles and think of the gun under the bed. When I go to stand up he grabs the edge of my sarong. Water keeps slapping against the rocks. I ask what happened when he saw Mel and he releases his grip.

. . .

DRIVING THE INLAND ROAD

I'm driving the inland road again. North to South this time. The truck steering wheel feels slippery in my hands but at least my wrists don't ache. It's warm enough to have the windows down and I'm taking it slowly. The moon is like a sliver of fingernail, white and thin with pointy ends. At Gunnedah my headlights shine on a billboard beside a stone church. Have faith. He loves you. But I keep driving south into the night.

. . . . . .

FOREIGN PARTS

In Barcelona

LAURIE CLANCY

Things go from bad to worse in the seething Spanish city.

It was the same in Barcelona. They would quarrel over something trivial, the value of a Spanish coin or the pronunciation of a word, they would make love, and then a few hours later they would begin to fight again. Wounds re-opening and bleeding.

'We can't go all through our lives quarrelling and then making up in bed.' John looked absurd, dressed in just a shirt and tie, and Maggie laughed. 'Why not?' she said. He was the only man she had ever known who dressed vertically.

'With naked foot stalking in my chamber.'

'What?' said John.

The studio over La Rambla, a yellow and blue, light-filled place, had cost them more money than they had ever paid for accommodation in their lives. Each morning they heard the city stumbling to life below them. At four o'clock they would be woken by the garbage trucks clanking. An hour later it was the turn of the delivery men, meat trucks, bakery vans, leathery tanned labourers staggering under loads of vegetables for the *marqueta*. Then came the early commuters, still yawning as the darkness changed to pale light, the first taxis, the occasional scream of a police siren or the strange, gooselike honking of an ambulance.

By mid-morning they could step out on their tiny third-floor balcony and gaze down at the flower sellers, the newspaper stalls, the buskers, performers and operatic beggars. 'Marvellous,' said John. He watched a tiny man dressed like some old Moorish warrior all in black, who posed motionlessly.

. . .

A tourist dropped a coin into his bag and the sword came down like lightning, was poised above the young woman for a second before the warrior resumed his position of immobility. 'Marvellous.' He made it sound, Maggie thought, as if he were personally responsible for the entire scene.

. . .

John Prescott and his wife Magdalene had been together now for over five years but this was their first honeymoon. 'Like Columbus voyaging,' said Maggie, pointing to the huge statue at the bottom of La Rambla.

'He's pointing in the wrong direction,' said John. 'Out to Egypt or perhaps northern Africa.'

Maggie looked at him.

It was the second marriage for both of them and like most people who marry a second time they struggled to adjust to a new set of rules, a new range of habits. Now Maggie had twelve months' study leave from her university to complete her book on Elizabethan love poetry in London. John had taken three months leave of absence from the different university in Sydney where he taught in the physics department to travel with her. Maggie had suggested they make love in as many European cities as possible. 'Get in *The Guinness Book of Records*, eh?' John suggested. He was almost fifty years old. Maggie was about a decade younger.

Back in the studio, Maggie was wrestling with a lock.

'John, darling, can you fix this thing? It's jammed or something. You're so good at these things.'

John fiddled with it, pressed it, tried to turn it. 'It's loose. There's nothing I can do. We'll have to see the agent.' He went downstairs, came back a few minutes later with his hands behind his back and presented Maggie with a huge bunch of carnations.

She smiled. 'Thank you, darling. But you realise we have no vases.'

. . .

Walking up La Rambla towards the agency later in the morning, John thought happily of how foolish it was for a couple in their middle age to be strolling hand in hand, like the pairs of young lovers they seemed to encounter all over the city, courting on park benches or sitting side by side on motor bikes, their helmets dangling from the bars. Once again, the sun was shining palely and the sky was clear except for the twin white streaks of jet aircraft flying too high above them to be heard.

He glanced sideways towards Maggie and was again intoxicated by her dark, almost gypsy-like beauty, her tanned skin and rich, luminous eyes, the tiny wisps of hair that hung over her forehead. There was a poem she loved to quote, that featured her hair. Something about black wires? He loved her voice, her throaty laugh, the delicacy with which she approached strangers and asked for directions in her minuscule and mangled hoard of Spanish words. Oblivious of this inventory of the affections, Maggie was pointing to the buckets of flowers in front of the stand.

'Come on,' she said. 'Quickly, just one more time we'll go through them.' Maggie had been trying to teach him the names of the flowers, especially the ones they had at home. John had at last developed a vicarious pride in their tiny garden. When he and Maggie had first moved into their terrace house in Paddington, he had been amazed to see her take a whole summer off from her book on Elizabethan love poetry to build a garden.

'I couldn't do that,' he said. 'I'd be overtaken by my own post-grads.'

'The book will be written when it's ready to be written,' she said. 'One can't work in an unharmonious environment.'

Was that what people in literature really thought? That books just got themselves written when they were ready? That scientific discoveries got themselves discovered when they were ready? John loved his work. To him, an equation like $F = MA$ was as beautiful and satisfying as a rose.

'Come on,' Maggie said. 'What are those blue ones over there?'

'They're . . . pelargoniums, aren't they?'

'Very good. And now those yellow ones, what can you tell me about them?'

They walked on, and were accosted by a dark-skinned woman, a scarlet sash across her chest leaving her shoulders exposed. She placed a carnation in the pocket of John's sports coat. She spoke frantically in Spanish. Then she turned to Magdalene with another carnation – *'Por la signora'* – but Maggie walked away, 'No thank you.'

John felt in his pocket and produced a 100 peseta coin. He had no idea what the rate for free carnations was.

'Ah, no, no,' she gave him back the coin. She was feeling all over him, touching his sports coat. *'Inglese? Americano?'*

'Australiano,' he said.

'Ah, *Australiano.*' She kept patting him with solicitude.

What did she want? He tried to give her back the flower.

Another woman, with a similar bright sash draped across her, appeared at his side. She seemed to know what the first woman wanted and gestured with great authority but again John understood nothing of what she was saying.

'Souvenir,' she said.

'Does she want souvenir?' John had no Australian coins but a friend had given him some English change when he left the country. '*Inglese* okay?'

'*Si Inglese.*'

He began to reach into his side pocket but the woman was there before him, her brown fingers, gnarled, delicate, feeling delicately in his pocket as she withdrew the coin. Then she handed it back to him.

'John,' said Maggie, a few metres away. 'Don't let them touch you.'

But even as she spoke he knew what had happened. He felt in his pocket. Gone, the 70,000 pesetas he had taken out of the bank to pay for the rent. He looked around, but even though it must have been only a few seconds ago the two women had vanished.

'Thanks a lot,' he said. 'You couldn't have mentioned that earlier, I suppose?' He looked at Maggie, who was silent, her cheeks aflame.

She said, 'You're not going to . . .?'

'Report it to the police? No, what's the use? It was all in cash.'

They walked on in raging silence to the agent's office.

. . .

The agent was a voluble woman of about fifty, with dyed hair, wearing a red dress and matching, heavily applied lipstick.

Although she had no English at all, that did not stop her from conducting an energetic conversation. They tried to explain what their problem was. Maggie had looked up the words for 'lock' and 'loose' in the tiny Spanish/English dictionary they carried about with them and tried them out.

The woman stared at them without comprehension.

John stood up, went to the door and began a pantomime of trying unsuccessfully to insert his key into the broken lock.

'Ah, *si, si.*' The woman lunged for the phone. As she dialled, the phone tucked against her cheek, she continued to speak. Then she suddenly stopped, spoke into the receiver for a long time without interruption, put the telephone down and held up both hands.

'Twenty minutes,' Maggie translated hopefully. 'Someone will be there in twenty minutes.'

'*Si, si.*' The woman asked them a question.

'She's asking us if we like the apartment.'

'*Si, mucho bueno,*' John answered for both of them. 'Very much. Excellenta apartimenta. Fine view. Vista.'

'Si, La Rambla,' the woman said. She pointed to a poster of La Rambla on the wall. She began a long speech about La Rambla.

'She's saying,' Maggie told him, 'that people come from all over the world to see La Rambla. They even come from all over the rest of Spain.' Although she had not much more Spanish than he did, Maggie was adept as picking up what people were saying. She smiled at him. 'Shall we tell her about the robbery?'

John turned to the woman. 'I have just been *pick-pocketed* on La Rambla.' He emphasised the word carefully, assuming it was the same in Spanish as in English. He took a piece of paper from the desk and wrote on it '70,000 pesetas.'

The woman had stopped in her tracks and was staring at him in consternation. 'Pick-pocket?'

'*Ladron,*' said Maggie, frantically looking up the dictionary. '*Carterista.*'

John began to pantomime the robbery for her, the movements of the women as they came up to him. He took a flower from a vase on the desk and stuck it in his own pocket. He patted himself all over. He was enjoying himself wonderfully. There was something about this absurd clowning that made him feel liberated.

'Ah,' said the woman. 'Gypsies.'

Of course. They had to be gypsies. They couldn't be Spanish.

The woman changed suddenly and produced a bag, showing them how it had, not one, not two, but three metal chains threaded through it, to make it difficult for thieves to cut through them. 'La Rambla very dangerous,' she informed them. '*Ladrones. Carterista.*'

'Thank you,' said John.

. . .

On the Thursday, five days after they had been scheduled to leave for Madrid, Maggie said, 'I'm leaving tomorrow. You can come or not as you wish.'

'Just one more day. One more.'

'This thing's become an obsession with you. You wouldn't go to the police and now you're doing this mad vigilante thing. The Rambo of la Rambla. You won't ever see those women again.'

'I will. I'm sure I will. They'll figure most tourists stay only a week at most and will come back then. It's only logical.'

'Well, I'm leaving tomorrow.'

John groaned.

They went next morning to return the key. As they passed a stall full of birds Maggie cried in delight, 'Look, yellow-crested cockatoos! Australian. Aren't they beautiful?'

'They're a prohibited export. I could inform on those people.' Maggie looked at him but said nothing.

He stopped suddenly, grabbed Maggie's arm and pulled her behind the stall. 'It's them. I knew they'd come back.' Maggie peered out. The two women were dressed as before except that this time the sashes were a bright blue and they wore a great deal of jewellery.

'See? They're using the same trick with the flowers.' They had approached a tall, elderly man carrying a suitcase and were offering him a carnation.

John sprang from behind the cart and ran towards them. 'Pickpockets,' he shouted. '*Carteristas. Policia!*'

The three figures turned and stared at him. The man began to feel his breast pocket.

'Pickpocket!,' snarled John, as he grabbed one of the gypsies by the wrist. 'Thief. *Voleur. Ladron. Putes. Hijas de puta. Unas zorras.*'

'Your Spanish is improving,' said Maggie.

The elderly man said, 'I don't think anything's missing but I thank you for the warning.'

'*Bartarda!*' cried John, hauling on the woman's wrist. She leaned back, resisting. He pulled harder, throwing her slightly off-balance. Somehow, it was no surprise when he saw the knife emerge from under the voluminous layers of blue, so tiny, glinting in the pale sunshine, the kind of knife one would use to cut up fruit or peel vegetables. He could see it had been carefully looked after, the way one looks after one's favourite tool. As it began to enter his stomach he saw the brown fingers again, such delicate artistry.

'John!' shouted Maggie.

His feet slipped from underneath him and he fell backwards on the slippery pavement, wet from where the flowers had been hosed down. He kicked over a pot and sent it skidding. I've kicked the bucket, he thought to himself, and wondered if it were the first joke he had made in his life. How absurd, he thought to himself. To die in Barcelona.

He was aware through a kind of pale haze that Maggie was bending over him and a policeman was pushing onlookers back quite roughly. He was the pot spinning along La Rambla in crazy movements and the names of the flowers in all the pots came back to him at once. Violets. Birdflowers. Calonchas. Maggie would be proud of him. He smiled as he closed his eyes.

. . . . . .

The Fellow Passenger

ELIZABETH JOLLEY

As his ship proceeds to Australia, Dr Abrahams goes on a parallel inner journey.

Dr Abrahams stood watching, for his health, the flying fish. They flew in great numbers like little silver darts, leaping together in curves, away from the ship, as though disturbed by her movement through their mysterious world. Nearby sat his wife with her new friend, a rich widow returning to her rice farms in New South Wales. The two women in comfortable chairs, adjoining, spoke to each other softly and confidingly, helping each other with the burden of family life and the boredom of the voyage.

'Who is that person your daughter is talking to?' said the widow, momentarily looking up from her needlework.

'Oh, I've no idea,' Mrs Abrahams said comfortably. And then, a little less comfortably, she said, 'Oh, I see what you mean. There are some odd people on board.' She raised herself slightly and, raising her voice, called, 'Rachel! Rachel dear, mother's over here, we're sitting over here.'

As the girl reluctantly came towards them, Mrs Abrahams said in a low voice to her new friend, 'I'm so glad you noticed. He does seem to be an unsuitable type, perhaps he's a foreigner of some sort.' She lowered her voice even more. 'And they do have such ugly heads you know.'

Their voices were swallowed up in the wind, which was racing, whipping the spray and pitting the waves as they curled back from the sides of the ship.

Dr Abrahams walked by himself all over the ship. The sharp fragrance from the barber's shop excited him, and he rested gratefully by the notice boards where there was a smell of boiled potatoes. The repeated Dettol scrubbing of the stairs reminded him of postnatal douchings and the clean enamel bowls in his operating theatre.

Whenever he stood looking at the front of the ship, or at the back, he admired the strength of the structure, the massive construction and the complication of ropes and pulleys being transported, and in themselves necessary for the transporting of the ship across these oceans. It seemed always that the ship was steady in the great ring of blue water and did not rise to answer the sea, and the monsoon had not broken the barrenness. Most of the passengers were huddled out of the wind.

When he returned to his wife he saw the man approaching. For a time he had managed to forget about him and now here he was again, coming round the end of the deck, limping towards them in that remarkably calm manner, which Abrahams knew only too well was hiding a desperate persistence.

Knowing the peace of contemplation was about to be broken, Abrahams turned abruptly and tried to leave the deck quickly through the heavy swing doors before the man, with his distasteful and sinister errand, could reach him. There was this dreadful element of surprise and of obligation too. For apart from anything else, the man had an injury with a wound which, having been neglected, must have been appallingly painful. It was something, if seen by a doctor, could not afterwards be ignored.

'All you have to do is to treat me like a fellow passenger,' the man had said the first night on board. He entreated rather, with some other quality in his voice and in his bearing which had caused Abrahams to buy him a drink straight away. Perhaps some of the disturbance had come from the unexpected shapeliness of the man's hands.

The Bay of Biscay, unusually calm, had not offered the usual reasons for a day of retreat in the cabin. Abrahams, excusing himself from the company of his wife and daughter, had again invited the man for a drink.

'What about a coupla sangwidges,' the fellow said, and he had gobbled rather than eaten them. A little plate of nuts and olives disappeared in the same way.

The two stupid old ladies, they were called Ethel and Ivy and shared the Abrahams' table, were there in the Tavern Bar. They nodded and smiled and they rustled when they moved, for both were sewn up in brown paper under their clothes.

'To prevent sea sickness,' Ethel explained to people whenever she had the chance.

A second little plate of nuts and olives disappeared.

'That'll be good for a growing boy!' Ethel called out. Like Ivy, she was having tomato juice with Worcester sauce. Already they had been nicknamed 'The Worcester Sauce Queens' by the Abrahams family.

Abrahams, with the courtesy of long habit, for among his patients were many such elderly ladies, smiled at her. His smile was handsome and kind. The very quality of kindness it contained caused both men and women to confide. It was the nature of this smile, and the years of patient, hard work it had brought upon him, that had necessitated a remedial voyage. For Abrahams was a sick man and was keeping the sickness in his own hands, prescribing for himself at last a long rest. He had been looking forward to the period of suspended peace, which has such tremendous healing power and is the delight of a sea voyage.

At the very beginning the peace was interrupted before it was begun, and Abrahams regretted bitterly the sensitive sympathy his personality seemed to give out. It was all part of his illness. It was as if he were ill because of his sympathetic nature. The burdens he carried sprang from it. That was what he allowed himself to believe but it was not all quite so simple. There were conflicting reasons and feelings which were all perhaps a part of being unwell, perhaps even a part of the cause. He tried to make some sort of acknowledgement, to reach some sort of inner conclusion in the all too infrequent solitary moments.

At the first meeting, Abraham's feeling was, apart from a sense of obligation or the good manners of not liking to refuse to buy a drink for the stranger, a feeling of gladness, almost happiness, perhaps even a tiny heart-bursting gladness which could have made him want to sing. He did not sing, he was not that kind of man. His work did not include singing of any kind. There was not much talking. Mostly he listened. His work kept him quiet and thoughtful. He often bent forward to listen and to examine and to operate. He had good hands. His fingers, accustomed to probing and rearranging, to extracting and replacing, were sensitive and capable. If he frowned it was the frown of attention and concentration. It was his look of kindness and the way in which he approached an examination, almost as if it was some kind of caress, which made his patients like him.

In the bar that first night, he reflected, he had come near singing. A songless song, of course, because men like Abrahams simply would never burst into song.

Once he did sing and the memory of it had suddenly come back to him clearly, even though it had been many years ago. Once his voice, surprisingly powerful, it could have been described as an untrained but ardent tenor, carried a song of love across and down a valley of motionless trees. Throughout his song the landscape had remained undisturbed. He had not realised how, in the stillness, a voice could carry.

'Heard yer singin' this half hour,' the woman had said, holding her side, her face old with pain.

'Oh? Was I singing?'

'Yerse, long before you crorsst the bridge, I heard yer comin'. Thanks to God I sez to meself the doctor's on his way, he's on his way.'

It was during a six months' locum in a country town. That day he sang and whistled and sang careering on horseback to a patient in a lonely farm house. He remembered the undisturbed fields and meadows, serene that day because he went through them singing.

'The stranger's voice in the bar, and his finely made hands taking the glass from Abrahams, brought back so suddenly the song in the shallow valley.

On the track that day he thought he'd lost his way and he was frightened of his surroundings. The landmarks he'd been told to watch for simply had not appeared. There was no house in sight and no barn and there were no people. He'd been travelling some time. Joyfully he approached some farm machinery but no one was beside it. He almost turned back but thought of his patient and the injection he could give her. In all directions the land sloped gently to the sky, the track seemed to be leading nowhere and he was the only person there.

He came upon the man quite suddenly. He was there as if for no reason except to direct Abrahams, though he had a cart and some tools, but Abrahams, in his relief, did not really notice. The man's eyes shone as he patted the horse and

Abrahams felt as if the intimate caress, because of the way the man looked, was meant for him. He continued his journey feeling this tiny heart-bursting change into gladness, which is really all the greatest change there is, and so he sang.

As he walked or stood on the deck he thought about loneliness. The crowded, confined life of the ship was lonely too.

'Give me some money,' the man said. 'It'll look better if I shout you.' So in the temporary duskiness between the double swing doors Abrahams gave him some notes and small change and followed him as he limped into the bar.

'What'll you have?' the man asked the old ladies. They were there as usual, before lunch, their large straw hats were bandaged on with violently coloured scarves. They sat nodding those crazy head-pieces, talking to anyone who would listen to them.

They were pleased to be offered drinks. Abrahams had a drink too, but it was accompanied by disturbing feelings. The thought of his illness crossed his mind. The man's hands had an extraordinary youthful beauty about them, out of keeping with his general appearance. As on the other occasions when glasses had passed between them, their fingers brushed lightly, but it was not so much the caress of fingers as of a suggestion of caress in the man's eyes.

Abrahams, with a second drink, found himself wondering had he been on horseback that time in the country or in a car. Had that other man touched the horse or merely put a friendly hand on the door of the car? With his hand he had not touched, only the expression was there in his eyes. This time, all these years later, it was a touching of exceptional hands together with an expression in the eyes.

In the afternoon there was a fancy-dress party for the children. Mrs Abrahams had been making something elaborate with crepe paper. Already the cabin blossomed with paper flowers. Abrahams discovered his daughter sulking.

'Look, Rachel darling,' Mrs Abrahams persuaded. 'You will be a bouquet, we shall call you "the language of flowers",' she said, holding up her work. 'White roses – they mean "I cannot" – and this lovely little white and green flower is lily of the valley. It says "already I have loved you so long" and here's a little bunch of violets for your hair, Rachel, the violets say "why so downhearted? Take courage!" and these pretty daisies say …'

'Oh no, no!" Rachel interrupted. 'I don't want to be flowers. I want to go as a stowaway,' and she limped round and round the cabin. 'Daddy! Daddy!' she cried with sudden inspiration. 'Can I borrow one of your coloured shirts, please? Oh, do say I can. Do let me be a stowaway, please!'

Abrahams took refuge among the mothers and photographers at the party. He joined in the clapping for the prize winners, 'Little Miss Muffet' and 'Alice in Wonderland'. 'All so prettily dressed!' Mrs Abrahams whispered sadly. A girl covered in green balloons calling herself 'A Bunch of Grapes' won a special prize. The applause was tremendous.

'They must have made a fortune in green umbrellas,' the rice-farm friend said with delight.

'Spent a fortune on green balloons,' Abrahams muttered to himself, almost correcting her aloud. He was unable to forget, for the time being, his sinister companion who was somewhere on the decks, waiting with some further demand. Silently he watched his little daughter's mounting disappointment as she limped round unnoticed in one of his shirts, left unbuttoned to look ragged.

He thought he would like to buy her a grown-up looking drink before dinner, something sparkling with a piece of lemon and a cherry on it, to please her, to comfort her really. If only she could know how much he cherished her. He longed to be free to play with her. She was old enough, he thought, to learn to play chess. But there was the fear that he would be interrupted, and she was old enough, too, to be indignant and to enquire.

'I am not quite well,' he explained to his wife after the first encounter with the man. 'It is nothing serious but I am not sleeping well.' He did not want her disturbed by something mysterious which he was unable to explain. So he had a cabin to himself and arranged for his wife and daughter to be together. Their new cabin had a window with muslin curtains and a writing table. Mrs Abrahams took pleasure in comparing it with the cabins of other ladies on board. Dr Abrahams called for her and Rachel every morning on the way to breakfast.

The children's fancy-dress party was depressing. The atmosphere of suburban wealth and competition seemed shallow and useless. The smell of hot children and perfume nauseated him. But it was safer to stay there.

The ship remained steady on her course and the rail of the ship moved slowly above the horizon and slowly below the horizon. There were times when Abrahams felt he was being watched by the stewards and the officers, and even the deck hands seemed to give each other knowing looks. These feelings, he knew, were merely symptoms of his illness which was, after all, nothing serious, only a question of being over-tired. All the same, he was worn out with this feeling of being watched. He avoided the sun deck for it was clear from the man's new sunburn that he lay up there, anonymous on a towel, for part of each day.

'You'd better let me have a shirt,' the man said. 'I'll be

noticed by my dirt,' he said. He took a set of three, their patterns being too similar for Abrahams to appear in any one of them. He needed socks and underpants and a bag to keep them in. The nondescript one Abrahams had would do very well. It was all settled one evening in the cabin which Abrahams had said he must have to himself. The fellow passenger slept there, coming in late at night and leaving early in the morning. It was there in the cramped space Abrahams dressed the wound on the man's thigh with the limited medical supplies he had with him.

'Easy! Easy!' the fellow passenger said in a low voice.

'It's hot in here,' Abrahams complained. He disliked being clumsy. 'It's the awkwardness of not having somewhere to put my things.'

'It's all right,' the fellow passenger said. 'You're not really hurting me.' He seemed much younger undressed. His long naked body so delicately patched with white between the sunburn, angry only where the wound was, invited Abrahams.

'I'm not wounded all over,' he said, and laughed, and Abrahams found himself laughing with him.

'Easy! Easy! Don't rush!' The younger man said.

That laughter, the tiny heart-burst of gladness was a fact, like the fact that the wound was only in one place. They could be careful. It was a question of being careful in every kind of way.

Abrahams knew his treatment to be unsatisfactory but there seemed nothing else to do in the extraordinary circumstances. If only he had not answered the smile in the man's eyes on that first evening; he should have turned away as other people do. Knowing the change and feeling the change, in whatever way it brought gladness, was the beginning and the continuation of more loneliness.

Incredibly the ship made progress, her rail moving gently up and persistently down.

Like many handsome clever men Dr Abrahams had married a stupid woman. She was quite good at housekeeping and she talked consolingly through kisses. Her body had always been clean and plump, and relaxed, and she was very quiet during those times of lovemaking, as though she felt that was how a lady, married to a doctor, should behave. Abrahams never sang with her as he sang in the cabin.

'Easy! Easy!' the fellow passenger said. He laughed and Abrahams put the pillow over his head.

'They'll hear you.' He buried his own face in the top of the pillow. He could not stop laughing either.

'And they'll hear you, too!' Abrahams heard the words piercing through the smothered laughter.

Always unable to discuss things with his wife, Dr Abrahams did not want to frighten her now and spoil her holiday.

'Your husband is a very quiet man,' the rice-farm widow said to Mrs Abrahams. 'Still waters run deep, so they say,' she said. That was very early in the voyage after a morning in Gibraltar, spent burrowing into little shops choosing antimacassars and table runners of cream-coloured lace.

'Did you go to see the apes?' Ethel enquired at lunch.

'Plenty of apes here,' Abrahams, burdened and elated by discovery and already bad tempered, would have replied, but instead, he smiled pleasantly and, with a little bow, regretted the family had not had time.

'You see Ethel and I have this plastic pizza,' Ivy was explaining to Mrs Abrahams and Rachel. 'At Christmas I wrap it up and go down to Ethel's flat, "Happy Christmas, Ethel," I say, and she unwraps it and she says "Ooh, Ivy, you are a dear, it's just what I wanted", and then next year she wraps it up and gives it to me. It saves all that trouble of buying presents nobody really wants. Thank you,' she said to the steward, 'I'll have the curried chicken.'

Rachel, accustomed to good meals, ordered a steak. Abrahams could not help reflecting that Ethel and Ivy had both the remedy and the method which simplified their existence. They appeared to be able to live so easily, without emergency, and without burdening other people with their needs. They could, of course, require surgery at any time, though he doubted that this ever occurred to either of them. Perhaps he too, outwardly, gave the same impression.

The fellow passenger's demand was both a pleading and a promise. At the beginning Abrahams had risen to the entreaty, but, as he understood all too quickly, his response was complicated by an unthought-of need in himself. Walking alone on the ship he was afraid.

The begging for help had, from the first, been a command. Abrahams knew his fellow passenger to be both sinister and evil. In his own intelligent way he tried to reason with himself what, in fact, he was himself. At the start, but on different terms, it was a matching desperation of hunger and thirst and an exhaustion of wits. The fellow passenger had certain outward signs. For one thing, he had a ragged growth of beard which in itself was dangerously revealing. He was dirty too. He needed help, he told Abrahams, to hold out till the first servings of afternoon tea in the lounge, and until such time when the weather would improve and cold buffet lunches would be spread daily in the Tavern Bar and on little tables on the canopied deck by the swimming pool. To be in these delightful places, in order to fill his stomach, he needed to mingle in the company.

'It's dangerous,' he said, 'being alone. Being on my own

makes me conspicuous and that's what I don't want to be.' A companion who was both rich and distinguished was a necessity and it had not taken him long to find the kind of fellow passenger he needed.

'I better have a bit more cash,' he said to Abrahams. 'I'll shout you and them old Queens. They know a thing or two about life, those two. I'll take care of them.' His words sounded like a threat.

They had, without laughter, been sorting out what was to happen next. The cabin had never seemed quite so small, quite so awkward. He had plans to alter a passport, he knew exactly what had to be done. He needed a passport and it only needed the doctor to produce one.

Like many clever men Dr Abrahams was easily tired. He had come on the ship, as had the fellow passenger, exhausted, already an easy victim. Now, more tired than ever, he hated the man and saw him as someone entirely ruthless. It seemed impossible to consider what might have been the cause. It was clear that there would be no end to the requests. Abrahams realised that soon he would be unable to protect his family and quite unable to protect himself. The voyage no longer had any meaning for him. Together, the two of them went to the bar.

Ethel and Ivy were there as usual.

'It's on me today,' Ethel cried and made them sit down. 'You must try my tomato juice,' she cried. 'It's with a difference, you know,' and she winked so saucily everyone in the bar laughed.

The fellow passenger drank quickly.

'Now it's my turn,' Ivy insisted. 'It's my turn to shout.' She watched with approval as the fellow passenger drank again.

'So good for a growing boy,' she declared and she ordered another round.

Dr Abrahams held his glass too tightly with nervous fingers. After the conversation about the passport he felt more helpless than ever. He could scarcely swallow. He should never have lost his way like this. Quickly he glanced at all the people laughing and talking together and he was frightened of them.

'More tomato juice for my young man,' Ethel shrieked. Her straw hat had come loose.

'Ethel dear, watch yourself!' Ivy shrilled. 'We're in very mixed company, you know, dear.' Their behaviour drew the attention of the other passengers.

'Steward! Steward!' Ethel called. 'Don't forget the-you-know-what-oops la Volga! Volga! It makes all the difference. There, dear boy, let's toss this off.' She raised her fiery little glass to his. 'Oops a daisy!' Her hat fell over one eye.

While the fellow passenger drank, Ivy retied Ethel's scarf lovingly. She rocked gently to and fro.

'Yo ho heave ho! Volga-Volga,' she crooned. 'Volga Vodka,' she sang, and Ethel joined in.

'Yo ho heave ho! Volga-Worcester-saucy-vodka-tommy-ommay-artah – All together now – Yo ho heave ho-Volga-vodka,' they sang together and some of the other passengers joined in. Above the noise of the singing and the laughing Abrahams heard a familiar voice, but it was much louder than usual.

'Go on, dear boy! Go on! Go on! Don't stop now!' Ethel and Ivy cried together, their absurd hats bobbing. 'Tell us more,' they screamed.

It seemed to Abrahams that the fellow passenger was telling stories to Ethel and Ivy and to anyone else who cared to listen.

Hearing the voice he thought how ugly it was. The ugliness filled him with an unbearable sadness.

'So you're wanted in five countries!' Ethel said. 'Why that's wonderful!' she encouraged. She bent forward to listen. Ivy examined the young man's shirt. She patted his shoulder.

'This is such good quality,' she breathed. 'Look at this lovely material, Ethel dear.' But Ethel would not have the subject changed.

'Rape!' she shrieked with delight. 'And murder too, how splendid! What else, dear boy? Being a thief is so exciting, do tell us about the watches and the jewels and the diamonds. You must be very clever. Ivy and I have never managed anything more expensive than a pizza and then it turned out to be quite uneatable.'

The fellow passenger did not join in the laughter. He began to despise his audience.

'Look at you!' he sneered. 'You two old bags and you lot – you've all paid through the nose to be on this ship. But not me, I'm getting across the world on my wits. That's how I do things. I've got brains up here.' He tapped his head with a surprisingly delicate finger. 'It isn't money as has got me here,' he said and he tapped his head again.

For the first time Abrahams noticed the ugliness of the head. He thought he ought to find the Purser and speak to him.

'It's all my fault about the head,' he would confide, and explain to the officer about the arching of soft white thighs and the exertion. 'It's like this,' he would say. 'When you see the baby's head appear on the perineum it's like a first glimpse of all the wonder and all the magic, a preview if you like to call it that, of all the possibilities.' The Purser would understand about the shy hope and the tenderness when it was explained to him. Abrahams thought the Purser might be in his cabin changing for lunch. He could find the cabin.

'What has happened?' he wanted to ask the Purser. 'What has happened?' he wanted to shout. 'What is it that happens to the tiny eager head to bring about this change from the original perfection?'

He walked unsteadily towards the open end of the bar. Really he should speak and protect his fellow passenger. He felt ashamed as well as afraid, knowing that he needed to protect himself. Of course he could not speak to anyone, his own reputation mattered too much.

He was appalled at the sound of the boasting voice and, at the same time, had a curious sense that he was being rescued. The fellow passenger was giving himself to these people.

Abrahams did not turn round to watch the man being led away by two stewards in dark uniforms.

'Mind my leg!' He heard the pathetic squeal as the three of them squeezed through a narrow door at the back of the bar. It was a relief that the wound, which he was convinced needed surgery, would receive proper attention straight away.

There were still a few minutes left before lunch. For the first time he went up on the sun deck. Far below, the sea, shining like metal, scarcely moving, invited him. For a moment he contemplated that peace.

'Yoo hoo, Doctor! Wear my colours!' Ethel shrieked. Turning from the rail he saw the Worcester Sauce Queens playing a rather hurried game of deck tennis. Ethel unpinned a ragged cluster of paper violets from her scarf and flung them at his feet. Politely he bent forward to pick them up.

'You must watch Rachel beat us after lunch,' Ivy shrilled.

The pulse of the ship, like a soft drum throbbing, was more noticeable at the top of the ship. To Abrahams it was like an awakening not just in his body but in his whole being. He stood relaxed, letting life return as he watched the grotesque game and, with some reservations belonging to his own experience, he found the sight of the Worcester Sauce Queens charming.

. . . . . .

Travelling

JOAN LONDON

Chaos in Laos.

There were four of them who had arrived in Luang Prabang that day, and now hung around the entrance of the Royal Air Lao office in light rain, waiting for a man called Ted Akhito. As far as they could make out (here Ruth for once had made the enquiries, her matric French promoted by Galen), this Ted was a Japanese English teacher who rented rooms to travellers on the second floor. Probably CIA. Who wasn't? An introverted, sleuthing silence fell among them, not helped by the rain.

Travellers were scarce in Laos that year, and they seemed to be sticking together, linked by a sort of professional pride. On the traveller's scale of values, Laos had an off-beat, quietly dangerous chic. Vietnam had lost its glamour even for the foolhardy, but in those days, Laos, with war flickering through its jungles so you had to town-hop in a battered DC3, and sleep in the curfew to the distant sound of planes and even gunfire, still had that nice edge of controllable adventure.

In Ban-Houei-Sai, the little border town on the Laotian side of the Mekong, shopkeepers had refused to serve them, and the one café that would give them a meal had been full of armed soldiers and beefy American men in laundered mufti. *The place is crawling with CIA,* Galen wrote to a friend back in Australia (he liked to write on-the-spot accounts in cafes), *it's probably only a matter of time before the borders are closed.* There was that Shangri-la savour of a soon-to-be-lost frontier.

But last night in Ban-Houei-Sai, while Ruth was dousing herself in a mandi bath, an unseen watcher had laughed at her from behind the window bars. There are peeping Toms everywhere, as Galen said, but there was something about the sureness and scorn of that laugh, its pause, its continuation, as she had clutched a sarong about her pink body and fled down the curfew-darkened corridors of the hotel, that she related to war. She wasn't sure that they had any right to be in this country at all.

It was nearly dark when Ted Akhito arrived, under a dripping umbrella. They followed him up a staircase that opened, loft-like, into a large rectangular room with shuttered windows at either end. It was bare except for the rows of bamboo mats along the walls.

'Five hundred kip a night,' said Ted Akhito, looking at his watch. He was young, as young as they were, dressed in Westernised tropical whites. There was no question of bargaining about the price.

'I must go now. I have a class. I'll be back later to check things out. Curfew is at ten o'clock.' He spoke excellent English without an accent, except he said 'class' like an American. What was he doing in Luang Prabang? Yes, almost certainly CIA.

Mats were already being claimed while he was talking.

'Here?' said Ruth to Galen. There were two mats together near the staircase. That tiny panic, like schooldays, when the gym teacher would say, 'Find yourself a spot,' and you'd jostle and circle to be at the back, near a friend. Galen shrugged. She took the mat that would be furthest from Bob, the Englishman, who as usual was hovering to see what Galen would do.

The Canadian was already striding up and down the room, looking out the windows.

'Wonder where you can get a meal in this town,' he said.

'Wouldn't mind a cup of tea,' said Bob. He was always ready to attach himself to a superior energy.

Galen was flicking through his *Student's Guide to South-East Asia*. 'Got the name of a café here somewhere,' he said.

There was a general movement to the stairs. 'Hold on,' Bob was muttering, arm-deep in his rucksack. 'I've lost my mac.'

Ruth hurried to join Galen, who with Canada was already at the bottom of the stairs.

. . .

Luang Prabang's wet empty streets did not seem under siege. The Student's Guide was pre-war, but the Melody Café still existed by the river, a dimly-lit little cave scattered with a handful of their own kind. A hang-out. Like the German Dairy in Chieng-Mai, or the Thai Song Greet in Bangkok. Made you realise that the trail had been well and truly blazed before you. Look at the menu. Along with all the usual rice and noodles, you could get roles and jam for breakfast, bolled eggs, stek fry, bananas milkshek. They wouldn't be quite the real thing of course, they were hybrid dishes cooked up for nostalgic Western palates.

'I'm gonna have me a steak,' Canada announced soon after they had settled themselves around a table.

'Steak!' said Bob, looking at the menu. 'That's eight hundred kip. It's a rip-off.'

Canada slapped the table lightly.

'This is a rip-off, that's a rip-off, *oh* you're having *steak*, I haven't had a steak since I left home.' He addressed the table in general. He was never personal. He went on. 'Why are travellers so god-damned *mean*? Like it's immoral to spend money or something. They haggle over anything to save five lousy cents. Me, if I want steak, I'll *have* steak.'

'All very well if you've got the money,' said Bob, still staring at the menu.

Ruth tried to catch Galen's eye. A taboo had been broken. They had been so conscientious about adopting the right ethos. If you let them rip you off they didn't respect you, and you were spoiling it for those who came after you. The less you spent, the more you roughed it, the better traveller you were. For some it was not just economical, it was spiritual. Working off some of that bad European karma, vaguely evening up the score. 'We lived just like villagers.' After India, there were some travellers who never used knives and forks, or a handkerchief, or a sit-down toilet again.

Canada was untroubled by the niceties of the sub-culture. He didn't look like the typical traveller either. Western males in Asia seemed to become feminised. Like Galen or Bob, or the travellers at the other tables, their muscles became wasted from dysentery, their bodies were lost within their own oversized clothes. Their hair grew, they adopted bangles or earrings or headscarves, their gestures were smaller, guarding their own space. Canada's denim shorts were tight around well-built thighs. He wore a heavy leather belt around his hips. He was square-featured and tanned like an old-time football star. The exchange of names didn't interest him. He called everyone 'Hey', they called him Canada.

The café owner's wife stood before them, smiling. Young, very upright and finely attentive though a child was hovering by her thigh. A grandmother held a baby, and an older child played around the kitchen door. They smiled at her as they gave their orders. Except Bob. He was deliberating over the omelette or the fried eggs.

'Excuse me, excuse me,' he called out after her as she had turned towards the kitchen. Again she stood before them.

'Look, do you mind, I'll have the boiled eggs instead, two soft-boiled eggs, two minutes each, understand? Two minutes.' He held up two fingers and tapped his watch. She nodded.

'Thank you so very much,' said Bob. He treated her to one of his weary smiles.

Ruth kept her head turned away as Bob subsided, satisfied, on the bench next to her. When they had first met Bob, in the German Dairy, a week and a country ago, she had not been sure whether in these transactions he wasn't trying to produce a comedy turn. He looked as if he was going to be funny, with all those schoolboy freckles and his hair barbered ruthlessly above his ears. He drank milkshakes for his health, he told them, by way of introduction, and his smile seemed benignly goofy under his milk-speckled moustache. Hepatitis, caught in India. Infinitely travel-worn, like all those emerging from the great sub-continent.

Like her, he couldn't seem to get the hang of foreign currency. 'This ... can't ... be ... right,' he had said to the German Dairy's proprietor. 'I ... will ... not ... pay ... so ... much.' He spoke in pained, deliberate tones, shaking his head slowly for emphasis. Galen had stepped in, and sorted it out for him. But he'd still felt aggrieved as he walked back with them to their hotel. Ruth's old hope, half forgotten in the serious business of travelling, of finding a fellow clown, died. He wasn't trying to be funny. It was a form of tantrum they were to see every time he had to part with his money.

'Nice place,' Ruth said to Galen, across the table. Galen didn't answer. He and Canada were picking their way through an abandoned Laotian newspaper, testing out their French.

'I thought you guys were supposed to be bilingual,' Galen was saying, laughing.

Their waitress brought them a pot of tea. Galen and Canada looked up, paused, motors idling over. Her swift fingers setting out the cups, her oval face …

'They take their time,' Bob muttered. 'I'm starving.' He reached a white freckled arm across her to pour himself a cup of tea.

Ruth's legs felt heavy as she crossed them. For a moment she thought of saying to Bob, 'Do you ever feel like you're an inferior physical species?' Like her, Bob was noticeably of Anglo-Saxon stock. Fair skin inclined to flush up in the heat. Blue eyes often sweat-stung. Beige teeth. Innocent knobbly white feet sprawling across thongs. But this was way beyond acceptable perimeters. *Too personal.* The sort of comment she used to make over wine at her own table, safe in that acknowledged femininity that she seemed to have left back in the West.

Was that what she meant? She felt she'd lost a whole persona somewhere along the trail. Become a mere trudging mate whom nobody seemed to hear. It wasn't just that mascara streaked down your face in the humidity and long hair was out of the question, you just tucked it back as best you could. She hated to catch sight of herself in shop mirrors. A large girl with a bare earnest face. Sexless as a missionary. And fat. Getting fatter. There were no shadows, no roles, no corners to hide in anywhere. Just the fact of yourself coming to meet you border after border.

'The women in these parts are supposed to be the most beautiful in the world,' Canada said to Galen. His steak had arrived. He was feeling convivial. 'Good grub, heh?'

'I wish I knew,' said Bob. His eggs had not appeared.

'It pays to order what they know,' Canada said, 'if you're hungry.' His eyes glittered at Bob above his busy jaw.

Ruth finished first. Galen worked slowly through his rice, his chopsticks moving in a ruminative way like the fingers of women crouched on doorsteps, searching through their children's hair. Galen had applied himself to the art of chopsticks as he did to everything, with the natural expectation of success.

Ruth preferred to use a fork. The way you could scoop and order and round up with your aggressive Western prongs. And the fork gave her more contact with the food somehow. Sometimes she felt that the closest relationship she had these days was with the plate of food in front of her.

'Ah, here we are,' Bob was saying, clearing his spot on the table. The eggs had arrived, lolling in a soup bowl. 'Not quite the usual presentation,' he had to add, but cheerfully enough, holding one down and tapping around its crown. He smoothed his moustache back, his spoon dived and was dropped clattering onto the table.

'Bloody concrete,' he said, reddening under his freckles. The eggs were both hard-boiled.

'He's infantile. It's embarrassing. It's so ... *colonial.*'

Ruth nudged Galen aside on the walk back to the hotel to share her anger with him in the dark. Bob had stood up in the café, waving his eggs at their waitress, calling out 'Look here.' They had left him personally supervising the timing of two more eggs in the kitchen.

'Well,' said Galen. 'So what?' He kept walking fast to catch up with Canada.

'I'm fed up with him. We've had him hanging round us since Chieng-Mai.'

'Oh God,' said Galen. 'Chaos in Laos.'

'Oh very clever.'

'Honestly,' said Galen, 'when you are just going to shut up and enjoy yourself like everybody else?'

'Don't lecture me,' cried Ruth. She wheeled off and sat on the steps of a building they were passing.

'I'm going on,' said Galen. She saw him meet up with Canada at the next corner and, both hunched over with hands in pockets, disappear into the shadows on the long avenue.

Ruth didn't sit there for long. The flap of a single pair of thongs was fast approaching. Like her, Bob had no sense of direction, and hated walking alone in the dark.

. . .

Back at Ted Akhito's, there was an hour left to them before curfew, but it was not inviting. A naked bulb hanging in the middle of the dormitory cast a subdued, yellowish light. Canada and Galen were making rapid male preparations for sleep. There was a flash of Galen's long hopping white legs, before he was magically prone, sheathed and flattened. It would have been indecent to watch Canada as he thrashed and muttered his way into his sleeping-bag and turned his face to the wall.

Galen re-surfaced. He lay half out of his bag, trying to read *Anna Karenin*; he maintained that he could not fall asleep without a dose of the printed word, but in this light he had to run his fingers under the lines like a ritual of prayer. Perhaps it was a gesture of waiting for Ruth. At home she always fell asleep to Galen's lamp and the soft turning of pages. She would have leaned across him, and said, 'Where are you up to?' Anna Karenin was her book; she had read it for four whole days in the hold of an Indonesian cargo boat.

She had been carried along by the book as much as by the boat, the story had unfolded to the rise and drop of the seas. Nineteenth century Russia would always be associated with the dazed hustle of their arrival in Djakarta.

Bob came panting up the stairs.

'There's not a soul to be seen out there. Do you think it's a sort of pre-battle hush?' He spoke loudly, as if he were rejoining a party.

'The light!' growled Canada from his corner. 'D'ya need that light?'

'All right, all right,' said Bob, 'it isn't curfew yet.' He lingered at the end of Galen's mat, ready to conspire. But Ruth had turned to unpack, and Galen was closing his book.

'Christ I'm tired,' said Bob. He flapped across the room to the door. They heard a hiss, 'Where's the ruddy switch?' and the light went out.

Ruth was left crouching by her pack, unresolved. Galen was still. She had intended to unpack, shake out her hair, write in her diary, all without reference to Galen, but within his range of observation: it would have been a wordless interaction that brought them to the conclusion of this day, and the battle between them that each day's travelling seemed to bring. Then one of them might have been ready to make a sign, that across these strange deprivations, their unity survived.

Darkness had pre-empted her. She was now a mere night scuffler. She moved like a thief, each sound was a betrayal. Unlayer her pack. Possessions as familiar as her hands. Book, sarong, diary, toothbrush. The layers descended in relevance. Right at the bottom, occasionally disturbed by the hands of customs officers, was a woollen sweater still smelling of home, and the photos of her family.

On the other side of Galen, Bob was crackling out his sleeping-bag. It was covered in a crisp papery plastic. For lightness. They had heard a lot about that bag. How it had been specially made for walking tours in Wales. Double thickness down, much too hot for Asia, with complicated aerations, all zip-controlled. Rolled up to the size of a giant green salami. A room-mate, French, had tried to rip it off in Calcutta.

Zip, crackle, deep sighs from Bob, more zips, more sighs. A final crackle. Enough to make the back of your skull crawl, Bob's horny feet manipulating plastic.

Galen had yawned, was turning over. Now to inch her way into her sleeping-bag, lay back her head. The big windows let in a grey translucence that had settled over the room. The night outside was silent. *You'd hardly know there was a war on,* she would write to her parents when they were safely out of Laos. She wrote them hasty air-letters of cool-minded reportage, casual feats of endurance. My goodness, they would write back, you have to be young!

Beside her, Galen had started moving, in a series of subtle, strait-jacketed shrugs. Ruth listened, and understood. He was taking off his passport pouch and money belt, and kicking them to his feet. 'Trust nobody,' they had been told. She shut her eyes. For yet another night, they were to lie side by side like brother and sister, burdened with old knowledge of each other. Galen, her husband for nearly half a year, had become a traveller, a different person to her. But he remained after all, like her, a well-warned child of the bourgeoisie. She turned over then, ready to sleep.

. . .

'Look after her,' Galen's father had said. Of course he hadn't had a tea-towel over one shoulder, down on the wharf, he was wearing his suit as he did whenever he left the farm, but that was how she saw him. Waving them off with a floury hand.

Every time Galen had taken her home, Norman would make scones. Rubbed butter into flour with trembling old brown hands. Cut the dough with an upturned sherry glass, up and down, swift as a process worker. 'Open the oven door for me darling,' he would say to Galen. Out the kitchen window, just beyond the chook sheds, you could see the bare brick walls of suburban houses. The poultry farm was in an outer suburb now. There had been nothing but bush and market gardens when Norman bought the place, and flatness, a convex landscape after England, Galen said. He'd been twelve. His mother died that year. He always called his home 'the farm'.

It took him an hour by bus to get to uni. He was always late for morning lectures. When she first knew him, he used to disappear mysteriously from pubs or parties. Slipping off to catch the last bus home. He got a lot of work done that way, he said.

Meeting Norman that first time, she'd been a bit breathy and overdone. She used to think she had to keep Galen entertained. She'd admired the scones, admired Norman's history book collection, pranced around the sheds and admired the chooks. Smoked like a chimney, dropping ash in her tea, but you couldn't do anything wrong in Norman's kitchen. As they were leaving (they were going to a party in Ruth's mother's Mini, Galen at the wheel), Norman had said then 'Look after her Galen.' Galen never answered.

In the humidity, Galen's face was very sallow. The acne scars across his jaw seemed to darken, reminders of an old battle. Now that he was so thin, he looked more like his father. Like this, from the side, his head bowed over the letter he was writing on his knee. She watched a tear of sweat escape his headband and linger in the hollow of his cheek. She could never imagine Galen with his mother. He seemed to spring straight from the mother and father both in Norman.

'Looks like rain,' Bob said.

They were sitting in the courtyard of a monastery, halfway up the hill overlooking the town. It didn't look like they would get much further. They were sated, even by rich smells that hung in the humidity, of dung and damp undergrowth, and rotting overripe fruit. Even Canada, having paced the circumference of the courtyard, was sitting down now, smoking, over by the gate.

That morning, their pace had quickened with the promise and strangeness of a new place. Luang Prabang, after a night's sleep, was a beautiful country town. There were red blossoming trees along roads that still gleamed from last night's rain. High above the town, a golden dome shone from a hilltop, like a fairy-tale turret. Townspeople smiled at them, curiously. They shared cigarettes and sign-language with a group of soft-faced, schoolboy monks. This was how they liked to be received, as a species of scruffy pilgrim.

'Stomach's feeling strange,' said Bob. 'Think I'm in for another attack of the runs.'

Galen wrote on, rapidly. *I am sitting on the steps of a tenth century drinking-fountain,* she read at the top of his page, *in thirty-five degree humidity.* Facts she hadn't been aware of.

A bell had rung and the monks had disappeared. The sky that hung before them over the town was now a luminous grey. Palm trees in the courtyard started to rustle and wave. Nobody else seemed to be around.

Canada stubbed out his cigarette and started back down the hill.

'Coming?' said Bob to Galen.

The four of them moved towards the town like an awkward beast whose legs wished to go different ways. Canada was off-hand, accompanying them this morning as if there were nothing better to do. He walked ahead, restlessly peering into doorways of the ochre-coloured buildings, disappearing up alleys, looking for action. His presence made Ruth uneasy.

She was used to travelling at Galen's pace. He always had an air of elation about him, discovering new territory. He loved to plan their route, and fit together the puzzle of map and reality. His passport pouch swung out and back to its bay within his hollow ribcage. The tails of the black and white scarf he wore as a headband flew out behind him. Travelling was a feast of the eye, he said. Was there such a state as pure vision?

While she trailed, glimpsing the backdrop through a web of thoughts. Like watching ants as a child, guessing at purpose and connection in a teeming other world. Distanced by the huge eye of the self.

Sometimes she found herself silently in step with Bob. He always seemed to be holding his words in check, until he caught up with Galen. Bumping together, they didn't even bother to say sorry.

'Ouch,' said Galen suddenly. She had walked into him and trodden on one of his thongs. He held it up by one dangling tentacle.

'Sorry,' Ruth said. Galen was very attached to those thongs. His Bangkok thongs. He called them art objects. The crinkled rubber was printed with a series of red and green music notes, gay inconsequential crochets and quavers, worn away now to the hills and valleys of his feet.

'Damn,' he said. His eyes, looking at her, were as dark as the black checks in his scarf. *'Why can't you keep up with me?'*

. . .

The rain didn't matter. Running in the rain had been one of her specialities in the old days. Theatrical liberation like moonlight swims and talking for a whole evening in her 'Juliet of the Spirits' voice. Funny, you couldn't see the rain falling. Just the puddles widening, dimpling, somehow connected with the descent of the huge grey sky.

Already the aisles through the market stalls were running miniature rivers, gorges, lakes. She had to hitch up her skirt, pry up each footstep, her shoulder-bag slapping against her hip. Not such a short cut back to the hotel after all. Galen in bare feet would be nearly at the Melody by now. Untrammelled.

Most of the stalls were empty, the mats rolled up where this morning's produce had been laid out. Just a few women under one of the big umbrellas, smoking and laughing. Probably at her, the only person out in the rain. Eyes down, picking her way home as fast as she could. Focus on that emptiness three paces ahead. Do not look at me. Alone, it was always like this.

. . .

'Hey,' Canada said, appearing at the top of the stairs and turning back to the others. 'D'ya hear about the two German guys? They hired themselves a boat and went downriver. Haven't been seen since.'

'Pathet Lao got 'em I spose,' called out Bob. 'Anyone know for sure?'

'Ask Ted Akhito,' said Galen, on his way to the dormitory. The other laughed.

Ruth looked up from the mat that defined her territory. It was late afternoon, they had taken what you might call a long lunch. Whenever she was not with them they seemed to come a little closer to the action of the place.

Surprisingly they came and stood around her mat. Galen crouched down beside her. Bob started moving his hands together and apart in a little concertina movement that she had come to recognise. He was shuffling an imaginary pack of cards.

'We've decided to play bridge,' he told her.

'I don't play,' Ruth said.

The three of them were damp and breathless, seemed to be sharing a joke. Boyos returning from the pub. Galen put a hand on her shoulder. He was still barefoot.

'Bob's going to teach you. Bob's going to be your partner.'

'You know I hate playing cards,' Ruth said to him.

Bob and Canada were already settling themselves around a spare mat under the window.

'Come on,' Galen said. 'We'll be nice to you. Promise.'

Bob was dealing.

'You sort them into suits,' he said. 'Descending order of value. Ace, King, Queen Jack – 4, 3, 2, 1.' He was frowning, busy, spitty-sharp. Bob came into his own when he played cards.

The faces on the cards were stern and mediaeval as they spilled out of her hand. Bob went on, about contracts, tricks, trumps.

'What?' she said to Galen.

'Just listen and play,' Galen said, not looking up from his own cards. 'You'll pick it up.' That's what he had always done.

On the other side of her, Canada lazily pulled cards in and out of the fan in his hand. He lay on his side, one heavy thigh lapping the other. His eyes had never flickered once in her direction. Why had she let herself be drawn into this? Listen. Keep up. Play.

'Nine clubs,' she offered, hopefully.

Bob flung down his cards.

'You haven't been listening, have you? You don't understand.'

Ruth couldn't help the slow smile spreading across her face.

'I can't seem to see the point of the game.' She heard Galen begin to laugh.

'Hey,' said Canada to Galen. 'How long have you been travelling with this chick?'

Galen couldn't stop laughing. He rolled onto his back and up again, his headband fell across his eyes.

'Oh boy.' He put a hand on Ruth's knee. 'This is for life,' he said.

. . .

'*Mais où est* Ted Akhito?' Ruth asked the clerk in the Air Lao office again.

Ca ne fait rien Madame, *vous pouvez payer ici*,' came the same reply.

Ruth turned back to the others. 'It's no good. We'll just have to give him the hotel money and hope for the best.'

'Ask for a receipt,' said Galen.

'Bloody irresponsible,' said Bob, counting out his notes. 'I think we have every right not to pay.' But they had already decided that it would be too risky just to leave the town without somehow paying the mysterious Ted Akhito, whom they had never seen since that first night. He probably had friends in high places.

'Hurry up,' said Canada. Outside, the Air Lao cattle truck that ferried passengers between the airport and the town had started up its engine. As before, they were to be its only passengers.

Ruth was the first to sling her bag into the back of the truck. The others hoisted themselves up while she climbed over the boards at the side and swung in. The truck lurched off. They held on to the cabin, standing up.

'All right?' Galen asked Ruth. She nodded.

After their long walk to the Golden Dome, Ruth and Galen had told the others that they would be leaving Luang Prabang the next day. Bob said it was funny, but he'd been thinking of leaving too. Canada just seemed to be with them as they were buying their tickets. You could get used to a place very quickly, they said, it was always a relief to be moving on.

From the truck they could see behind their street now, to paddy-fields spreading under water, islanded with palm-trees and bamboo huts, dotted with bending, slow-moving figures. The truck was speeding up. Now, in their final glimpse of the town, they could grasp its strictly civic plan, its streets and squares set out under the Golden Dome, the steaming river that curved around it and disappeared into alien hills. Like the two Germans, who had never been found. A flock of camouflage-splattered helicopters rose like smoke in the distance. In those hills and jungles there would be the sort of scenes you see in newsreels at home.

'Hey!' Canada was pointing across a square. There, surely, hurrying out of a building, was the neat white figure of Ted Akhito.

'Well I like that,' Bob said. But they were all smiling. They had rightly been judged not to be security risks. They were too lazy. Too cautious. You'd hardly know there was a war on. If you played by the rules.

The town was behind them now, shadowed by its own hills.

. . . . . .

September 11, 2001

KEN HALEY

Wheelchair travel is hard enough, but when you're on the road on September 11, 2001, it can get a lot harder.

*E**ven they* [Americans] *may one day know fire and… the sword… for it is hard to believe that when one half of the world is living through terrible disasters the other half can continue… learning about the distress of its distant fellow-men only from movies and newspapers. If something exists in one place, it will exist everywhere.*
— CZESLAW MILOSZ *The Captive Mind* (1950)

. . .

SEPTEMBER–OCTOBER 2001
Day 134 (11 September): TBILISI
On this beautiful autumnal afternoon I wander through the picturesque quarter of Zemo Kala. In a sun-dappled park, two old men play chess under a tree while others watch on intently. The world is at peace.

At seven o'clock this balmy evening I take my seat to the back of a private box at the glittering Paliashvili Opera House. The curtain is about to rise on a performance of *Turandot* by (drum roll please, maestro) the Batumi Children's Opera and Ballet Company. Billed as the world's only juvenile troupe presenting works from the standard repertoire, the Batumi is an ensemble whose accomplishments I await with a dull dread. 'Puccini by six-year-olds?' I wonder condescendingly as the recorded orchestra strikes up.

I need not have feared. The singing is pitch-perfect, the costumes are resplendent. Who care if 'Summertime' and 'I Could Have Danced All Night' do not seem entirely of a piece with Italian tradition? American themes divert our attention, but inclusion is not the same thing as intrusion. 'If something exists in one place, it will exist everywhere.'

Batumi, on the Black Sea coast, is the capital of Adzharia, virtually a breakaway province of Georgia. Whatever their motives, the Adzharian government and other sponsors of the company, comprising 250 performers between the ages of six and sixteen, invested A$150,000 in the dream of a children's opera.

If a dream can become reality, the reverse also holds true. The odd aria still coursing through my mind shields me from all thought of the real world as the taxi drops me back at Nika's pension. On the stroke of midnight I press the buzzer, the gate swings open and Nika's niece, looking more pallid than usual, whispers, 'Have you heard what has happened in America?'

Day 135 (12 September): TBILISI
Nika appears on the balcony, her grey hair Electra-wild. 'This is the end of the world!' she exclaims, hands flailing. I tune into the BBC on shortwave while her niece fetches a black-and-white TV from the first floor. An incredulous onlooker is describing the fall of someone from the 104th storey of the World Trade Center, but already the 'live' report is taped history. The images I see, when the old set sparks into life – including the one of that airliner banking round to register its fatal impact on the temporarily spared twin tower – are spectral, like those long-ago images of Neil Armstrong planting white boots in moondust. These images,

too, appear to come from another world: certainly not the one we have lived in until now. The times have lurched us forward, or maybe backwards, and it occurs to me that – even if Nika was being more hysterical than historical – the crevasse between yesterday and today is so jagged that those seven words she uttered may prove to be right.

This is the day my distant fellow-men have come to know fire, and the 'sword', at least in the form of the box-cutter. My heart goes out to the victims, and not just the dead. Being caught in the crosshairs of history is something I can identify with – even if the analogy is imperfect (I, at least, am alive to tell the tale). Their lives were cut short in an apocalyptic second; my own trauma extended over months.

The acute and eternal pain inflicted on those hundreds of thousands of Americans related to those who perished, or who knew them as workmates, church-goers-mosque-goers, come to that – reminds me that behind the gruesome pictures and war-size banner headlines lies a deeply disturbing fact: for these people, the world has gone mad.

Weltschmerz engulfs us all today but, while others gaze on scenes from Dante's Inferno for hours on end, I spy the madness through a keyhole. A world gone mad is something I have comprehended since 1990, because that's when mine did. Madness is being disconnected from everything you expect. One thing in my life – but nothing in my lifetime – was as unexpected and horrible as this. I sleep, but fitfully.

Pre-dawn TV, BBC for breakfast, more Fukuyama pronouncements from Nika. The need to travel – to escape the 21st century, to grasp something permanent in a river swollen with flotsam – bears down on me. By a quirk of historical timing, my original plan to visit the town of Mtskheta,

Georgia's spiritual centre, now seems far-sighted.

Only the religious trinket-sellers outside the cathedral compound detract from the timeless peace of Georgia's Westminster Abbey. Past the sadly solitary bronze bell lying on the ground, I enter the vast dark interior of the church between age-weathered sandstone pillars. If Catholic rites seem dramatic to one raised amid bare-bones Protestantism, Orthodox churches can only be described as melodramatic. Priests clad in all-black soutanes glide noiselessly to and fro, lighting candles which glow mesmerically in the gloom but do nothing to lessen the sepulchral atmosphere of the great vault.

Even with the silent tread of a wheelchair tyre, I alter course to avoid trampling on the grave of an elder of the church, or the tombstone of a king.

A stocky woman wearing a coloured headscarf rhythmically sweeps the slate floors and marble-topped resting places of the great and glorious. At the far end of the nave I can make out the fresco of a haloed Christ. A single speck of sunlight strikes the open palm, for all the world like his own votive candle held out as a timely peace offering to the 'real world'.

In the afternoon I am back in Tbilisi, wading through a deluge of shell-shocked emails at a suburban Internet café, when I turn to the cubicle behind me and see a big strong man blubbering like a baby. 'Are you all right?' I ask, foolishly in the circumstances. He is an American, a law student on an exchange of some type. The details escape me; his shock is with me still.

Day 137 (14 September): TBILISI
This evening is spent in a bar frequented by expatriates, a rendezvous arranged before September 11 with the couple who gave me the lift from Azerbaijan. Now, with quite a

knot of Americans among the clientele, the Friday-night get-together has the air of a wake. The TVs, which would normally be screening sports matches, are tuned to the memorial service from Washington. The sound is off, but pictures convey all the essential information: Bush speaking to the mortified crowd, the flag at half mast, Billy Graham at public prayer. To break up the sombreness, we get – instead of ad breaks – incessant replays of those grisly, now eternal, moments of impact.

Day 138 (15 September): TBILISI
For the first time I consider the impact on my own plans. Do I carry on regardless? Should I wait and see how things develop? An email arrives from a Canadian friend living in the Philippines. 'GO HOME, KEN!' it screams. That's one option I dismiss out of hand. As my travel plans don't include New York, where's the danger? Reason counsels me to note down the trend of events, and take my cue from that. Intuition isn't so sure.

Day 139 (16 September): GORI
After 70 rollicking kilometres, the morning train from Tbilisi judders to a stop in front of the station entrance in this ancient town, now best known as the birthplace of one of the biggest mass murderers of the 20th century, Josef Stalin. A large oil portrait of the original Man of Steel keeps guard over the entrance.

Well over half those of working age in Gori today are unemployed. A group of louche youths with swastikas tattooed on their forearms hang about outside the museum dedicated to Josef Vissarionovich Dzhugashvili, worker's hero. His childhood home is a humble log cabin. The clear impression is that young Joe learnt early on how to get by without the necessities of life, an attitude he would strive diligently to pass on to the masses in later years.

This man, or monster, arguably influenced more lives in the 20th century than any other, keeping in mind his mass deportations of whole nationalities as much as his purges and diabolical pact with Hitler. So it is fitting that the Stalin Museum, erected in 1957, is a 'palace' on a grandiose scale. Today the museum is officially closed but a security guard opens it up in return for a vodka-money bribe and somehow summons Larissa, the English-speaking guide, from only he knows where.

I take five minutes to haul myself up the grand marble staircase while the guard carries my empty chair to the first floor with cavalier inexpertise. Here, restored to my perch, I see the life of Stalin unfold through several memorial halls. The most remarkable exhibit of all is Larissa's unshakable belief in her hero as 'the most popular figure of the 20th century'.

'But what,' I confront her, 'about the 60 million people who met a violent end during his quarter century in power?'

Larissa will have none of it: 'He is pictured as a very cruel man in films but he was not a harsh man. He was a very plain, ordinary and modest person, and used to listen to people.'

Day 141 (18 September): KOBULETI

I have taken a bus to the Black Sea, which means I have now crossed the Caucasus from sea to shining sea in just under a month.

Here at Kobuleti I have planned a two-week halt to work out the following five months' itinerary. For the next fortnight I will map out the route ahead, country by country, choosing in what order to visit them, where I will need to seek visas, where not. But now there is no way to know what lies around the corner: pleasant and stimulating times, a jihad or a fifth Crusade that will imperil the life of any Westener who sets foot – or wheel – on the Arabian Peninsula.

On calmer reflection, the best course becomes clear: wait to see where the Americans, or their enemies, strike. If the Middle East is too dangerous to contemplate, switch the original order and go to Eastern Europe first. Perhaps after a few months the Middle East will have stabilised and the way will be open to make it the last leg of the voyage.

Day 142 (19 September): KOBULETI

Dining tonight at a corner table on a pavement outside a local restaurant, the soup course is interrupted by a car ramming the pillar a metre in front of me and threatening either to come crashing into the table or explode. The driver keeps revving the engine until smoke pours out of the cabin, forcing him to eject while there is time to do so. Waiters hover, warily, but before they can usher me away to a less exposed table the driver – a wild-eyed man in a ragged wine-drenched shirt – rushes into the restaurant and starts yelling incoherently. The waiters disappear, replaced by the apologetic owner offering a word of explanation: 'Morphinisti', which I assume means 'drug addict': Kobuleti is clearly not quite the backwater I'd imagined it to be.

ARMENIA: 3 – 23 OCTOBER
Day 156 (3 October): VANADZOR

At the Armenian border a Georgian immigration officer, spotting that I had spent exactly one month in his country on a 30-day visa, muttered something about 'overstay'. His mental calculator could almost be heard clicking over and dollar signs gleamed in the reflection of his stare. But, after ten seconds of suspense even he had to concede the truth in the old rhyme: 'Thirty days hath September ...' I will say this for him: he managed a gracious chuckle while bestowing my exit stamp.

The most gripping thing about Vanadzor is that everyone, it seems, wants to leave it. On the main street a large crowd of grim faces mills outside the police station day after day. I am told they are there to pay bribery money for the next step in the emigration process that will take them, they all hope, to one of the promised lands: France, the US, and I suppose Australia.

The only guesthouse that can accommodate me is a real find: family-run, its elderly owners ply me with tea and homemade cake. This is my introduction to Armenian hospitality, and after a whole night of undisturbed sleep I am in for a hearty breakfast and a welcome surprise: the grandparents run a bakery out the back that makes my first morning in Armenia the sweetest-smelling of the entire journey. I head for the bus station laden with fresh gifts.

Day 157 (4 October): VANADZOR TO DILIJAN

A fellow passenger on the bus strikes up a conversation. His English is of the barest minimum but persistent, and eventually I make out that he is asking where I will be staying in Diligan.

As I can never be 100 per cent sure in advance, my vagueness encourages him. Pointing to his chest, and then to me, he says, 'Home!'

How can I say no? While it will be very embarrassing all round if it turns out I cannot use the toilet – we are in the sticks of western Asia so I don't even know if it is a Western-style fixture – neither of us has enough language in common for me to broach the matter diplomatically. So, I accept.

My new friend Samuel, it emerges, is one of the bus drivers on this line, but today he is returning home as a passenger. I needn't have worried about creature comforts, as I discover soon after our arrival in the ex-mountain resort of Dilijan. Samuel, Susan, Fruzik, Alva, Mane, Marie and Samson are an extended family. From the first hour when I am respectfully left to rest in the hammock on their porch to the moment four days later when I catch a Yerevan-bound *marshrutka* (minibus) at Tsakhadzor, these are days that travellers live for, to write home about and recollect years later.

Four days is long enough to meet the cousin who teaches English and comes for what I would call dinner, if the richest banquet ever laid before a non-head of state can merit such a mundane description. It is also long enough to discover that the Saruhanyan family own four cows (one of them kept in the garage, exposing Samuel's car to the elements) and that, from their bountiful milk supply, the grandmother of this extended family, Alva, makes the world's best, tangiest cheese. Scoured into tongue-tempting kiss-curls, it goes with the creamiest of butter on the most enticing of bread rolls.

The Saruhanyans may live a long way from the big smoke but they are as clued up as anyone in New York or Sydney. The TV is tuned into Moscow these nights and they glance at it sidelong from the dinner table, as if Frankenstein's monster has taken up residence in the living room. Once their thoughts are translated, I know they await the outbreak of hostilities in Afghanistan any day now. They are quiet Christians, and the invasion of their land by Muslims–Arabs and later Persians – is unforgettable folk memory.

Day 158 (5 October): LAKE SEVAN

Samuel drives me an hour across verdant valleys – we're still following the Silk Road thousands of kilometres west of Uzbekistan – when suddenly, as if viewed over the rim of a silver goblet, the blue-green waters of one of the world's highest lakes take the breath away.

We skirt the shore south-east to Moraduz, a stunning lakeside cemetery of ancient, medieval and modern stone crosses. Known as *kachkars*, these highly decorated crucifixes are uniquely Armenian works of art. In one instance, several *kachkars* line the walls of a tomb vault reminiscent of a small house, complete with its own doorway. Writing with a stick in the sand, Samuel indicates it is a thousand years old.

Day 160 (7 October): YEREVAN

Down a winding mountain our marshrutka snakes its way towards Yerevan, Armenia's ancient and modern capital.

I'm in luck finding a room at the Hotel Erebuni, smack in the centre of town. The hotel faces onto Republic Square; and backs onto a car park that doubles as the pick-up point for buses to what may still be my next destination, Iran. The manager interrupts a meeting to greet me personally and offers me a complimentary bottle (not a glass, mind you) of cognac, the country's most famous product (not counting emigrants). The message is coming through loud and clear: Armenian hospitality never fails.

I remember to ask for a room with a view of Mount Ararat and, once inside, lie down on the bed for a quick rest. Two hours later I lift my head from the pillow and begin unpacking my bags. After a modest drop of the smooth liqueur, I tune in to cable TV. 'This is CNN.' The 'war on terror' has entered a new phase. Bombs are dropping on

Kabul. The campaign to oust the Taliban, and hunt down Osama bin Laden, has begun. Propped up by pillows, I sit transfixed till midnight.

— From *Emails from the Edge*

. . . . . .

CLOSE-UPS

The Last Visit

PADDY O'REILLY

Amanda has gone downhill in the three years since her sister Georgie has seen her, but Georgie hasn't a clue: 'You're not anorexic are you?
Aren't you hot in that cardigan?'.

My sister Georgie tells me she's coming to visit. I haven't heard from her in three years. My first thought is, what does she want? My second thought is, she can't have it.

The cafe tables are packed so tight the waiter has to rise on his toes to pass between the customers. He eases his buttocks past my head and delivers plates heaped with eggs and bacon to three men at the table beside us, who raise forkfuls to their mouths as they eye off Georgie. She's always had this effect. She is a double D cup. I stare at the men and they look quickly back at their plates. Everyone sees me and knows. Everyone except my sister.

'Anyway, Georgie, have to head off,' I say. 'Heard a friend of mine's sick, so I'm going to visit her.'

'Do you want me to come? When will I see you?' she asks and I put her off by saying we'll go to the movies together before she leaves. I'm still thinking, what does she want?

I drop my sister at the door of her friend's house and go back to work. Joe's waiting for me on the corner.

'What the fuck are you wearing?' he asks.

'I'm about to change,' I say, and I strip off my cardigan and duck behind the fence to change my skirt and stockings. The strip of mouldy concrete between the fence and the flats reeks of piss and vomit and I hop around trying to make sure my bare feet never touch the ground.

'Did you hear Cherie's sick?' I ask Joe when I come out with my pretend clothes stuffed into my shoulder bag.

'Cherie's on the way out,' he says.

'What do you mean "on the way out"?' I say, but Joe shrugs and heads off down the road.

For the rest of the day I keep thinking about what he said and I sit and smoke cigarettes on my corner and chat a bit to the girls hanging around on the corner opposite and take a couple of jobs, just quickies to the beach carpark and back. Every now and then I shiver.

That night, I go round to Cherie's flat. No-one answers my knock but the door swings open when I push it. The place stinks. Two cats sit on the kitchen table lashing their tails and further inside, in the bedroom, I can hear Cherie moaning.

She's coming off, I can tell right away. She's yellowish and sweating and mumbling and when I say, 'Hey Cherie, it's Amanda, I came to see if you needed anything,' she looks straight at me but she doesn't seem to know who I am.

'Everyone sends their love,' I tell her, even though she probably can't hear me. I back out of the room, which also smells pretty bad because Cherie hasn't moved off that bed in days.

I take a look around the flat before I leave. When I open the fridge the cats jump off the table. They twist around my legs until I pull out a crusty piece of pizza and drop it on the floor. In the lounge room is an ancient record player and four records, and a bunch of CDs but no CD player. I take a couple of the CDs since they obviously can't use them.

As I pull the door shut behind me Cherie's flatmate appears at the top of the stairs.

'Is Cherie trying to get clean?' I ask her.

'No-one knows,' Maree says.

The last time I saw Maree she was wearing a brand new shirt that I offered to buy off her, a paisley shirt with big purple buttons. But she must have sold it to someone else because I didn't see it in the flat and now she's back to wearing the same old slutty tube top and hot pants with her fat thighs hanging out and her boobs sagging down to her knees. I can't believe half the girls who get tricks down Grey Street. Are the johns blind?

'But at least she's stopped screaming,' Maree says. 'I think she's over the bad bit.' She puts her key in the lock and realises the door is open.

'Fuck,' she says. 'Did fucking Cherie leave this door open again? I'll fucking kill her. I've got valuables in there.'

'Well, I'll see you later,' I say. I take the stairs two at a time on my way down.

I don't like to leave Cherie there like that, with no-one knowing what she wants, but what can I do? On the way up Jackson Street I run into Joe.

'See, I told you. She's on the way out,' he says. Joe always knows where I've been, even when I'm too out of it to know myself.

'You're giving me the creeps. Do something.'

'What am I supposed to do?'

'Where's her bloke?'

'I told you, she's on the way out. He knows that. No point throwing good money after a dead loss.'

I rest my hand on the arm of Joe's leather jacket. The leather is cracked and dry. 'Is that what you're going to do to me? Tell everyone I'm on the way out and leave me to lie in my own shit?'

Joe brushes my hand away. He pulls a smoke out of his breast pocket. A score falls on the ground and he bends over and picks up the silver packet, saying 'Whoops,' and laughing.

'Of course I won't,' he says, lifting the lighter into his cupped hand and lighting the smoke. 'It'll be the best care for you, baby.'

'Baby? You've been watching too much TV.'

. . .

At home Kareen's eating fish and chips out of a box and watching TV.

'Seen your sister?' she says.

'Went to see Cherie.'

'Oh yeah? How is she?'

'They say she's on her way out.'

'Shit,' she says, and lifts the box toward me. 'Want a potato cake?'

We watch *The Simpsons* and the news on a couple of stations and *Sale of the New Century*. I know all the answers except three hard ones.

'You should go on that,' Kareen says. She keeps wandering in and out of the bedroom and the lounge room as she dresses for work. She drifts through wearing a bra and no panties, then a bra and panties and a pair of shoes, then a pair of shoes and panties and no bra.

'Are you going to put something else on top of that, or are you in the mood to get booked?' I say to her.

'Can I wear your leather jacket?' she asks.

'No.'

'Well, what about that green skirt – the short one?'

'No.'

She goes back into the bedroom and comes out wearing her jeans and a tight jumper. Kareen is only sixteen and very pretty with a soft red mouth. She could have been a model.

'That looks all right,' I say, tucking the label of her jumper in. 'Why did you want to get dressed up anyway?'

'Oh, you know. I dunno.'

She's blushing. I heard she's got a crush on a john, some older guy who cruises on Friday nights. He's picked her up three weeks in a row. He drives a sporty Lexus and gives her an extra tip each time. I've seen her hiding the money in her tampon box, as if she thinks that will be safe from Joe. Joe's only known her a few weeks. He asked me to let her stay in my flat while she got on her feet.

'She's been abused,' he said. 'She needs a bit of kindness. I know you'll be good to her.'

'So name me one of the girls who hasn't been abused. Big deal. You get her a flat. I don't want to share, I've told you that a million times.'

Like I had a choice. She moved in the next day and I got a punch in the kidneys for my attitude. 'You're smart, Mandy, and you're not out of control like some girls, but you're gonna be a victim of your own attitude one day.' That's what he always says to me when he's angry.

They used to tell me the same thing at school. 'Young lady, mind your attitude. Why can't you be more like your sister?'

Because I'm someone else, I wanted to answer. Because things happen differently for me. And because you have no idea who we are.

. . .

Next day at the needle exchange van, Maree stands in front of me in the queue.

'How's Cherie?' I ask.

'Gone,' Maree answers through a mouthful of dim sim.

My heart lurches. Well, I think it's my heart but it might be my liver or my stomach or my bowels. Anyway something inside does a kind of hip hop because I think she means Cherie is dead.

'When? How?' I'm standing quite still, holding my needles. Someone shoves me in the back and tells me to get a move on.

'Last night. She went quiet and I thought I'd better look at her and she was real pale, Casper, you know, and twitching? So I called the ambulance and they took her to the Alfred.'

'And what did they say?'

'I dunno. I had to get my videos back before twelve. I get home and I think, great, I can have my bed back now, I'm so sick of sleeping on that fucking couch, but the bed's gross. She shat in it!'

'Well she was sick, Maree. Get it? Sick? No-one to look after her?'

Maree slumps off, stuffing another dim sim in her mouth. I pocket my syringes and walk around the corner to where Joe's waiting.

'I'm going to get off this stuff,' I say as he hands me a deal.

'Go for it,' he says.

'I mean it.'

'Yeah well, I hear it's been done, but I sure don't know any of them. Unless you count the ones in the morgue.'

'Very funny,' I say, and I set off up the hill in Grey Street toward my corner on Burnett Street. There's a lunchtime rush.

'What's your secret?' a girl calls out from across the road. 'I'm getting nothing.'

'My charm and sophistication,' I call back.

Joe's not due back till three. I figure I've made enough money to take a short break.

The green cool park rolls by outside the tram window. Joggers sweat it out around the track and a couple of teenagers are pashing on the grass. I lean my head against the warm glass and relax until I remember I'm going to the movies with my sister tonight. She wants to have a drink afterwards and talk. After all these years she wants to talk. I know she's a good person. Everyone likes Georgie. But it's too late for talking.

I was happy this morning when I realised Cherie wasn't dead. Now that's gone pop and the good mood has shot out of me like air out of a balloon. I can't believe I'm going to visit her in the hospital. She ripped me off on a deal once and I was sick for days thanks to whatever she'd cut it with. On the street these things happen all the time but you always hope the other girls won't do you over. They do. You have to let it go.

Last summer Cherie and I caught the train to Sovereign Hill theme park. We panned for gold. In the first handful of gravel she found a speck of gold and got all fired up.

'It's a sign. My luck's changing. I'm going to get clean and get out of this crap life.'

'A sign? A sign from the management,' I said. 'They put gold in the creek every day.'

'You didn't get any,' she pointed out.

The first thing we did when we got back to town was score. But maybe she is finally getting clean.

At the hospital reception desk I realise how stupid I really am. I don't know Cherie's second name. I don't even know if Cherie is her real name. Amanda isn't mine. The woman behind the desk keeps putting her hands out in front of her like a mime, making a wall between her and me and saying

'I'm sorry I can't help you, but without that information ... I'm sorry.'

By the time I've finished making a fool of myself there I've been gone for an hour already, so I take a taxi back. I offer the driver a couple of CDs as payment and he leaves the meter off and drives me back. As we pull up at Burnett Street I see Joe sitting on the fence, smoking a cigarette and chatting up the girls on the other corner. He smiles as I cross the road and I know I'm in trouble.

'Been having a lunch break?' he asks.

'Look,' I say, 'I just wanted to see Cherie–'

'What do you think this is? An office job?'

'I didn't ... ' I can feel myself coming right down. My body is starting to ache, hungry for a fix.

'Well?' Joe says.

'Joe, please. I just went to see Cherie, that's all. I was only gone half an hour.'

'But you didn't get to see her, did you,' he says.

I'm not surprised he knows. He knows everything about me. I sit down beside him and pull a cigarette from my bag. Joe lights it for me with his Zippo, the oily smoke curling up my nostril. At least he's not going to make me pay for leaving my corner.

'I am sorry about Cherie, all right?' he says. 'But life goes on. Anyway, what did I tell you about the ones who get clean being in the morgue? Was I right or was I right?'

Early that night after I get home and fixed up, Kareen runs in the door crying and trying to hide a bruise on her left cheek. I pull her hand away. The bruise is red, but tomorrow it will be purple and round and swollen, like passionfruit.

'Was it Joe?' I ask.

She shakes her head.

'Who was it?' I say. Kareen doesn't answer. 'Who was it?' I shout.

'Joe,' she sobs. 'It was Joe. He heard about my extra tips.'

Kareen goes for a shower and comes out of the bathroom in her pyjamas and with her hair in a towel. Warm soapy steam follows her into the lounge room. She flops on the couch and pulls on her slippers, great fluffy things with bunny faces on the toes.

'I don't want you in this flat anymore,' I tell Kareen. 'Go and get a job. Get a life. Get out.'

Spit bubbles to the corners of her pretty red lips as she blubbers.

'Please Mandy. I'll clean up the flat. I won't…'

'I don't want you here anymore. Go back to your family.'

My mobile rings. Georgie starts talking about which film we'll see and I let her run on while I watch Kareen gingerly dab her face with a wet dishcloth. I think about what I should wear to the pictures. When Georgie arrived in Melbourne I went to her friend's house wearing cargo pants and a woolly cardigan I'd bought at the op shop that morning, the kind of clothes she'd always worn and I never had. She hugged me and asked if I was eating properly.

'You're not anorexic, are you?' she said. 'Aren't you hot in that cardigan?'

This was the kind of thing she'd always said to me. Full of judgement – without a clue about what was going on. I tugged at the sleeves, pulling them down over my knuckles and shook my head.

'You look tired,' she said.

I knew what I looked like.

...

Georgie buys the movie tickets.

'You must be doing it hard on a kitchen hand's salary,' she says. 'Hey, how's your friend, the one who was sick?'

'Cherie? Oh, she's all fixed up.' Kitchen hand. I wonder if my sister is an idiot. Everyone else takes one look at me and knows – how can she miss it?

We sit in the dark cinema watching the heads on the screen nod and sway. Fleshy mouths open and shut too fast. I can't listen to what they're saying. The shooting starts and when the screen explodes with bullets and bombs and screaming I turn to my sister and say, 'I'm a whore and a junkie, sis. I'm a whore and a junkie.' I stare at her profile, saying it over and over, but she's caught up in the world of the movie and she can't hear. We stay until the last credit has faded and the house lights come up. Georgie looks around blinking as if she has just woken up. She laughs and says, 'It's only the film tragics like us who stay till the end.'

I leave her outside the theatre. 'Great to see you. Won't have another chance before you leave. Take care, big sis.'

She frowns and tries to grab my hand but I pull away.

'I thought we could go to a pub,' she says. 'I wanted to have a chat. About Dad. I never–'

'Maybe next time,' I call back over my shoulder. I have to force myself not to run.

When I get home I take a Valium and try to think about Cherie again. I can picture the flake of gold stuck to her fingertip. The man in old-time clothes put the gold in a glass vial for her to take home. Her lucky charm. I drink a few shots of whisky and have a cry in the bath.

At midnight I wake Kareen and show her where to hide money so Joe will never find it.

. . . . . .

The Worst Thing

PHILIP CANON

*A separated father's desperate attempts
to stay close to his son.*

I have a therapist. Once a week, I sit in front of him and tell him how I feel. He starts each session with 'How has your week been?' and I spill over with anger and hurt at what Jenny, my ex-partner, has done this time. I first went to him when she stopped my mid-week visits to our son Luke. She said they were too disruptive. Since then it has been one incursion into my relationship with Luke after another. Phone calls are 'disruptive' too. If I write him letters she returns them. Not so long ago, he spent half of every week with me. Now, when I drop Luke back to Jenny's, I have to park out the front of her house, say goodbye to him at the foot of the drive and watch him disappear through the gate with his little backpack. Under no circumstances am I to drive up her driveway. This decree is in her latest letter.

'It's like fucking Hitler,' I say to the therapist. 'Before anyone knew it he had half of Europe.'

Last weekend I took Luke to the football. When he got up, I made him put on his Carlton jumper. I pointed to the flag I had bought him. 'You can wave that whenever they score a goal.' Luke shrugged and said, 'Der.' He started playing with his warrior spinning tops. He was writing in a little notebook, keeping trace of which top won the most battles.

The last time I took Luke out into the park to play kick to kick, I tried to teach him how to hold the ball for a drop punt and a torpedo. He preferred to drop the ball lengthwise across his foot and kick it high in the air so that he could mark his own kick. I pressed him to make leads and have shots at goal, but he lost interest and said he was tired. When I insisted, he got upset and I felt like a bad father as well as being an every-second-weekend one.

Around midday, I was ready to head to the ground, only a short walk across Princes Park. I tempted Luke with the promise of chips and hot doughnuts. 'We can kick the footy on the ground after the game,' I'd said. 'We'll get in a bit of practice in the park beforehand.' Luke didn't acknowledge what I'd said and I fought the fear that he was already a casualty in his mother's war against me. He was looking through a pair of binoculars at all the activity around the stadium, visible from his bedroom window. 'I can see someone under a truck,' he said, 'he's been there for ages.'

At the last minute Luke told me that he didn't want to go to the game. He said he was tired and wanted to watch all the people for a bit. He was sitting in a chair with the binoculars around his neck. His feet were swinging. He looked like Jenny. I ruffled his hair to erase the resemblance, but he pushed my hand away and said, 'Don't.' I got angry and pulled the tickets out of my wallet. 'We have to go, mate.' He shrugged and I knelt down beside him, still wrestling with my anger. I gave one of his tops a spin, but it died on the carpet.

'Come on, I reckon the Blues might win this one.' I put my hand on Luke's shoulder, guided him towards the door. He shrugged off my touch, walked ahead of me and yelled from the doorway, 'Dad, it's raining.'

'No it's not.'

'Are you blind?'

'Spitting. Won't kill us. Anyway, the seats are under cover.'

In the park, Luke stood under a tree and when I kicked the ball to him, he let it drop rather than trying to mark it. There was not even enough rain to wet the grass. He kicked mongrel punts that I had to chase. Out of the corner of my eye, I watched a boy who couldn't have been more than six take an overhead mark and then hit his father on the chest with a perfect drop punt.

'Hold it straight up and down, mate – laces out.'

I kicked a long ball to Luke. It was a low, straight drop punt that spun perfectly. He was too slow to get out of the way and it hit him on the chest quite hard. His arms wrapped reflexively around the ball so that when he fell he had hold of it. It dropped out when he hit the ground. When I reached him, he was crying and clutching at breath. I rubbed his chest.

'It's okay, mate, you're just winded. You took a great mark.'

I laughed and gave him a hug.

'Stop laughing at me.' Luke twisted out of my embrace and started running towards the house. I gave chase and stopped him just before the road.

'Hey, that's enough! Take a few deep breaths and you'll be okay.'

'Let me go! I wanna go home! I've got a headache.'

'You'll be right.'

'I wanna go home.' I didn't dare ask him where home was in case he meant his mother's place.

'We're going to the footy,' I said.

. . .

Luke was five when Jenny and I split up. She and I remained friends. We said we didn't want lawyers and acrimony. I used to sit in her kitchen while Luke bounced on his trampoline or hammered nails into a piece of wood. Jenny seemed to like teasing me. 'Found yourself a good woman? She would want to know how to cook!' I would smile and say, 'Not yet. What's for dinner here tonight?' In this way, we pretended our relationship was over. Now we can't even talk without hostility. I tell the therapist how she baits me, says things like *You're not in a position of power* and *You're becoming angry, I am going to hang up now*. I imitate her deliberate, complacent tone.

'Of course I'm fucking angry,' I scream at the therapist. 'It's my son, my fucking son! How dare she –' The anger chokes me. I shake my head, hammer my fists into the chair. I think I might cry but the thought of crying prevents the tears from coming. The therapist asks whether I tell her this, tell her I'm angry, that she's stealing my son away from me. I shake my head and say that I can't. 'She never gives me a chance. Anyway, she's right, I have no power. She's got the big weapon and she'll use it.'

. . .

Luke and I took our seats just as the Carlton players were lining up to run through the banner. The club theme song filled the arena. The rain had stopped. Luke surprised me by waving the flag when the team sprinted towards the goals in their warm up. I felt a sense of hope and pointed out the players to him. I explained who would have to fire if the Blues were to win. When the opposition emerged from the race, a woman directly behind us screamed, 'Go, Sydney!' Her voice was loud and at such a pitch that it entered my ear drums and set up a vibration that made me shudder. Luke put his fingers in his ears and we looked at each other and laughed.

'We're in trouble if Sydney has a good day.'

Luke nodded his head with his fingers still in his ears. 'It's like a sound-torpedo.'

I put my arm around him and pulled him to me and gave him a tickle. He laughed the way he used to as a toddler. A deep chuckle. He was right. It was exactly like a sound-torpedo.

By half-time the game was as good as over; Carlton had capitulated. Luke said he wanted to go to the toilet. 'Can we get some doughnuts?' We left our seats and made our way through the crowd. I kicked myself for not making him go just before we left the house. Jenny would not have forgotten. Nor would she have bought him a bottle of lemonade or a bucket of chips on the way in.

At the toilets there was a constant flow of people going in and out. I towed Luke behind me so that he wasn't swallowed by the crowd. He looked over his shoulder a couple of times while peeing. He was so small standing next to the men. When he was finished, I made him wash his hands and we joined the doughnut queue.

'In my day they were cheaper,' I said. 'We used to buy them from a purple van outside the ground. I think it was six for a dollar twenty.' This impressed him because his maths was good enough to work out the difference.

We made it back to the seats and ate the doughnuts, which were oily and sugary and not as nice as they were when I was a kid. When the players ran out onto the ground, I told Luke to sit tight while I went for a leak.

'Why didn't you go when I went?'

'Just didn't.' I made to leave. 'Won't be a sec.'

Luke stood up to follow me. 'I'll come too.'

'You'll miss the start of the third quarter.'

He shrugged and reached for my hand. I stopped. You

only see him every second weekend, I told myself. *You get to spend two days with him every fortnight. You hardly know who he is any more.*

'C'mon.'

The people who hadn't already made their way back to their seats were almost all Carlton supporters. The siren blared out a few times, filling me with a sense of urgency. The toilet block was not far from where we were sitting. When we got there Luke said, 'I'll wait here, it stinks in there.'

'Come on, you can't wait outside a toilet.'

Luke didn't move and shrugged his shoulders again, a habit that was starting to annoy me intensely. 'Can I've another doughnut?'

I swore under my breath, but dug into my pocket and pulled out five bucks. 'The doughnut place is just there.' I pointed to a sign just off to my right.

'I can read, Dad.'

'Yeah. I'll meet you there.'

. . .

The therapist practises somatic psychotherapy. During the body work, he tells me that I can share any thoughts that arise. I lie on the table and remember a time before Jenny and I split up. We went to a barbecue at a friend's home in the suburbs. Jenny reluctantly agreed to come. People weren't her strong point. My friend, Jim, had mounted a marquee in his huge backyard and wedged speakers in a sunroom window. Luke played happily with Jim's boy who was roughly the same age. They had a set of plastic golf clubs and they took it in turns belting a fake ball around the yard. They stopped occasionally to grab a sausage. Jenny said she wasn't hungry and stood by my side all through lunch and frowned.

Halfway through a game of backyard cricket, Jenny took Luke home. She had been standing, arms folded, at extra cover. I hit a ball that Luke chased and Jenny gathered him up and said, 'Well done, it's time to go home now.' Luke shook his head vigorously and played dead to slide out of her grasp. He ran to pick up the ball. Jenny looked at me, eyes hard and glaring. She was standing in the middle of the pitch with everyone in suspense around her.

'Jenny,' I said, incredulous, 'he hasn't even had a turn at batting.'

'He's tired,' she said and gathered Luke in again.

I thought I was being a good parent, not getting angry in front of my sone.

I stood on Jim's nature strip that afternoon holding the cricket bat, watching Jenny buckle Luke into the car. I knew I should be doing something. 'I'll get a taxi.' I said, but Jenny said nothing. Luke looked miserable in his car seat. I waved goodbye, 'See you at home, mate.' It was only four o'clock. I went back to the barbecue.

I tell the therapist the story haltingly. He says, 'Mmm' and 'Right' to let me know he's hearing me.

'Should I have stopped her going?'

'How did you feel?'

'Robbed. Ashamed.'

'Do you think *you* should have stopped her?'

. . .

Luke was nowhere to be seen when I arrived at the food bar. I stood amazed, then pirouetted frantically hoping that my desire to see him standing there clutching a bag of doughnuts might make him appear. There were only a few people and none of them was small and blond. A pit opened in my stomach.

'Luke!' I yelled, not quite loud because I still didn't believe he was not there. The crowd roared. The whole stadium vibrated. I pushed away visions of Luke, distressed and unseen, looking up at all the faces.

'Have you seen my son?' I said to a woman cleaning greasy chips from a bench. She looked at me stupidly. I rephrased my question. 'A boy, this high, blond hair?'

She raised her eyebrows.

'Fuck off,' I said unfairly and sprinted back to the toilets. There was no way he could be in there, but I called his name urgently. An old guy taking a leak said 'try the cubicles.' I kicked each door open, fearful of what I might find, but found nothing. I punched the wall of the last cubicle. The crowd roared and the sound moved through me, from my feet to the top of my head.

The ground manager's office. I knew I had to report my son missing. They would make an announcement, call the police. Jenny would have to be told. I ran back towards the seats to get my bag, took the steps two at a time. The Carlton fans all rose to their feet when I hit the landing. *Goal!* There was a frenzy of noise and movement and then everything subsided. I slid along the aisle to our now empty places. People craned their necks to see past me. I felt like crying. I jammed everything back into the bag and stood up straight. My ears were buzzing and I was dizzy. The crowd breathed and murmured around me. I stared out across the field as if I could take in every indifferent face. Someone yelled 'Sit down!' but I stood breathing heavily, unable to move. Tears welled in my eyes. If I moved, Luke was lost.

A woman sitting to my right held up Luke's coat. 'You dropped this.'

That's when I saw him. At the front of the stand, on the

bottom step, leaning out over the rail, waving his flag. There was a bag of doughnuts at his feet. At first it looked as if he was celebrating Carlton's last goal. Then I realised that he was looking at the flag itself, transfixed by its movement. He waved it in big, arching circles.

I put my hand on the back of his neck and massaged it gently. He looked up at me with sugar crusting his smile. We didn't return to our seats, but stayed leaning over the fence looking down at all the people, the field, the players. Carlton's resurgence was enjoyable but short-lived. Sydney kicked a goal and Luke continued to wave his navy blue flag in among all the red and white.

. . .

Jenny is afraid of the world. When we were together, she would lie in bed with me and put a name to all the things that we needed to fear. Cot death, falls, choking. High temperatures, meningitis. There was the fear that some innocent kitchen product left in the wrong place could steal our son away from us. Worse than this, there were wolves in sheep's clothing. Little playmates who were really vicious bullies. Incompetent teachers who could kill our son's desire to learn. Well-meaning adults whose values might be poisonous. Strangers bearing sweets.

The therapist asks whether Jenny was a good mother. I tell him I suppose she was but can't say any more than this. 'She's not a good mother now,' I say. 'How's she going to live with herself? Knowing she destroyed her son's relationship with his father.' I am smouldering, smoking. The therapist waits for me to continue and I sit out the uncomfortable silence. I stare at his bookshelf and hope that he says something before I do.

'Do you tell her these things?'

'How the fuck can I?' I explode. The therapist shits me. He doesn't even have kids of his own. 'If I say anything to her, she'll punish me by taking Luke away,' I say, emphasising each word.

'Isn't she already doing that?'

. . .

I didn't bother kicking the footy on the ground with Luke after the game. We left when the final siren blew and walked across the park kicking the late afternoon chill off the grass. There were people everywhere; we got caught up in a group of young Sydney supporters walking arm in arm singing the Sydney theme song.

… lift that noble banner high …

Luke let go of my hand and ran along in front of them waving his Carlton flag. One Sydney supporter said, 'Ball, Kouta!' and lifted Luke up in the air. Seeing me he dropped him at my feet and continued singing with his mates. I raised my hand in a gesture of acknowledgement and thanks. 'Go, Blues!' Luke and I yelled after them. We stood laughing while the day draped shadows all around us.

. . .

I tell the therapist that I am not the father I wanted to be. There was a time when Luke and I would go for 'walks'. He had a trike with a trailer. I had attached a rope to the handlebars so that I could pull him up hills. He used to call me 'Da' and he'd pick up rubbish and put it in the trailer. We'd post it in the bin when we got home. 'He's here to clean up the world,' I would say because he'd said this to me in a dream when he was still in his mother's womb.

'I was his father then.'

'And you're not his father now?'

'No, I'm just someone who gets to borrow him every second weekend.'

The therapist does his silent, nodding thing, so I am compelled to keep speaking. I listen to my own voice as if from a distance. It's a tirade full of fury that trails off. I shake my head at the floor. The carpet is brown, threadbare. I hate it.

'What's the worst thing that could happen?'

I look at the therapist. He's a big man. He could have been a ruckman or centre half-back. Every time I see him, I wonder if he played footy.

'What if you told her how you feel? What's the worst thing that could happen?'

I can see Luke's face. I remember how he used to come running in and bounce on our bed, bounce on me. I can't bear to lose him.

'She might do a runner. Go to Daylesford or something and – home-school him. I don't know – she might smother him and he'll turn into a wimp.' I laugh at how stupid I sound.

The therapist doesn't laugh. He asks me to move my seat to the right. He's going to talk to a part of me I've disowned. He speaks to me as if there is someone else living inside me. He asks the other me questions and it tells him what it thinks about me. 'He's soft,' my disowned self says. 'He's got no balls. He's a girl. He's a pathetic soft-cock, useless piece of shit. That slut – she needs a good fucken slap!'

When I am me again, I can't stop crying. The therapist makes it worse. 'It's okay to be angry,' he says. 'It's okay to feel whatever you feel.'

'But I want to kill her,' I blubber. 'If I get angry, I'll kill her.'

. . .

Long after the game was over, there were still many fathers in the park kicking the footy with their sons and daughters. They were there until the light faded. I watched them from Luke's bedroom window. When it was too dark to see outside, I drew the curtains. Luke was playing on the bedroom floor. An urge to talk to him rose up in me. I saw myself squatting beside him, speaking. His head was turned in my direction.

. . . . . .

Fear of Flying

DANIELLE WOOD

She's a geologist with two loves: her partner, and the pristine southern island where she does her field work. Can she have both?

The wandering albatross, Diomedea exulans, *breeds in extremely low numbers on Macquarie Island. Numbers of breeding pairs have declined since the 1960s, reaching a low of only two breeding pairs in 1982. Over the past decades, wandering albatross populations elsewhere in the Southern Ocean have also been declining, and incidental mortality associated with long-line fishing has been implicated as the major cause.*

— Dr Aleks Terauds, 'Field report on Albatross Conservation', 2000–2001

It is the night before she leaves, and Leif knows precisely how it will be. He can see the events of the hours ahead like a pattern ghosted onto tapestry fabric, just waiting to be stitched in full colour. He will cook, and they will eat, not at the kitchen bar as is usual, but at the table in the dining room. A candle will be lit, to signify that it is an occasion, and during the meal they will be tender with each other. But all the while Leif will feel time leaching away. In the hallway, Petra's pack on its metal frame will lean against the wall, its drawstring mouth ready to be fed with neat stacks of thermal tops and pants, wet-weather coats and over-trousers, torches and spare batteries, notepads and pencils.

Then, after dinner, she will run a bath. Just as they have

sides of the bed, they have ends of the tub, hers the closer to the taps. She and he will pass the soap and flannel between them, and she will talk of small things, as if she were not, tomorrow, taking herself away. And Leif will feel that there ought to be more of everything: more significance, more gravity, more weight.

He even knows how they will make love, it is by now so well-rehearsed: this finger here, then that tongue there. They are set in their ways, like skin that cannot help but fall into the same creases at the corner of an eye, or receding waves that cannot help but take the grooved pathways of a tessellated rock. Tonight he will try to stretch it out, hold onto her a little longer by prolonging each stage. But after a while, she will grow impatient, and finish it.

He can always tell the precise moment at which she is gone from him. It is not long after he holds her long-waisted body where it straddles his, and feels it shudder and then slacken. Then, time dips into a shallow curve like the one between the base of her rib cage and the rise of her hip, and although his hand will cling, there in the curve, he will not be able to hold her. Her mind will already have flown.

. . .

It seems to Leif that if the course of the evening is set, the small details are still within his control. What, for example, to cook for dinner. He can't decide. Even in the recently renovated corner shop – ceiling festooned with dried herbs, shelves bearing pyramids of glossy fruits – nothing inspires him. He replaces an avocado, carefully, thumbprint side down.

Across the store from him, Petra is shopping for herself. Her basket contains small things: the little, light luxuries that she can carry on her back the length of the island, squirrel away and eke out over an entire summer. She joggles a jar of conserve in one hand, and he knows she is trying to judge the pain of its weight against the pleasure of its contents. What are the units, he wonders, in which pain and pleasure would be measured? He doesn't know, but he does know that if anyone was calibrated to measure this with precision, it would be his wife. She wears this exactitude of hers in the blunt cut of her straight hair and the mild severity of her light-framed glasses. He sees it, too, in her tailored proportions, the way her body fills her clothes precisely, without the puckering or pleating of either fabric or flesh. He thinks of her naked, and of the way her strong bones and muscles inhabit her skin with the same perfect accuracy. She hasn't even left yet, he reminds himself, and already the longing has begun.

A week ago, Leif brought up the question of when Petra might give up going to the island. The idea of their having a child lurked in the spaces between his words, but he couldn't bring himself to break the taboo and name it. The subject of children lies on the other side of Petra's boundaries, and hers are not lines drawn in sand, or roped curves in the outfield. Petra sets her limits like a tidy pensioner with concrete kerbing around her flowerbeds and, after almost a decade of marriage, Leif knows only too well that if he kicks at her edgings, all he will do is stub his toe and make her laugh.

The shop begins to fill with after-work shoppers and Leif sees a woman with a full fleece of peppery curls greet Petra and kiss her on both cheeks. Petra is not fond of this kind of social touching, but only someone who knows her as well as Leif does would detect her tiny flinch. The woman is a friend of Petra's parents, although Leif knows her best from a fading photograph above his in-laws' fireplace, taken in a time when she had darker hair and a small child at foot, when it was still possible to stand on the pink-sand fringe of a lake long since drowned in the name of hydro-electricity. These days, the woman has the frugal, earnest look of an ageing greenie – one of a generation that had relinquished the front line and placed its faith in people like his wife. Watching Petra in conversation it is easy to see why they trust her, the bright young doctor of biology, to bear their fragile flame into the future. She tilts her head to listen, and Leif can imagine the intensity of her flecked hazel eyes behind glass.

When the fleecy woman moves away, Leif goes to his wife and reaches an arm around her waist, kissing the space of bare neck between her hair and collar. He might not usually do this, not so publicly anyway, but tomorrow she will be gone and the only touches he will have left will be those he has managed to hoard.

'Russian Caravan or Earl Grey? This is the question we ask,' Petra murmurs to a colour-coded display of Twinings tea. She squeezes Leif's hand where it lies just above her hip, then unclasps it like a seat belt. And he hates that he is so easily undone and left behind.

. . .

They walk home with shopping bags in their outer hands and the fingers of their inner hands entwined. The streets they follow skirt a hillside to the west of the city, and through the gaps between the houses, Petra can see the inner suburbs sloping down to meet Hobart's modest CBD. She can see the Lego-block angles of the docklands and the ship that will tomorrow take her south, resting on a square of blue like a bright orange crustacean. The river is the pathway it will follow, Petra knows. She has made the journey many times before. But the island where she spends each summer seems the kind of place you might only reach through the back of a wardrobe, and there is part of her which cannot credit that anything as tangible as a river could join her two worlds.

The evening sun warms only those things it can touch directly, and Petra feels the chill in the places where trees stripe the pavement with shade. She enjoys the shiver that crimps down her spine, feeling it like a faint prelude to the island's sub-Antarctic freeze. She likes this feeling of her mind turning: a globe that will soon stare out into a new sector of the sky. In a week's time she will be half an ocean's sail and two full days' walk from here, and the extent of her world will be a small timber hut, one field assistant, a web of narrow tracks, a dozen nest sites, a dome of sky and its birds.

Already the island will have begun to draw the birds back to its shores. Most often it is the males who come first, taking up their positions. Petra should reach the south of the island in time to see the females come in from the ocean to join them. She will watch the antics of the non-breeders, whose flirtatious displays fill the amphitheatre with beating wings and noisy cries, and she will observe the swift reunions of the established pairs who gently fence with their yellow-pink bills for just a moment before an unremarkable copulation. She will sky-watch and wait, her heart like an egg in her throat, with the birds whose partners return late, or not at all. And she will curse the long-liners and the flinting, silvery promises of their baited hooks.

She feels how her thoughts are drifting ahead of her, out on a racing current, into tomorrow. Tightening her grip on Leif's hand, she pulls herself closer to him, as if the momentum could return her fully to the present moment. Over the last few days, she has been watching him closely, measuring the dejected angle of his shoulders in an effort to quantify just how much worse he is, this year, than usual. She expects him to be a little needy in the weeks before she leaves, more possessive of her time, more demanding of her touch. But not like this.

'Your hands are always warm,' she says, kissing his folded fingers. 'How do you do that? Could you do without a hand, do you think, for just the summer? Just one? I could take it with me, and keep it in my pocket, like a hand-warmer.'

'That's your way of telling me you'll miss me, is it?'

She does not entirely believe his smile.

'Silly. I don't have to tell you that.'

. . .

Through dinner, through the running of the bath, and for the time it takes for the temperature of the bathwater and the temperature of their bodies to reach equilibrium, Petra makes safe passage, keeping the conversation close-hauled.

'Have you made up your mind?' she asks, making whorls with her fingers in the strands of his wet hair.

Rather than face her, as usual, Leif lies between her parted legs, his spine pressed onto her belly, the back of his skull resting between her breasts.

'What about?'

'What you're going to do? This year's project?'

'No.'

'You're not going to do the top room?'

'No point.'

'It's the only room left, though.'

'It's not as if we need it.'

'There's lots in this house we don't need.'

'You know what I mean.'

Does she? Yes, she supposes that she does. The top room

is across the narrow landing from her office and she sees into it each time she climbs the stairs. As hard as she tries to ignore it, there is, she knows, a message of reproach in the threadbare carpet and patchy plaster. She knows that she is supposed to understand that, for Leif, there is no point repainting the room, if not in pale pink or pale blue.

'I sometimes wonder what you'd do if the house were finished,' she says, squeezing a sponge full of water over his chest and watching wispy dark hairs stream away like seaweed in the tide. 'I suppose we'd have to sell. Buy a new disaster.'

'You think?'

'You'd be bored without anything to fix.'

'This is it, then? We go on like this, indefinitely?'

Will you sacrifice your marriage for a handful of birds?

More and more frequently, Petra asks herself this question and feels the point of its blade. To give up the island would be to tear the flesh away from the bones of who she is. But she has only to think of a life without him to bring on a flood of panic, and of tenderness for him. At times she is sorry for her insistence on her independence, and always she is sorry for the ways in which she knows it hurts him. She cannot imagine that she could ever bear to be with anyone else. She would always feel the nothingness where one of his qualities had been, or the something where there ought to have been a space.

'I don't want you to go,' he says, and she responds by holding him tighter with her arms and with her knees. She can feel the heaviness of his heart. It is sinking, drowning. Like a surf-lifesaver, she cups her hand beneath his chin where it lies just above the waterline and wonders if she has the strength to keep them both afloat.

. . . . . .

Matrimonial Home

BEVERLEY FARMER

He was desperate to leave her, and now he's desperate to come back again.

He rang an hour ago, so his wife is expecting him, or he would turn back. The verandah lamp is on for him, throwing lights and shadows like a fire behind the rainy branches and the black iron fence, and the door is propped half-open. The gate squeals as he shuts it. A black cat sprinkled with rain strolls past him into the house. Not knowing if he should knock or call or go straight in, he dawdles on the verandah. Among the branches gold fruits are hanging. He remembers the persimmon tree and fondles one, cold and glassy and squat, heavier than it looks. And not gold, it was the lamp, but as dark as a ripe apricot.

'Hullo.' Margaret, in shadow by the door.

'Hullo!' He turns with a stiff smile.

'You're wet.'

'Il pleut doucement sur la ville,' he recites.

'I know how you hate the rain. Well, come in.'

'I was just admiring the persimmon tree.'

'Yes, it's never had so many. You must take some home with you.'

'Home.'

'Doesn't Sandra like them?'

'I told you. I'm at my sister's.'

'Your sister loves them.' She waits for him to follow her in and latches the door.

'No wonder Annie called it the Persimmon Tree House,' he says, for something to say.

'What did you say?'

'Annie. The Persimmon Tree House.'

A log fire burning gives the sitting room its only light. In front of it the wet cat sprawls and preens its belly. It makes a smudge of black among flames that the floorboards mirror.

'Oh,' his wife says, 'When she was little. We don't call it that any more,' she adds after a moment.

'Why not?'

'It's the Matrimonial Home these days.'

'I wrote to the solicitors, Marg. I told them to call it off.'

'They wrote, yes.'

'You know I don't want the divorce.'

'It was the marriage you didn't want the last time I saw you. Now it's the divorce. No pleasing you, is there.'

'I wasn't really expecting to be welcomed with open arms.'

'I wouldn't put it past you.' She takes his sodden coat and hangs it up. 'Come and sit down.'

He sinks into the velvet chair that used to be his, spreads his legs out to the fire, lights a cigarette. Blinking scornfully, the cat jumps up and sniffs the seat of the other velvet chair, but his wife pushes it off.

'New cat.' He hates cats. She knows he does.

'He was a consolation present. He has a nasty nature but he's beautiful, or the other way round.' She feels awkward too. 'Coffee, or wine? You've had dinner?'

'Yes, thanks. Sorry, I meant to bring a bottle.'

'No need. These are yours. There's a chardonnay in the fridge, or there's red. French, or are you tired of French wines? There's some Napa Valley red.'

'The chardonnay, please. I'll open it.'

'No you won't. I will.'

He laughs. 'Why?'

'I can fend for myself. You're my guest. Not that you're not legally entitled to be in the Matrimonial Home, if it comes to that. I assume it won't tonight.'

'Margie, don't.'

'I'm behaving badly.'

'I deserve it.'

He stands by the fire until she comes back and pours green-yellow wine into two glasses.

'Cheers.' He raises his glass.

'Cheers. Well, welcome back. I thought the idea was to stay in America till June.'

'I wound things up earlier. I just had to get back by Easter. I wrote to you about all –'

'Yes, I got it.'

'Oh.'

'I started to answer it but I tore it up. It seemed more sensible to wait and see, considering.'

'Considering?'

'How much your letter didn't say.' A log shifts, covering itself in eddies of flame, and cuts off what she is saying next. For the first time he looks back at her. 'Annie,' she says. 'Our *daughter*. Have you seen her yet?'

'Ah, she met the plane. She didn't tell you?'

'She rang and asked me your flight number. She must have found out somehow. I thought she wanted to stay neutral.'

'Annie? Oh, come on. She's on your side all the way. Never once wavered.'

'Is she?'

'She's *dying* to see us back together again.'

'Oh. That's my side? Well, it *was*, of course. Before you turned up in Paris. You and Sandra.'

'I see.' He takes a deep drag of his cigarette, finishes his wine too fast and chokes. He can feel his face reddening. 'Then it's my side she's on.'

'As always. Poor Annie, she a romantic. So are you, I suppose.'

'I suppose.' He splutters and ducks his head. 'Well, I can do with any help that's going.'

'Thump your back?'

'In a general way, I meant.' He pours more wine.

'We're to live happily ever after, is that the idea?'

'No good?'

'And what about Sandra?'

'All over. Ages ago.'

'Ages?' She is staring into the fire. 'What do you mean, ages? Have you been to her place since you got back?'

'She wasn't there, I just took my things. I think she's going to stay in the States another week or so. She said she might, at the airport. She has a friend she wants to see in Boston.'

'How's her thesis? Finished?'

'Nearly. As far as I know. She was too depressed to work on it much, she said. It has passages of real inspiration.'

'Praise from you, Praise indeed. So she saw you off. Is last week *ages* ago?'

'We were under one roof. Domiciled, is that the word? – under the one roof. Even that was bad enough, after we got back from Paris.'

'Why was that?'

'I told her I'd go home to you. If you'd have me.'

'You didn't tell *me*.'

'She said she'd go whenever I said. She didn't want to go.

She wouldn't admit we'd failed. She sat tight and wouldn't be provoked into a quarrel –'

'That's weak.'

'I know. She's a totally passive woman. Dogged and deadpan no matter what you do or say. She won't argue. Won't fight.'

'Weak.'

He nods. 'What I think myself.' Then he catches her eye. 'You're leading me on, aren't you? What am I saying wrong? You're trying to trap me.'

'*You* were weak, that's all. Go on.'

'*I* was? It was deadlock, we were barely speaking, a disastrous paralysis of the will. I was dying for a showdown and dreading the thought of it. I couldn't throw her out in cold blood, could I? And it dragged on and on.'

'Of course you were sleeping with her.'

'Oh Margie.'

'No right to ask?'

'Of course. Every right.'

He watches her stroke the cat as it winds itself round her ankles. Both of them are dark-haired and glazed by the firelight, their eyes almost shut.

'Well? Were you?' she says.

'Now and then.'

'You *see*.'

'*You* don't. She was just there. That's all it was. It didn't mean a thing to me. Even to her in the end, I think. It was even shocking, how little it had come to mean.'

'You'd say that, of course.'

'No credit for owning up to it?'

'How else could she have stayed? Of course you were sleeping together.'

'I'm trying to tell you what happened. The truth, as a matter of fact.'

'Same old story, isn't it? I hope she's over it by now. More likely she's hoping you'll go back to *her*.'

'All I can say,' and he winces at his own pomposity, 'is that I've never given her the slightest reason for hoping that.'

'What will you do?'

'It seems to be out of my hands now.' This is petulance, when resignation is what he's trying for. Angrily he gets up and pours more wine. The bottle has lost its jacket of frost and feels warm, but the wine chills his mouth. She sips and sits staring through the quivering wine in her glass at the flurries and pools the fire makes. He lights a cigarette. 'Not smoking?' he says.

'No.' She grins at him. 'I've given up.'

'More willpower than I've got.' He blows out smoke.

'I should hope so.'

'Isn't that the black dress you bought in Paris?'

'That you bought me in Paris.'

'That you finally let me buy you in Paris.'

'*Enfin* – yes. As it happens.'

'You said you'd never wear it again. When we quarrelled in the Brasserie Lipp. You said it had brought you bad luck.'

'I wonder if Sandra wears hers.' But he doesn't follow. 'Whatever you bought *her*, and don't tell me you didn't.'

'To tell the truth, I did –'

'Of course. To restore parity.'

'I did offer to buy her a dress. I'd let slip about yours and she hadn't said anything but I could sense it was on her mind. She turned it down, though.'

'Silly woman.'

He shrugs. 'She'd rather have books, she said. So I never bought her a thing to wear the whole time we were away.'

'Why the triumphant tone?'

'Why? I did buy her *books*. Lots of old Colettes. There we were in our hotel under our two lamps in a dark little room in the rain, reading Colette and blaming our misery on each other.'

'On each other.' That makes her smile.

'And on ourselves.'

'It never changes anything,' she says wearily. 'Let's not talk about it. I used to think about it all the time. You'd kept me in the dark and I'd never know the whole story. But it's so long since –'

'Not so long, is it? You said –'

' – It's so long since I cared what your life with Sandra was like. Is it just sour grapes? I don't think so.'

He is staring from a face suddenly still and grey.

'Are you sure of that?' he says at last.

'You think I want to hurt you, get my own back, don't you? It's not that. Why meet at all now, if we won't be honest with each other? Don't look like that. What *can* you have been expecting?'

'Not a life sentence.'

'I'm not the judge. I was the victim. That's how *I* felt on the morning you packed and went to live with Sandra. You had sentenced me to despair. I was left wondering how to live through even one day of it.' She stands, rustling her black dress. 'I'll make coffee.'

Clumsily he stands and puts his arms round her, his head in the hollow of her neck. His hair tickles her. 'Coffee already?' he murmurs.

'Please,' She wipes her eyes. 'Listen to me. You haven't been listening.'

'Is there someone else? Is that it?'

'We're at cross purposes, aren't we? There's no one else. There's no one.'

'All our years together. Surely –'

'That was what I said. Did it make any impression on you?'

'Of course. It did on Sandra too.'

'You went and told Sandra what I'd said?'

'Only that. She was always bringing it up. "We've been together for twenty-one days," she'd say, "to your twenty-one years with Margaret." Things like that. Darling, is your hair still black? It looks like honey in the firelight.'

He moves strands of her hair in his freckled hands. It is still black, with here and there a glint of white. Like the cat with raindrops on it, he thinks, and strokes her hair.

'No, don't.' She sits down. 'What did *you* say?'

'Not much I could.'

'She was asking for reassurance, or so it sounds.'

'Reassurance! Exactly.' Sitting, he runs both hands through his own greying ginger hair, a new mannerism of his.

'Why not? You were sure enough before.'

'That was before.'

'She didn't come up to expectations.'

He shakes his head.

'Why did you think *I* would? What do I have to gain by a reconciliation now? Except financially, of course. Obviously we both have a vested interest in staying married.'

'That's not why. At least have the fairness to –'

'How fair were you?'

'Okay, sorry. You know very well that money has nothing to do with it, though. Don't you?'

'What has?'

'Love?'

'Security?'

'Love and security, fine. Not financial security.'

'Why, though, would I represent security?' She frowns. 'Unless it's because I represent the past. There's nothing so secure as the past, I suppose. We're like crabs that have had to fight their way out of their old shells. We wish we could crawl back into them. We're afraid the new shells won't harden.'

'*What* new shells?' He pours more wine. 'In a sense you are the past, of course. You're the future as well. The only future that makes sense. As present, I'm stranded.'

'Like me. When I got back from Paris –'

'Oh God. You didn't understand. I *had* to go to Paris.'

'I couldn't face coming straight home. I stopped off in London. I was only away six weeks, but you'd have thought it was six months, to look at the house. Of course it was summer here. But the past! Nothing stays safely the way it was. I'm not the same.'

He says nothing, his gaze on the glowing floor, on the cat nodding, rasping one shoulder with its sharp tongue.

There was such a chilliness, a scum of neglect over everything, she could hardly believe it. Dust sticky on all the glass. The lights blurred and strung with cobwebs. In the bath was a dead baby mouse, stuck there by its black tail, its ears curled and its eyes glinting, its body as light and dry as a moth. In a cupboard potatoes had shrivelled and put out white and purple shoots, two of them long and jointed like feelers. It was as if the house was underwater and in its recesses silent creatures flickered, crabs, lobsters.

'Even the garden,' she says aloud. 'Weeds and slugs, white spiders in white webs. A crow always grating and swooping, even wasps. Am I imagining this? I thought I might go mad, I was so alone. You were never out of reach before. There were other women, but you lived with *me*, they never lasted.

When an affair was over I always knew, you were so sorrowful. Anxious for comfort – reassurance – which you got. And I could comfort myself while you slept with the thought that you were at least *here*, and you couldn't go on betraying me for ever. Little enough to look forward to, wouldn't you think? But you're falling harder all the time. You've even left me.'

'Marg. I *wasn't* out of reach.'

'Oh! Not out of reach in America? And before that, all the nonsense about your secret hideaway? Not telling a soul her – *your* – address? Ringing me every few hours from public phones to make sure I hadn't slit my *throat*, for God's sake –'

'I know I behaved irrationally –'

'Confessing and then hurtling out with your bags in that *head*long rush –'

'It was the only way I could go –'

'Of course people were very kind. Most people just thought you were overseas as planned, on your study leave. The ones who did know said not to worry. He'll be back, dear. It's only the male menopause. Keep his dinner hot. Here's a lovely kitten for you. It'll be company.'

He grimaces. 'I shaved and showered and got dressed in the middle of the second night. I was on the point of coming home. She was so devastated I couldn't do it.'

'She got you to leave *me*. It would have served her right.'

'She did and she didn't. She never had much faith in it. God knows, I soon lost mine. It was as if some other clown in my skin had taken over. While I looked on in horror.'

'That lets you out, then.'

'I know it doesn't. I'm trying to explain.'

'Why didn't she have much faith in it?'

'We hardly knew each other, she said. It was too soon.'

'True enough. Four or five months, wasn't it?'

'I knew I'd lose her if I went to America without her. She'd she wouldn't stay faithful. And I can't share a woman, you know how I feel about that.'

'Did she say she wouldn't?'

'Virtually.'

'If she was at all honest, she must have known – oh, never mind.' She picks up her glass, but it's empty. He tips the last yellow trickle into the glasses.

'She was honest,' he says doubtfully.

'Up to a point, perhaps.'

'Aren't we all.'

'Oho! You're a special case. So's she, if honesty can handle sneaking off with married men.'

She never thought I'd leave you. She knew all along that I was letting infatuation carry me away. She was always saying that.'

'How annoying.'

'Oh, it was.' He gives a short laugh. 'Still, since she was right …'

'How smoothly you say it. I was always saying it too.'

'I know it's unforgivable.'

'It would be, for you. We both know that. 'It annoys her that he won't look straight at her. 'I always trusted you absolutely not to leave me. That was my security.' She picks up the glasses and the bottle, all empty. 'What's the use? It's getting late. Let's have coffee.'

'Late?' He looks amazed.

'I have class in the morning.'

Lately, she thinks, I've made a ceremony of going to bed. I turn off the lights and break up the embers in the grate. I consign myself carefully to bed, now that I sleep alone. This is late for me.

She leans close to the kitchen window to make its gold reflections vanish when her shadow touches them. A wet moon lies over the shallow garden. Its light is not moving in the milky puddles. The rain has stopped. She can see scrolls of lilies and a bowed white tree, no taller than she is, its long red branches spilled like hair brushed up from a white nape. The pear tree with its fruits against the whitewashed wall. At the top of a column of spines, one many-branched stalk in midair, clustered with pale bells. She steps back. Now the yellow room settles on the glass again. She fills the copper kettle and lights the gas.

He comes out and puts his arms lightly round her from behind. She stands away stiffly, but he pretends not to notice. 'I let the cat out,' he says. 'Okay?'

'Yes.'

'It wanted to go.' She just shrugs. 'Margie?'

'Mmm?'

'*I* don't. Can't I stay?' He presses his face against her hair, patient. 'For old times' sake. Just for tonight.'

'Just for tonight.'

'I'll go quietly in the morning. Anything you say.'

'Tell me the truth: where *are* you staying?'

'At my sister's. At Sheila's. I told you.'

'I'll ask her.'

'Go ahead and ask her.'

'You didn't exactly rush here. What's the rush now?'

'I've walked past here at least ten times in the last four nights.'

'Why's that? Nostalgia?'

'I don't believe I can live without you.'

'Let's talk some other time. I'm tired.'

'What if you get into bed and I bring the coffee in?'

Shrugging, she goes without a word to undress by the slanted light of the lamp by her bed. She brushes her hair, making it swing and crackle in the mirror. She is a pillar of wax, tufted in three places and melting, dwindling, on her arms and shoulders and yellow hips. Look at my hands, she thinks as she pulls back the covers and slips underneath: like hens' claws. We grow old and none the wiser. She hears him light a match; sigh, as he breathes in smoke. He makes a deft clatter of spoons and cups. He feels at home now. A cigarette in his demurely smiling mouth, he pads in naked, with one hand holding the coffees and an ashtray and with the other cupping himself shyly.

'*Where* are your clothes?'

'By the fire.'

'*Why?*'

'I'm *freezing*. Ow. I'll *drop* something.'

'All right. Get in, then. Come on.'

He shakes the bed and the table beside it, spilling the light of the lamp on his back. He looks like a swimmer in sunny water, spotted with light and faded freckles, reaching for the cups once he is in bed. She smells his sweat, like hay, as she remembers, or like wattle flowers, sweet and yeasty, overripe.

The telephone rings in the kitchen.

'I bet that's Sandra.' She crashes her coffee down and drags her bathrobe over her shoulders. 'If it is, she'll be sorry.'

'It won't be,' he says blandly. 'She wouldn't ring here.'

'Anyone's capable of anything, I'm finding.' She hurries out. He smokes quickly, sipping his coffee; he can just hear her murmuring, then a sudden laugh and the bell as she hangs up.

'Annie,' she says, crawling in next to him. 'Being daughterly.'

'Ah.'

'She did at least try to sound surprised that you're here.'

'Ah, well.' He smiles. 'I may have mentioned –'

'So it would seem. At this time of night, too. I've hardly seen her since I got back from Paris, but she's always ringing up. I told her all about it, of course.' She makes a face. '*Joyeux Noel à Paris*, and there you were on the doorstep. With Sandra in tow.'

'My worst Christmas. Three days of hell.'

'When did you know you *had* to go to Paris? You never told me.'

'When you wrote that *you* were there. I had to see you. Sandra knew, I suppose. She insisted on coming with me.'

'I wouldn't have told you which hotel if I'd imagined you'd do that.'

'Wouldn't you really?' He has finished his coffee already. She signs. 'Did you have lots of snow? Back in America?'

'Snow, ice. Everything was white. It wasn't as cold as Paris, though. It never stopped raining, remember?'

'*Il pleut sur la ville –*'

'*Comme il pleure dans mon coeur.*'

'I'll never forgive you, you know. Not as long as I live.'

'No, I know. I'll make it up to you.'

'Not the *temps perdu*.'

'Everything.'

There is a book face-down under the lamp on the table. He peers at the title: Colette's *La Naissance du jour*. She is looking away, so he says nothing. At the edge of the golden light, on the dressing table under the mirror, he notices a deep wooden bowl of persimmons from the tree. The tree itself is outside this window, dripping and moving its tangle of shadows slowly on the blind. 'The Matrimonial Home,' he murmurs reproachfully. She says nothing. He puts his cup down and stubs out his cigarette. 'Peel you a persimmon?' he says.

'No!' she smiles. 'They're too messy to eat in bed. Those aren't even ripe, they're sour. They're for looking at.'

'I'd rather look at you.'

'Don't overdo it, now.'

'Me? When I've missed you so unspeakably?' He takes her empty cup and then lies on his back beside her.

'Turn over,' she says, 'and I'll hold you.' She puts her arm along the curly bulk of his thigh and doesn't speak for so long that he thinks she's asleep, her breath warm on his back. Then he hears her murmur, 'You'll only leave me again.'

'I won't.'

'Don't, please.' And her lips warm on his shoulder.

'Darling, I won't.' He hides his exultation. Turning, he lifts her hair and runs his thumb along the damp white skin of her throat, which is like a lily as the songs say, or like a camellia petal, pale and faintly crazed. Her pulse flickers in it. Two red mounds rise on it like nipples where a mosquito must have bitten her. He licks them. 'Asleep?' he whispers. But she makes a long turn and lies on her back, one arm over him, her eyes in shadow, lightly closed.

All the familiar women with their long white throats and breasts, he thinks. Their soft thighs, where they're warmest, and the rough wet hair between.

With a swish and a rattle of blinds the rain starts again.

'*Il pleut*,' she whispers. 'I can't send you out in this.'

'Good.'

'What were you thinking just now?' Her eyes are open now, dark and wet. He kisses them to close them, then kisses her mouth. 'You were remembering *her*,' she says. 'You can tell me the truth.'

It's not really the truth.

'But Marg, I *wasn't*,' he cries out; too despairingly, because he feels her start and recoil. He lights a cigarette. He breathes the smoke in heavily. They move apart in their bed and lie listening to the loud rain.

. . . . . .

MYTHICALITIES

Ithaca

LUKE SLATTERY

*Was this the place that Odysseus called home –
this island 'tilted in the sea'?*

WELL MET BY MOONLIGHT

It's twilight before the *Kefalonia* slips out from the grimy port of Patras, on the north-western Peloponnese. With pastel fittings and televisions in every corner, the ship seems more airport departure lounge than the Greek ferry of my dreams. Local families and tanned island hoppers dwell below in climate-controlled comfort, or queue for drinks at the bar. Out on the open deck, though, is a world untethered from time. And as we steam west across a sea so unnaturally flat it seems to have been beaten down, I keep watch for the islands wreathed in myth.

Beside me at the stern rail is a chain-smoker thickly stubbled to his cheekbones, gazing wistfully after the cigarette ash he dabs relentlessly overboard. On a blue plastic seat a girl with corkscrew curls berates a cell phone the colour of her glossy red lips. Otherwise I'm alone. I feel as skittish as the infantile, as obsessive as the elderly. The stories I've grown up with are no longer bound to the page in serried rows of black on white; they are somewhere out here, dancing across the zinc tabletop of the moonlit Ionian Sea.

To this day there is barely a river, a mountain ridge, or a moonscaped Aegean isle untouched by the tales of the ancients. But of all the songs that were sung in high-roofed archaic feasting halls by honoured bards, or rhapsodes, only two went on to shape the course of Western literature in their image: the *Iliad*, and its more approachable sequel, the *Odyssey*. If the former is the mother of all war epics, the latter fathered the adventure story. It relates how Odysseus, most cunning of Troy's besiegers, returns via circuitous sea-lanes to Penelope, archetype of the long-suffering wife, and their budding sweet-natured son Telemachus. It's a story of separation and reunion, love and temptation, courage and guile – of strong men who weep for home.

Aristotle, in the *Poetics*, boiled this spacious 12,000-line epic down to a spare but still serviceable outline. 'A certain man has been abroad many years; he is alone, and the god Poseidon keeps a hostile eye on him. At home the situation is that suitors for his wife's hand are draining his resources and plotting to kill his son. Then, after suffering storm and shipwreck, he comes home, makes himself known, attacks the suitors: he survives and they are destroyed.' The kingdom of the homesick hero lies on the far western fringe of Greece. The island's name, etched into the literature of exile and homecoming, is Ithaca. And it's to Ithaca that I am headed now.

After a short stop at the Kefalonian port of Sami the ship sets a fresh course into the night. We are now so thoroughly encircled by silhouetted mountain crags, speckled here and there with stabs of light from villages high in the hills, that the constellations seem to lack for space. A ragged lump of black velvet looms broadside. 'At home we have no level runs or meadows,' sang Homer, 'but highland, goat land – prettier than plains, though. Grasses, and pasture land, are hard to come by upon the islands tilted in the sea, and Ithaca is the island of them all.' These lines, fashioned some 2700 years ago from a poetic tradition of even greater antiquity, seem to fit the thrusting shadows. The *Kefalonia* cuts a crescent around the nearest of these tilted peaks and stills its engines. Ahead is a welcoming necklace of lights strung around Vathi, the taverna-lined capital of this Odyssean isle.

ITHACA – AT LAST

To Greek poet C.P. Cavafy, whose 1911 poem *Ithaca* is much loved by wanderers everywhere, the island was less a place, a physical entity, than an emblem of peregrination. Better then not to hurry the journey:

> *Better if it lasts for years,*
> *So you are old by the time you reach the island,*
> *wealthy with all you've gained on the way,*
> *not expecting Ithaca to make you rich.*

The arrival, for Cavafy, is as nothing compared to the journey; especially the arrival in an Ithaca so poor by the wide world's standards. But the poet's fine conceit is lost on me this warm early autumn night. I prefer the words set down by a reputedly blind bard in an age when the best men were god-like and the gods as weak-headed as the worst of men. Homer heralds Odysseus the lost king's arrival not with a trumpet blast but a sigh of relief:

> *'…the deep sea-going ship*
> *made landfall on the island … Ithaca at last.'*

It has taken Odysseus, pursued from Troy by an aggrieved Poseidon, 10 years to reach native ground. But the hero's homecoming, so richly deserved and deeply desired, is anticlimactic. The tight narrative coils of the quest seem to slacken as Odysseus looks blankly at 'the winding beaten paths, the coves where ships can ride, the steep rock face of the cliffs and the tall leafy trees'. All he has yearned for these many years is before his eyes. But this shrewdest of Greeks has lost his bearings. He sees only another stepping stone in the sea, another staging post on the journey home.

The fog of forgetting turns out to be a providential gift from Pallas Athena, daughter of Zeus, to settle the king and cool his nerves before the two of them, goddess and mortal in cahoots, hatch a plot to restore the kingdom. Athena, disguised as a shepherd, breaks the good news and the great wanderer's heart races with joy. But as he has landed with treasures – 'gorgeous tripods, cauldrons, bars of gold and lovely robes' – the canny Odysseus keeps his emotions, and his identity, concealed.

The master of deceit spins a fanciful story to cover his tracks, little knowing that the friendly Ithacan shepherd before him is a goddess of guile. Athena smiles, strokes him with her hand, drops her rustic mask, casts off her sheepskin, and reveals herself as a woman tall and beautiful. They make a good match, as the goddess herself will recognise:

> *Come, enough of this now. We're both old hands*
> *at the arts of intrigue. Here among mortal men*
> *you're far the best at tactics, spinning yarns,*
> *and I am famous among the gods for wisdom,*
> *cunning wiles, too...*

Athena is the deity in the narrative machine. She makes things happen; makes everything possible. First she implores Zeus to free her favourite from the clutches of the goddess Calypso, who has ensnared him on her island hoping to marry him into immortality. Athena then shepherds Telemachus in search of his long-lost father. Only through her covert intervention does Odysseus endure his trials, and it's only by her celestial guardianship that the wanderer has managed to dawdle home. Infused with a kind of sub-erotic energy, theirs is a remarkable pact. If Athena were not herself a model of chastity – she was born fully-formed from the head of father Zeus, untainted by Eros – her attentions might even have raised eyebrows at Olympus.

One tradition connects Homer with the Greek island of Chios – home of a group of rhapsodes called the Homeridae, claiming descent from him – and another with Smyrna in present-day Turkey. A later Roman source wryly notes that half the Mediterranean claims descent from either Homer or his near-contemporary, Hesiod. Ithacans and romantically inclined scholars still speculate that Homer must have visited the island, and perhaps even lived here.

On my first morning a dawn as 'rosy-fingered' as anything in the Odyssey breaks over the limestone cliffs beyond Vathi harbour. The mountain face, as if quarried from the sunrise itself, blushes a gentle rose. There and then I sway towards the islanders' dream: yes, it seems possible that Homer passed this way. But as the sun lifts above the first bright peak I regather my doubts. There is magic in myth – intoxication too.

ODYSSEAN ECHOES

A slow bus spirals north from Vathi along the island's coiled spine, past villages that cling to those limestone cliffs, above white-pebbled coves. In the hill town of Stavros stands an idealised bust of Odysseus with falcon gaze, and beside it a map of his improbable wanderings across the length and breadth of the Mediterranean. At one point he arrives within sight of Ithaca – close enough to see rising smoke – only to be blown backwards when his men untie an oxhide bag containing the world's winds, a gift from Aeolus the keeper of gales, gusts and breezes.

Perched high above Stavros is Anoghi, once the island's capital, now home to some 40 people who pray at a tiny church filled with luminous thirteenth century Byzantine frescoes. From eagle height the narrow road swoops down to a coastline of scalloped limestone. The road ends at Kioni. On one side of its sweet horseshoe harbour stands a string of cafes and restaurants; yachts and brightly coloured fishing boats swaying at their moorings. Over a lunch of beer and fresh fried anchovies I study a cat lying in wait for the fish that thrash at the water's edge whenever a diner throws a crumb. Sometimes, explains the waiter excitedly, he 'makes catch'.

Kioni is an enticement to linger, and soon I'm doing precisely that. I return to Vathi, throw together my possessions, and brave the next bus back. By late afternoon I'm padding along the seafront at the pace of an astronaut. The pale seabed hereabouts is terraced and with each few steps the water turns from liquid jade, to opal, to cerulean blue; and then to cobalt out where the lazy white Mediterranean cruise ships drift. The water that laps the island's pebbled fringe, the first thing to cool the toes, is something else again: neat gin, martini on the rocks. Ithaca turns out to be a fine place to dip into Homer, then into sea, and back again; the island and the verses seem to collude in awakening the senses. The fabulous epic is richly glossed with the beauty of the sea and seafaring; of banqueting and beguiling tales, of lust and lustrous women. Aside from Calypso, the 'nymph with lovely braids' who ravishes Odysseus while he pines for home, there is the 'white-armed' princess Nausicaa, who spies the shaggy hero at the river bathing. The Odyssey is the most sensuous of classical works.

Later in the day, under a fading sun, I stroll to a nearby cove. I'm joined by a couple of these celebrated Italians, who arrive on an over-powered motor-bike. The woman, thin and deeply tanned, stretches out a leopard skin bikini; her thickset partner wades out to his waist. Eyes fixed on the horizon, I'm dimly aware of his bulky presence. I catch a neat 'hiss' and a large 'splash'. He paddles off, leaving a cigarette butt spinning on the sea's polyester skin.

The 1953 earthquake that devastated the Ionian islands – and sent many Ithacans literally packing to Australia, South Africa and the United States – failed to spare Kioni. Where once there stood well-tended olive groves and weary villages, now there are modern bungalows with shuttered windows and white plaster walls. But for every new holiday cottage, there is an abandoned stone ruin with a forest springing from its floorboards. Goats roam the hillsides. Donkeys still bray at the moon. It's just that the people are gone. The island's post-war generation led the Greek exodus – Ithacans were among the first migrants of the 1950s to flee from destitution and civil war. Today there are only 3000 permanent residents, and few hold ambitions to farm the land. 'This year for the first time I buy imported olive oil,' thunders an ancient Ithacan whose hospitality I accept one night. 'There are no *hands* left on this island!'

If Homer did in fact visit the island some 2700 years ago, as some dreamers maintain, then perhaps he fell a little in love with it. Athena, lifting the mist from Odysseus's eyes, prods his memory: *'There's plenty of grain for bread, grapes for wine,/ the rains never fail and the dewfall's healthy./ … there's stand on stand of timber/ and water runs in streambeds throughout the year.'* This sounds more like Arcadia, just across the sea in the mountainous Peloponnese, than Ithaca the island abandoned by its own. The rhapsodic tone could be explained by Homer's fondness for the place – or his ignorance of it.

The Homeric echoes are never quite silenced on Ithaca; you cannot, like Odysseus's crew as they sail pass the lair of the Sirens, stop up your ears to the song. It's a short walk from Vathi to the Cave of the Nymphs, where legend has it that Odysseus hid those treasures he landed with (gifts from the friendly Phaecians), before purging his palace of suitors in an orgy of bloodletting that would delight any Tarantino fan. Many of the island's restaurants, cafes and bars carry the names of Penelope, Cyclops, Calypso or Odysseus himself. It is tempting to see all this Homeric self-consciousness as a mere marketing drive for a slice of the tourist cake, yet the yearning runs deep in the island's psyche. Was Odysseus, perhaps, a mere mythical figure? I ask a local hotelier. 'Boh!' he snaps, as if I've just raised doubts about his paternity. 'He was the King of Ithaca.' Penelope his Queen is something of a secular saint on Ithaca. She was a role model for island women, a template of feminine and maternal virtue, well into the last century.

The local cult of Odysseus is harder to fathom, as the mythical king is in truth easier to admire than to love. In the *Iliad* it is Odysseus and Diomedes, 'lord of the war cry', who lure the pathetic Dolon into false security, prise from him his secrets, then lop off his head. Odysseus, like Achilles, is not above berating his victims as they bite the dust. But as one of the two Achaeans sent to appease the sulking Achilles (the other is Ajax) he is at once subtle, noble, and tactically astute. His counsel is unfailingly prudent. In Book 19 of the *Iliad* he checks Achilles's rash call to arms: 'Achaea's troops are hungry: don't drive them against Troy...' The matter settled, Odysseus dictates the terms of a truce between Achilles and Agamemnon. The tone is brazenly confrontational: '*And you* [Agamemnon]/ *great son of Atreus/ you be more just to others, from now on.*' Remarkably, he gets away with it. Odysseus, architect of the Trojan Horse ruse, has a talent for survival matched only by his gift for deception. 'You terrible man,' Athena taunts, 'foxy, ingenious, never tired of twists and tricks.' It sounds like an insult. But then again virtue, as the Swiss historian Jacob Burckhardt once remarked, never was an attribute of heroes. Cunning, he wrote, 'is perfectly permissible, and even deceit; Odysseus is the incarnation of it'.

In later Greek literature, however, Odysseus's human failings are sharply caricatured. By the war-weary fifth century his duplicity is reviled and he becomes, for Euripides, a '*monster of wickedness/ Whose tongue twists straight to crooked, truth to lies,/ Friendship to hate, mocks right and honours wrong!*' The transition from the Homeric to the Classical age sees a shift in attitudes towards Odysseus. A battle-weary Athens (Euripides was writing in the middle of the three-decade long war with Sparta) seems to have developed a moral awareness as if it were a new tastebud.

On first reading the *Iliad* is the more archaic and distant of the two Homeric epics. A tightly focussed war story, its chief concern is the conflict among men, between men and gods, and the contest among the gods themselves. The Odyssey on the other hand is a mature-audience fairy tale of delayed homecoming. Even though the journey is played out against a fantastical and spectacularly varied backdrop, the poem's emotional landscape is domestic, familiar. Odysseus is Everyman in an extraordinary world. He longs for the dream to end, to wake in his own bed. He longs for home.

The *Iliad* in its closing chapter invokes war's shared burdens and is, ultimately, ennobling. Odysseus' homecoming, on the other hand, culminates in a bloodbath that rivals the great Trojan battle books and exceeds them in this one sense: it seems, to us, entirely nihilistic. The *Odyssey* has none of its predecessor's thematic largeness of heart. After revealing his true identity the reborn King of Ithaca, with Telemachus and two allies by his side, slays every one of the suitors while their former ally, the goatherd Melanthius, is cruelly dismembered and his genitals fed to the dog. The suitors' mistresses are then herded together, made to clean the halls of blood, and ritualistically murdered. 'I swear I will not give a decent death,' declares Odysseus, 'to women who have heaped dishonour upon my head, and on my mother's, and slept with members of this gang.'

He has them hanged – 'like doves or long-winged thrushes caught in a net across the thicket where they came to roost, and meeting death where they had only looked for sleep, the women held out their heads in a row, and a noose was cast around each one's neck to dispatch them in the most miserable way. For a little while their feet kicked out, but not for very long.' The poem seems to be written for a male audience beset by acute anxieties about long absences from home: an audience of seafarers and traders. It culminates in a truce between Odysseus and his enemies; but the real unknotting of the plot comes with this grisly revenge sequence.

It is difficult to imagine the perpetrator of these murders as the sage and prudent Odysseus whose counsel brings peace to the Achaeans at Troy, and almost impossible to picture him as the emblem of a civilisation that values self-restraint, proportion and balance as counselled by Apollo's priests at Delphi. And yet Odysseus, embodiment of a universal biological principle – survival – is a worthy ideal for an island of hard times whose misfortunes stretch in an unbroken chain to the present. As he says himself: '*I am like those men/ Who suffer the worst trials that you know,/ And miseries greater yet.*'

There are, it soon emerges, a few uncertainties about Ithaca's Homeric lineage. These rivalries continue to flourish because there is no firm evidence that Odysseus dwelt here, if he existed at all. Compounding the confusion are the vagaries of Homeric geography, which suggest that the kingdom of Odysseus could have been centred on neighbouring Kefalonia or Lefkas. Despite centuries of questing by archaeologists and scholars, nothing conclusive has emerged from Ithacan soil. Curiously, considering the potency of the Odysseus myth, the island seems unlikely to support the sort of archaeological evidence that would stamp it the centre of a notable kingdom. The historical record, too, is threadbare: although a likely staging post along the trade route to Italy in Homer's time, it seems to drop below history's radar before the Golden Age of Greek civilisation in the fifth century BC.

Heinrich Schliemann, the German amateur archaeologist who unearthed the many-layered ruins at Hisarlik Hill and the proud citadel of Mycenae, dug at Ithaca in 1868 with only modest returns. He found no evidence of an Odyssean palace but plundered from his trenches what he could. A British archaeological team followed in the 1930s, focussing its efforts on a sunken sea cave at Polis, below the hill town of Stavros. That dig yielded the remains of several wheeled tripod urns used for votive offerings – perhaps for colonists en route to Magna Graecia, the Greek colonies in Southern Italy. Retrieved too was a vase depicting Homer's wandering hero flanked by his son and Athena, and a theatrical mask bearing the words: 'a wish for Odysseus'. But such was the prestige of the Homeric tales right across the Greek world that these lines prove little. Nevertheless, when I ask the caretaker at the Stavros Museum if Odysseus was the king of Ithaca, she smiles and says very simply: 'Of course.'

A DISPUTED INHERITANCE

Soon afterwards, at a restaurant in Stavros one rain-thrashed night, I meet an Ithacan-Australian environmental chemist and local historian, Denis Sikiotis, who has had the temerity to challenge the island's Homeric dreaming. Sikiotis argues, citing one ancient tradition, that Penelope was a woman of dubious morals. 'Why else were so many suitors hanging around?' he asks. Odysseus, for his part, was merely a 'piratical chieftain', unworthy of heroic status. Sikiotis has been howled down by local Homericists for apostasy.

The next night I'm invited to the home, recently built on a rare pocket of level land, of Dimitri Paizis. The most passionate of Ithacan antiquarians, Paizis has written a book defending Ithaca's Homeric paternity from the rival claims of Kefalonia. He offers me a copy. 'Denis has offended us,' he explains as we take coffee on a porch with views that would flatter a fortress. 'He has insulted the island.'

Bluff and unguarded, Sikiotis seems more firmly stamped with the culture of his migratory home, Australia, than the mores of his birthplace. In contrast Paizis, a retired sea captain and autodidact, is feline, courtly and complicated. He sends out darting slanders about his rival as we discuss Ithaca's contentious paternity claims. I leave that night with the two antagonists – Sikiotis, the archetypal sceptic, and Paizis, the model believer – installed in my memory like unwanted and quarrelsome boarders.

Ithaca's losses have been great. Without the *Odyssey* myth prosecuted so forcefully by Paizis the island would be quite bereft. In an atavistic world obsessed with identity, the *Odyssey* connection is a link to the past, a commercial brand, and a touch of glamour. More, it's a way of belonging. Sikiotis, on the other hand, offers a much-needed antidote to the intoxications of myth. If he has 'insulted' the island, then so too did Herodotus, who claimed that Pan was the issue of an affair between Penelope and Hermes. As Pan means, literally, all or everything, the story has a sensationally barbed point: he could have been fathered by *anyone* during Odysseus' twenty year absence; the first half spent on a tour of duty at Troy, the second on a wayward and much-delayed journey home.

Boarding the *Kefalonia* in Patras I'd set out in pursuit of a dream. The philhellene and travel writer Patrick Leigh Fermor, based just across the sea in the rugged Mani of the Peloponnese, would have called it a 'retrospective hankering'. But it was more than that. Antiquity never dies; in some respects we grow closer towards it. And so I'd relished the chance to view myth-drenched Ithaca for myself. But after a week on the island I found myself embroiled in a heated provincial controversy about the Odyssean connection.

THE WESTWARD ROUTE

Homer is such potent magic, of such venerable antiquity and enduring cultural prestige, that the temptation to read his world onto the ruins is almost irresistible. Robert Fitzgerald, author of the most richly poetic of modern verse translations, fell victim to this urge when he came to Ithaca in the 1960s while researching his *Odyssey*. Fitzgerald struggled to reconcile Homeric geography, literary tradition, and the evidence of his eyes. He was travelling, he came to believe, in Homer's footsteps.

A dawn approach on a ship from Piraeus has Fitzgerald convinced that Homer knew the island first-hand. 'He too, I felt sure, had looked ahead over a ship's bow at that hour and had seen those land masses, one sunny and one in gloom, just as I saw them. An overnight sail from Pylos would have brought him there at the right time.' Fitzgerald's conjectures are not unlike those of archaeologists on the other side of the Mediterranean who speculate that Homer must have made the journey from Chios to the ruins of Troy, like a writer of historical fiction soaking up local colour.

How, at a historical distance of 2700 years, can we make any assumptions about Homer's possible travel itinerary? Scholars now believe it much more likely that the poet was weaving mythical material from an older maritime adventure – the basis of the story known to us as Jason and the Argonauts – into descriptions from Greek traders and colonists of their journeys west across the Ionian Sea.

After first consulting the oracle at Delphi these seafarers, mostly landless young men, but in some cases exiles or vanquished parties in clan disputes, set out in search of arable land, and freedom from both wealthy landowners and those Hesiod derides as 'bribe-taking' magistrates. The colonies they founded were *apoikiai* – the Greek word *apo* signifies a detachment; *oikos*, a precursor of our word economy, means a household. Or else they were trading posts called emporia. The *Odyssey* seems to bear the trace of these westward migrations, which began in Mycenean times and continue through the so-called Dark Ages (1100–800 BC). Many of Odysseus's adventures seem to take place in southern Italian waters, sites of the first Greek colonies in the west founded in the mid eighth century. The famous story of the Sirens – one of these bird-women played the lyre, another the lute, while yet another sang, and together they lured passing sailors – is believed to elaborate some collective memory of the difficult passage around the gulf of Naples to Ischia.

The Harvard classicist Bernard Knox suggests that long before these organised colonists set out, traders and explorers must have returned with tall tales of wonders and dangers. The currents and whirlpools encountered in the waters between Sicily and the mainland are good candidates for the treacherous Charybdis, who sucked in water and spewed it out thrice daily, while the sheep-herding Cyclops 'may be a memory of the indigenous populations who opposed the intruders landing on their shores – a demonised version of the native, like Shakespeare's Caliban.' He also finds in one particular speech of Odysseus the 'authentic voice of the explorer evaluating a site for settlement', and thus a clear memory of Greek voyages to the west. Recalling a small uninhabited island near the land of the Cyclops, Odysseus describes it as,

> *... No mean spot,*
> *it could bear you any crop you like in season.*
> *The water-meadows along the low foaming shore*
> *run soft and moist, and your vines would never flag.*
> *The land's clear for ploughing. Harvest on harvest,*
> *a man could reap a healthy stand of grain –*
> *the subsoil's dark and rich.*

So began a process of cultural transplantation that would give rise to Magna Graecia, or Greater Greece. South of Rome in the fifth century BC flourished a sophisticated Greek world, both commercially and culturally powerful. Naples began life as Greek Neapolis. Subdued by Rome in the fourth century B.C, it remained a vibrant outpost of Hellenism (Greek was still widely spoken) four centuries later. Perhaps the most splendid Greek achievement of all was the prosperous Sicilian port town of Syracuse. Colonised in the eighth century by Corinth, it became Athens's great rival in the Western Mediterranean. The *Odyssey* seems to bear witness to the earliest stages of this rich cultural pollenisation; the creation, no less, of Roman high culture. As John Boardman explains in his seminal work on the subject, *The Greeks Overseas*, it was the 'reports of merchants' that gave colonists the knowledge of possible sites for settlement. These reports, combined with the memory of much earlier Mycenean trade in southern Italy, flood the *Odyssey* with its wonders – and its terrors.

THE SCHOOL OF HOMER

'A Blind man he is, and dwells on rugged Chios,' claims the *Homeric Hymn to Apollo*. Blind or not, Homer was a weaver of oral tradition, poetic formulae, hearsay and personal invention into a powerful art. So powerful, in fact, that his epic poems had managed many centuries after their composition to sow discord among the denizens of a peaceful island of rare beauty in a quiet corner of the Ionian Sea. Who was right? Sikiotis the sceptic? Or Paizis the believer? I wanted to know. And on a morning after autumn rain has turned the ground to terracotta paste, I decide to track the Homeric dreaming to its source.

The mountain path to Agios Athanasios, known as the School of Homer, is drying fast under a fierce sun. The valley below is a tumble of silver olive trees, arrow-headed cypress and red-tiled rooftops. Cut into the encircling hills, like gaps in a curtain, are views of a serene sea and the bony peaks of northern Greece far beyond. I catch the gentle tonk-tonk of goat bells and the scent of wild thyme on the air.

Further along the path up Pelikata Hill this mood of rustic tranquillity is shattered. From somewhere above comes the dull percussive pounding of hammer-on-wood. At the side of the path two bare-chested youths hoist a wooden plank onto their shoulders and tread carefully up the rain slicked hill.

'School of Homer?' I ask, pointing upwards. 'School of Homer,' they nod.

The holy grail of archaeology in Greece is the lost palace of Odysseus. After inconclusive excavations elsewhere on the island, this is considered the site most likely. It's a no-go zone for tourists – an archaeological work in progress. But a tall, thin man with wind-tossed white hair welcomes me. For Thanasis Papadopoulos, professor of prehistoric archaeology at the University of Ioannina in northern Greece, the Homeric connection lies somewhere between an article of faith and a frustrated hope.

'I think this is the place,' he says with an imploring smile. 'What do you think?'

I am looking at an exposed cliff face, perhaps five metres high, and the ancient ruins at its feet. At the summit stands the remains of a lichen-encrusted Cyclopean wall – so named because it was thought only one of Zeus's armourers could quarry rock of this size. Olive trees press in at all sides. Nature has reclaimed the stones.

From this wooded mountain eyrie the views exceed my fantasies. It may be the most beautiful – certainly the most romantic and mysterious – ancient ruin I have seen in Greece.

No photographic image or inherited expectation stands between the School of Homer and the eye; it has a kind of innocent 'lost-world' quality. It's also a little dangerous: stand looking too long at the view from these stones and you begin to see the ships of the colonists under sail in the straits. License those fantasies any further and you might catch sight of a panting herald with news of a challenge; or replay in slow-motion a king's bloody revenge as he returns to a house sullied by drunken yokels who covet his wife. You might start to *believe*. Spend too long with your head in Homer and your feet among ruins and the imagination unseats reason. One begins to understand how Homeric fantasies have inflamed many a good mind even before the time of Schliemann.

Under the shade of a venerable olive tree with a Marlboro packet wedged in its trunk, Professor Papadopoulos speaks for the stones. 'We are looking at a two-storey palace connected by a staircase,' he explains, picking at a string of silvery worry beads. 'There is an outer protective wall, an underground spring and well. From here you have commanding views of the sea. It seems to fit the description from the *Odyssey* of a two-storey building with rooms for commodities.' Some palace or citadel stood on this site, but is there a positive link to Homer's Odysseus? 'We are not yet in a position to tell,' says Papadopoulos. After ten summers working on Ithaca – the last three at this site – his money is running out and the islanders are growing impatient for proof of their Homeric paternity.

By the time we finish exploring the site the sun has climbed to an anti-social height and a meal with his crew of archaeological students and labourers awaits the professor in Stavros. On the leisurely walk downhill he relates how archaeologists, though trained to see the *Iliad* and the *Odyssey* as forms of mythic poetry – mere invented things – tended now to view the epics as fantastical reworkings of lived history. The world of Odysseus, according to this view, is in many ways Homer's world. The poems, then, are a little like treasure maps directing archaeologists to rich finds. Summer after summer, this faith draws Papadopoulos back to Ithaca.

'And why not?' he says, wiping sweat from his brow. 'We have the evidence that the kernel of the myth was truth. So why not here in Ithaca?'

. . .

In literature, as in life, the *Odyssey* is a synonym for the travails and delights of the journey; a byword for peregrination. Yet for the inhabitants of the Odyssean isle the tale is about a golden inheritance coveted by neighbours. The Homeric wanderer and his loyal queen are, for Ithacans, the ancestral first couple. And Homer, whose 'school' lies mid-way up Pelikata hill, is the poet who visited these parts and consecrated their homeland in the annals of myth.

The *Odyssey*, in an inversion of meaning peculiar to Ithacans, has come to mean home.

. . . .

Stone

LIAM DAVISON

Western Victorian explorers bring back strange stories, and from these even stranger ones arise.

There's a story told, and I have no reason to believe it isn't true, about a low stone wall which used to run in an unbroken line across the entire width of western Victoria. Not much remains of it now, though in places small piles of stones can still be found, looking more like the tumbledown remains of cairns or campfires than part of a great wall. Still, local people will take you to them and point them out as the remains of a structure of monumental proportions. There's something smug about the way they'll do it, as if by identifying the wall they're laying claim to some privileged link with a lost past from which you are excluded. In some places there are free-standing corners of stone such as remain when all but the strongest part of a house has fallen into ruin. These, you will be told, mark those points where the great wall intersected with lesser walls to form an intricate network of stone which divided the land into equally sized squares.

Most of what remains of the main wall – the original line of its foundations and the occasional mile of waist-high stone still standing against all odds – is now hidden beneath tall grass or is so overgrown with weeds that it is all but invisible to the untrained eye. Much of it has been taken away, stone by stone, for the building of farms or houses. In places, whole paddocks are so strewn with stones it's difficult to believe they were once part of the same wall. For those men well versed in the history of the area or with knowledge of walling, the wall is still there. They can't look out across their land without seeing the straight line of it running unbroken between the seemingly random outcrops of stone and the sorry little cairns which other men see.

Occasionally these men will meet to tell stories about the origins of the wall and the legendary wallers who built it. They will talk about the division of land in Europe and the Enclosure Acts of Scotland and Ireland, and of how the great wallers of those countries brought with them not only walls but a whole way of looking at the land. They'll tell stories about what parts of it still stand, building their own importance as they lay claim to a new piece of knowledge or a newly identified section on their own land. Some tell of how the whole incredible length of it was supported by the weight of each stone resting in such a way against its fellow stone that gravity held it up, and that the deliberate removal of one of the stones led to the gradual collapse of the wall, section by section in a process so slow that it was mistaken for the random falling of stones or the effects of wind and rain. Sometimes the story-telling will go late into the night as the men argue over whether a particular group of stones is part of the main wall or simply the remains of an unimportant subsidiary wall built by an unskilled farmer. Sometimes the men will come to blows, exchanging punches until their faces are bloodied and one of them concedes that he was mistaken in his judgement. None of the stories are written down. It's the telling that's important, as if each story is further proof of the wall's existence.

One of the stories however is not about the wall itself but about a pile of stones which may not have been part of it at all. Some hold the stones were a small outcrop just to the north of Byaduk. Others argue it was one of the many piles to be found in the Stony Rises close to Camperdown – stones which many regarded as one of the finest stretches of wall still standing. Whatever the case, the story is the same. It tells of a journey west by a party of men attracted by stories they'd heard of the land which could be found there.

The party set out on an overcast day in August, a straggling line of eight horses, a dray and thirteen men. They passed unceremoniously behind the small huts which made up the outskirts of the settlement and disappeared around the edge of the swampy ground under a sky already low and heavy with rain. There was no emotional farewell, no crowd of well-wishers to see them off. Few of the settlers even noticed they had gone. By nightfall on the first day out, tensions had started to surface. Arguments arose over who should ride on horseback. There were disputes over rations. One of the men, an ex-convict by the name of Brent, was suspected of stealing food and the party was soon divided by mistrust and petty jealousies.

Mathieson, who led the party, was a man who could not tolerate division within his ranks and had always sought to resolve it by imposing his will on others. He punished Brent by reducing his rations and threatened the lash for any man found stealing or suspected of speaking with an uncivil tongue. The men resented his harshness and the division became more deep-set, with those who had made no financial commitment to the expedition threatening to leave and to set out on their own. Mathieson was forced to place a constant guard on the horses and rations. When he had one of the surveyors lashed for failing to keep the guard, even those closest to him turned against him and the party became less and less purposeful in its actions. They covered fewer miles each day and made increasingly less accurate observations until it became clear that the whole expedition was likely to fail.

Slowly the men deserted it. Each day a few more wandered off into the bush or turned for home in the faint hope of retracing their steps. Sometimes a horse went with them, or one of the compasses, but mostly it was food they took, or guns. By the end of the fourth week there were only three men left – Anderson the surveyor, whose eyes were constantly set on the horizon, Soddards, an ex-convict who fancied himself a naturalist, and Mathieson himself. The horses were gone except for the two harnessed to the dray. With each day the weather grew worse and the ground beneath their feet became so heavy with water that the horses found it all but impossible to keep the wheels of the low cart turning. Mathieson cursed them and resorted to the whip.

The country they moved through was mostly flat with occasional outcrops of stone, barely covered by thin grass. In places, water collected in shallow puddles, flattening the grass and turning it black beneath the surface. There was no sign of the land they'd expected to find – no rolling hills of green pasture, no brooks as such or wooded glens, nothing pleasing or appealing to the eye. Yet they continued on, each with a clear picture in his own mind of the land which must lie a day or two's journey further west.

Anderson saw a land dotted with small stone villages such as he remembered from his childhood. Not that the villages would be there of course, but there would be the places where they might have stood, the lines which roads might have followed, as clear in his own eye as if they were actually lined with hedgerows. Soddards saw the harsher landscape of his Pennine home, sharp ridges of stone falling away to deep lakes, townships with names like Stonesdale, Cotherstone or Stonehouse which would grow there as confidently as they had at home. For Mathieson, it was a picture of the flat land giving way to hills, the hills to mountains, and great boulders of stone piled each on each like a natural wall with rolling pasture land on either side. He saw his Scottish Grampians, towns with names like Balmoral and Hamilton.

But, at the end of each day's journeying, it became clear that the landscape had refused to change. The trees they camped beneath were twisted parodies of what they'd hoped to find. The land itself whistled with the sounds of insects, and each time they tried to drive a stake into the ground, they struck on stone. Soddards collected skins and the bones of animals which he packed away in boxes on the dray. One contained the bodies of a dozen birds, and their stench travelled with them, attracting flies and tainting the rations. Mathieson demanded that the specimens be left behind, but even with the worst ones gone, the smell remained. It was as though it came from the land itself.

In the late afternoon of what was to be their last day out, Anderson came across the stones. They formed what appeared to be a low wall no more than two yards long which joined at right angles with another wall, barely visible beneath the grass. The stones rested comfortably against each other, interlocking at the corner as if they'd been deliberately placed. Stepping up on to the stones, with one leg placed solidly on each of the walls, Anderson looked down at the ground and saw, beneath the thin grass, the clear outline of what looked to be the remains of a stone house.

By nightfall, the men had located the sites of another five houses, all of roughly the same dimensions. Together, they formed an irregular circle. Some were no more than depressions in the earth where the weight of stone walls had made their mark. Others comprised half-buried stones so that only after scraping at the earth or pulling the grass from it in clumps, could the tops of them be seen and the familiar shape of another stone house be revealed. Mathieson ordered that their camp be set up in the centre of the stone village and instructed Anderson to survey the area. For his own part, he recorded the dimensions of each structure in his journal, describing the type of stone used and making detailed sketches of how the stones interlocked or, in some cases, protruded from the earth like a set of broken teeth.

The horses were tethered outside the ring and, every now and then, as the men sat huddled round the fire, they heard them snort or rub their flanks against a corner of the dray. Beyond them it was quiet and dark. Inside the circle, with the reassurance of stone walls against their backs, the men felt as if, after all their travelling, they had finally arrived home. In the silence, they could hear the night sounds of their own country. In the darkness, they saw rolling fields partitioned by low walls of what looked like stone.

Only Soddards felt uncertain about what they'd found. He told of how, some years before, he'd travelled with a man called Thomas and of how they'd heard stories about natives who lived in stone houses in the Victorian Alps. Although they'd never found the houses, Thomas had filed official reports of what he'd heard. He made a detailed sketch in his notebook of how he imagined the stone villages to look. His sketch showed an irregular circle of stone houses, each of roughly the same dimensions, with the stones interlocking neatly at the corners.

As Soddards spoke, Mathieson became less settled, as if by telling the story, he was somehow destroying what they'd travelled so far to find. Occasional noises came to them from outside the circle – unfamiliar sounds of insects and night birds which Mathieson couldn't accommodate. He poked at the fire with a stick, scraped his boots across the ground. Eventually he ordered Soddards to be quiet. Feeling the stones hard across the small of his back, he turned to his journal again.

Late in the night, long after the others had fallen asleep, Mathieson heard a disturbance near the horses. He heard the wheezing of breath from one of them and a heavy thud as its legs folded beneath the weight of its body. In the first light of morning the men could see it lying near the dray with a spear wedged solidly between its ribs. Mathieson tried to wrench the shaft from its side, cursing the natives and swearing to take revenge. When it wouldn't budge, he broke it off, bracing his legs against the flanks of the horse and leaning his weight against it. He threw the broken shaft at the ground, lifted his gun from the dray and ordered Anderson and Soddards to load their own.

They came across them about mid-morning camped near a stony creek. Despite Soddards' attempts to stop him, Mathieson quickly opened fire, scattering the group and bringing down a man. He fired again, from close range, into the man's back and ordered the other two to bring in as many blacks as they could find. Anderson and Soddards made a half-hearted search of the area and, when they returned, they found Mathieson on his knees attacking the body of the dead man with a blunt stone. He went about it as if the man alone had been responsible for the death of the horse and the failure of the expedition. Anderson called to him to stop but the stone came down again and again against the broken skull. He moved towards him, reaching out to draw him away when Mathieson turned, caught Anderson by the arm and brought the stone down hard across his face. Soddards took aim from where he stood. He fired a single shot at Mathieson and threw the gun away.

They carried him slumped across the back of the horse and, by the time they arrived back at the stone village, he was dead. Soddards dug a shallow grave inside the first two walls they'd found and built another pile of stones above it, the same height as the walls but shaped like a cairn to mark how far they'd come. Taking what they could manage from the dray, the two men turned the horse and headed back across the flat land towards their homes.

Back at the settlement, they told of the memorial they'd built – how Mathieson had been taken by surprise by blacks and had never stood a chance. Soddards mentioned the arrangement of stones they'd found, how they could be mistaken for houses, but Anderson cut him short.

'It was a natural escarpment,' he said. 'Just the way they'd arranged themselves.' He described how they'd built their cairn, interlocking the stones the way good wallers did. 'There was nothing like that before,' he said. 'Nothing properly built.'

But already in the minds of the settlers, the image of a great wall was stretching across their land, traversing creeks and linking explorers' cairns. And when Soddards insisted on the order he'd seen in the original stones, the wall became even stronger. As the settlers went about their work of clearing and planting, it became more firmly fixed in their minds, as much a part of the land to the west as any other permanent feature. And each time a party travelled west to take up land themselves, it was a natural thing to fence their land with stone, digging it out of the ground and stacking it, waist high, in straight lines along their boundaries. Each new settler joined his wall to the nearest corner of his neighbour's, locking the stones in tight. At times, they uncovered what looked like sections of a wall already built. They thought of the stories Soddards told and incorporated the older walls into their own, interlocking the stones so it was impossible to tell them apart. The sons of settlers built walls as if it was in their blood.

As you drive west between Colac and Hamilton today, you can still make out what look like the remains of walls lining the roads or standing for no apparent reason in the middle of thistled paddocks. Some sections run down gullies and can be seen continuing on, following the same line, up to a kilometre away. Piles of stones, the same height as the walls, appear and disappear between trees and it wouldn't be hard to imagine that they were once all part of the same wall, or monuments left behind by innumerable expeditions which crossed and recrossed the land, closing it in, locking it tight. It wouldn't be hard to build the wall yourself, stone by imaginary stone, lifting the stones from the soft earth and dropping them into place. It wouldn't be hard to see an unbroken spine of stone surfacing from the ground as though it had been there always.

. . . . . .

Rite of Spring

MARGO LANAGAN

He's only a boy, and he's up on the holy mountain in a golden robe calling for the blizzard to stop and the spring to come.

This wind doesn't shriek or moan – nothing so personal. When the river took Jinny Lempwick last spring and half-killed her while we watched, it was doing what the wind's doing now, racing so strongly that a little thing like a person was never going to matter. All I can do is keep myself out of the main force of it, because it doesn't know how to care.

It's madness to be here at all, up on Beard's Top in an end-of-winter blizzard – and I'm near mad. I'm past thinking about soup, about fire, about sleep; I can only gape at how dumb, what a stupid idea, who thought of this? My mitted hands grasp and fumble ice and rock in front of my eyes. How do they keep going? How do these legs keep pushing me up the mountain as if I believed, as if I were as mad as my mad mother, or my mad, holy brother? Don't they realise I'm not made of the same stuff?

I don't know how my scrawny brother managed last year, with this robe in his pack. I feel as if only my hunting, my built-up muscles and my good lungs, stop me toppling off into the darkness. Sappy little Florius is stronger than I thought. I knew Mum was strong; Mum's the kind of person who can move a strapping great hunter like Stock Cherrymeadow aside with a word, with the force of a single lifted eyebrow. If she were in good health she'd be laughing now, thinking of me up here. Hellfire, she'd be here herself, not letting a big brawnhead like me go about her important business.

But she's not in good health. Felled to her bed, our mum, coughing, and raging at the cough. 'Don't come near me, thick boy! Just stop still and listen for a change!' And between her instructions I could hear Florius trying to breathe, in the outer room by the fire. He sounded like a hog caught in a pricklebush. It hurt just to listen. Mark Langhorne's lost all his five daughters to this cough.

Here we are, the cairn. This is where it all starts to happen. 'Don't get changed up top,' Mum said, 'or the wind'll snatch the robe away and we'll never afford another.' *And I'll not forgive you, ever, she may as well have said, and neither will anyone else in the village. Anything that goes wrong from here until king's-turn will be your fault and no one else's. May as well throw yourself off after the robe, for your life won't be worth living if you come back without it.*

So I use what small shelter the cairn gives to wrestle the robe out of the pack. The cold has stiffened it into great gold-crusted boards – I'm afraid it'll crack apart in my hands.

It's a wondrous treasure. I've only seen it the once, when Parson Pinknose shuffled in with it, autumn before last. 'It's all yours now, Ma'am,' he miseried. 'They won't let me do the thing again, after three summers' drouth.'

'Neither they should,' crabbed my mum. 'You Pinchnazes always do sloppy work, for all your prating about tradition. Next time *your* lot breeds a Deep One, do us all a favour and let its cord strangle it.'

You could tell the parson was too low-feeling to fight her back as she liked. He sighed as he pulled open the cloth bag, and the robe – well, nothing like that had ever been in our house before. Like bagged-up dragon-fire, it was, all full of danger and brightness. It pulled me out of my corner as on a trap-loop.

'You keep your mitts off,' my mum said, smacking me away and pulling the drawstring tight. 'What do you think you're up to, Parson, opening that here?' She glared at him.

'Just a last look, I thought,' said Pinknose wetly.

'A look for every boy and his dog? You know that's only for the Deep to see.' She shook her head and tut-tutted at the hopelessness of him and his ilk. 'You!' she added, shouldering me backwards. 'Stop gawping and bring some wood in.'

And here I am wearing the thing, Mum, I said to her in my mind, as neither you nor I would ever have imagined. Here's your thick boy, trying to keep side-on to a wind coming from every way, so it doesn't catch the blessed robe like a sail and blow him off your holy mountain and splat into Beardy Vale.

A terrible glumness settles on me. The thing is too big – not just the robe, which gets between my knees and presses on my shoulders like a pair of filled hods, but the whole damn weather and task and nonsense. *I'm* not Deep – everyone who knows me would laugh at the idea, loud and long.

'I can't do that sort of thing!' I whined in the sickroom. 'I'm not like Flor... I can't even –'

'"Can't" sets no blossom, boy!' Mum snarled, holding back a cough, looking all witchy with her slept-on hair and her bared teeth. '"Can't" melts no snow. You get your boots on and take that pack out of my sight. And *now!*'

And I got out, thinking I'd just stay out overnight, go down the old Brimston mine and come back and say I'd done it.

'But she'll know,' I said to myself, in the forest-green, in the mild and ferny places I can hardly remember now. And she will know, if I ever get back – ha!, it's a big *if* – she'll know if

I haven't done it all, and done it exactly right. She'll see it in my eyes.

So I clump up, towards the top of the top, wonky with the robe, drunk with cold and misery.

'Keep your thick head together,' Mum said. 'Say it back to me again.' And she made me say it and say it, the whole long clanging unrhyming poem, tricky as a blade-fish playing the white water, inning and outing and teasing you to beggary. And me realising I'd have to remember it on the bawling Top, with a cowing blizzard at me, with a damn millstone on my shoulders: 'Get off my back! I know it!' I shouted at her, and I slammed out of the house past wheezing Flor.

And now I'm not so sure. *Do* I know it? Do I know it *all*?

I've felt savage the whole way. 'Not my job!' I've shouted at the trees, at the Top's foot, which pokes out low and flattish to lull you before you hit the hard stuff. 'I do the hunting, remember? I bring in the food! I'm one of the dogs, going out to fetch!'

And speaking of dogs, I miss Cuff. I haven't been out without Cuff at my heel since I was tiny. 'But there's no beasts on the Top, not for this,' Mum said. 'This is a human thing only.'

'I'll tie her up to a tree down the bottom,' I said.

'You'll box her up like I tell you,' said Mum.

The look on Cuff's face when I put her in that box! Pull my heart into fish-bait, why don't you? So I was all aggrieved and misbalanced along the way. Cuff would have stopped me shouting, with her worry, with her wet nose at my hand.

And no I'm in such a rage with this bastard wind, that won't let me get to any kind of rhythm, that scours my face with coldness and bangs my nuisance hair in my eyes, and with the snow, that crusts up the gold on my shoulders and plasters itself to the front so that the mirrors won't shine away, awful wet snow that'll soak in and make the wretched burdensome thing even heavier, I tell you —

And all those years of Mum saying I was thick and people looking on Flor, with his spindly legs and his moon eyes, as the one to treasure and to butter up and to bring soup and sweets to and little gewgaws from Gankly Market! All those years of jealousy, but of relief, too, for who wants to be carrying all these people's hope — who wants to be Deep and different? Yet here I am *anyway* — all the years of putting up with me *not* the one and getting *nothing*, and yet it's me doing the grind, completely without anyone's thanks, only Mum yelling in my head: 'Get a word wrong and you'll know about the flat of my hand, young fella!'

So *many* words! I'm stuck somewhere in the first third of the thing, murmuring the wrong words over and over. I'm not a words persons by any imagining — I like places where it's unwise to speak, in a hide beside the grazing field with the deer coming in from all around, among ferns watching a boudoir-bird darting and doubting at my snare. I like to walk in of an evening with a brace of cedar doves, lay them by the pot and go to wash. That way Mum keeps quiet; that's her thanks, her silence. Now there's a wordswoman. Talk you into a hole, my mum would. And she's always right, as well. Wears a person out.

So. I'm here at the summit. Not that it feels like I've arrived, when I have to stagger and throw myself against the ground to keep from blowing away. 'You must stand for part of it,' Mum said, 'but you might have to start off sitting.'

So I get seated, with the robe ends tucked under me, and my face into the wind, so I don't eat hair, and I start the gobbledygook.

I'm fine until I get to the first list. One Father's name

dangles off my lips and I can't remember the next. Then comes the wind and smacks me over backwards with what feels like rocks in my face, a clump of snow-slop. 'They won't want you to do this,' Mum said. 'Don't ever think things want to change. It's a battle to make it happen. Now start at the top again.'

So I go back to the head of the Father list and I have another stab at it. Trouble is, our Fathers only had about three different names – then they'd add 'the Seventh', or 'the Strong' or 'with the Askance Eye'. It's a beggar to remember.

But, surprise, I do in the end. And then it's Beasts, which was a list I knew anyway; everyone gets taught the animals when they're little, just for fun. Then come the Mothers – another hard one, all those old witches with their sharp tongues coming out of their sharp brains. And then the Herbage – quite a lot of people know the plants, too, and I knew all of it except the herbs for beauty, which Mum taught me last night. There's only a few of them; I don't know why I didn't learn them before. 'Useful to know for your wife,' Mum grumped, 'or for when you're going after a wife.' Wife? I think of a wife sometimes. A kind and quiet wife, not Deep, nothing fancy. A wife like me, except rather more beautiful, thanks.

I carve the words out of the icy air with my snow-blown lips. Amazing – I'm getting it all out! It's like Mum's here, coughing and scowling at me in the lamplight, propped up on one elbow. That look on her face stands for no carry-on, no wandering away. 'Put your whole brain to it, boy!' she said, and now I see what she means. Even that part of my brain that's usually there at one side, knocking the rest into line and stopping me moaning against what I have to do, even that part's in on the job, passing me the words, worrying ahead for the next ones.

Now the lists are over and I'm into the wild stuff. *Get up, boy!* says my phantom mum. *You can't command the wind and weather when you're huddled on your bum, however fancy the robe you wear.* So I struggle up, shouting words that I mumbled, embarrassed, in front of Mum last night. They sounded powerfully pompous in our rough little home, but they suit this strong weather. They're something to throw at the wind; words seem like nothing, but they're tiny, fancy, *people's* things. Who cares whether they do anything? What else can we put up against the wind except our tininess and fanciness? What else can the wind put up against us but its big, dumb, howling brute-strength? So *there!*, I tell it with my miniature mouth, my tiny frozen pipe of a throat, my stumbling tongue (and even the stumbling is good, for the wind never stumbles, never goes back and rights itself, don't you see?). *All you've got is your noise – and I've got noise, too! And mine's a thing of beauty!*

On through the verse I go. I'm moving through all the world now, crop and town and ocean and sandhill, river and forest, rock and mist and tarn, describing the springtime we need for each. ('Miss one and I'll lob you,' said Mum. 'Better to say some twice than miss one.') I can't even *hear* the words, except in my head; my ears are full of the hooting and tearing of the wind. A gust nearly thumps me over the edge, and I fall to my hands and knees. The wind drags on the robe, grinding me backwards across the Top's top. I throw myself flat, still shouting; if I keep on, I might get through this alive. But the wind is trying to tell me otherwise. *Shut up and I'll stop*, it says, pounding me with hail-rocks. *Stop now and I'll let you go.*

The wind doesn't know my mother.

I'm glad of the words of that last verse; they save my life. They fill my mind and stop me thinking. *How can a living soul get through this?* They give me a thread to cling to as the storm beats its sodden laundry on me. I get to the end and there is so much strife and thrashing weight against my back, I start the verse again, yelling it into the rock, wrapping my arms around my head against the beating.

Mindless minutes pass. I hang on, I shout, I wait for the wind's fingernail to lever me off the Top like a scaly-bug egg off a leaf. If I move, it'll only happen sooner: that sickening lift, that awful drop into nothing, that crash, those last seeping few seconds of smashed pain. I've seen a raddle-cat's face in between the two hard bashes it takes to stave in its skull; I think I have an idea; I think I know what's in store.

At least I got the thing done. And done right, hey.

Oof! This is the gust that will do it. No – this, this is the one. This one's got the lift, this one's got the fingernails – that's right, under the forearms, under the shoulders, flip me up, toss me in the boiling storm, then let me drop –

. . .

It's the robe that saves me. Saves my head being stove in like a cat's, anyway.

I wake up rather elegant, in a cradle of rock. The breeze taps my face with a robe-corner. A lazy blueness, from a whole nother age, is spread all above me. A pair of keo-birds twindle solely up into it, higher and higher to dots, and then gone.

Lovely quiet. I don't want to move.

But things start moving without me. Feels like a new arm, stiff and not quite set in its glue. A lump of a leg, gone dead from lying so funny so long. And then very nervously my head, heavy as a river-rock. Everything hurts, from skin through innards to my aching cold bones.

I'm sitting up, though I don't remember deciding to. The

robe is soaked, heavy as plate-armour. I crawl out of it, and fold it after a fashion. The breeze, bright and brisk and icy, is trying to pretend it's not embarrassed about all that carry-on last night. If last night it was; I feel as if I lay there through a full round of seasons, and woke in a whole new life.

I glance down through the clouds and there's Gankly town, embroidered red on its green vale. Gankly's north of Beardy, and the cairn and our home are south. Clutching the lumpish robe to my chest, like an old madman all his worldly goods, I slide and scramble around the mountain.

Even weighted with those stones, the pack has been dragged right across the cairn's clearing. I empty the stones, and stuff the robe in, and lift the whole soggy bundle onto my back.

It's a long, long way down – and quiet, the cautious, damaged quiet that comes after a big blow. I walk alone through the warming world; I step over wet black branches torn to the ground by the wind; I leap from side to side of the brook that yesterday was my dry path upward. All these months the Top's been without colour, but now the winter grass is flushing greenish-gold before my eyes, the rocks are flecked violent and blood-red and patched with bronze lichen, and the sky is a deep, cloudless blue. I did it. I took hold of the mighty millstone of the seasons, and moved it, grinding and squeaking, onward in its circle. I hauled the words out of my memory one by one, and they stilled the winds, and brought this spring.

'Cuff?' I call, when I get home. In the shed, her muffled bark is immediate and mad, and she throws herself about in her box. But no person comes to door or window of the house. Everything is too quiet.

I prepare myself to find Mum and Flor, calm as calm. Everything dies. Look at those Langhorne girls. Look at every deer and cat and bird and fish that ever I hooked or trapped. It's no big thing. I've been so alone these last hours, I can't imagine the aloneness ending, can't imagine other people, their speech, their eyes. That's marvellous stuff, lost to me now.

On the driest grass I can find, I spread out the robe. It's still a feast for the eyes, even after all the feasting I've done on the way down. It's a different kind of feast, not grown by itself from seed or spore, but worked by people, for people's reasons, for people's use.

The house is dark, and smells of dead fire and the nettle-pulp for the coughs. Flor lies very still, his mouth open, his eyes slits of white. He's got the red quilt over him, that we only use for guests; Mum must have struggled to get it onto him, being so sick herself. My little brother, always so thin and pale and smiley. He turned the seasons beautifully for us last year. He did what I did, and I don't know how. I remember it rained on and on, and Mum paced up and down and swore as she peered out the window waiting for him. I remember the little drowned rat that came home in the end, his eyes brilliant with what he'd done, all the fear and seriousness gone from his skinny, joyful frame.

I go over to him, for it's not often in your life you get a good close private look at a dead person; there are always funeral people about, making it rude to stare. I have a good long stare at Flor, long enough for Cuff to stop bothering to bark. Still as a log, still as a stone ... and then there's a tremor of eyelashes, a glimmer on the eye-whites. I put my face closer and feel the warmth off him. A soft snore comes from the other room and I startle, and nearly laugh out loud. The two of them, both still here! Instead of struggling like before, Flor breathes deeply and silently – now I see the rise and fall of his chest under the motionless quilt.

'You great, soppy fool,' I mutter to myself, sniffing back the sudden tears. 'All they needed was bed-rest, and a bit of nettle.'

Mum is curled up like a possum, her face away from me. I go in, around the bed, with some half-baked notion in my head of waking her, of telling her, of claiming from her some kind of a blessing.

But then I go right off the idea. Her sleeping face is like punched-down bread dough; it's as creased as the rock of Beard's Top, and as polished, with the sweat of her broken fever. She's a sick little old lady – for now, at least. Before she wakes and starts pelting me with accusing questions and making me wish I'd never gone to all the bother. She needs sleep more than anything else. And the spring will come, whether she believes I brought it or not.

The shed smells of dog-pee and wood-damp. It's dark, and I find Cuff's box by following her scratching and whining, the brush of her nose on the splintery wood.

'Cuff, Cuff, my girl!' I whisper.

She throws herself against my side of the box and barks twice.

'Shall be go up to Highfields, shall we?' I murmur, feeling along the bench for the jemmy I left there. 'Shall we get ourselves a snow-hare, you and me, and put it in the pot for the invalids? I think we shall, girl. I think we shall.'

And murmuring so, I ease up the box lid. Before the last nail's free, Cuff pours out the opening into my arms, all tongue and toenails. Then she's in the shed doorway, looking back, her raised paw saying, *When you're quite ready* ... And beyond her is all the dampness and the dazzle of the first day of spring.

. . . . . .

GETTING TO THE END

What do I 'Do' with Cancer?

STEVE J. SPEARS

'I was, overnight, a 150-year-old man.'

'Depend upon it, sir, when a man knows he is to be hanged in a fortnight, it concentrates his mind wonderfully.'
— Samuel Johnson

I got it. How do I deal with it? By which I mean: (1) as a man – to wildly paraphrase Dickens – will I turn out to be the hero of my story? Brave chappie? Sook? An it's-my-life-it's my-death-suicide? Or will the hero be somebody else? Or cancer? These pages must show. And (2) how do I do cancer in another of an endless line of 'a journal of my disease' articles we've read before. I have no cancer answers and the only two big questions I have are not 'Why me? Why me?' but a political one, 'Why the health system?' and a theological one, 'Why cancer?'

. . .

SUMMER: In the list of life's nasties, needles, lameness, having stuff rammed up my bottom or down my throat, a catheter shoved into my penis, death, operations that aren't part of a *House MD* episode and Being Totally Enclosed Inside A Machine would head the list. The good Lord, with his usual savage wit, seemed intent on my experiencing all of them real soon (except the 'death' one, hopefully).

For a month or two before C-Day, the simple joys of

looking at sunsets-over-the-sea, walking the white sands of Always Bay, writing, swimming et al had become increasingly dominated by the realisation that, after a hearty 10-hour sleep, I would take to bed for late-morning and early-afternoon naps of the more-a-hearty-sleep-than-a-nap kind. Nauseous. Ashen. Breathing shallow. Both knees hurt. Jesus, did they hurt! Shuffle. Wheeze. Ouch. Nap. Wake up. Vomit.

I was, overnight, a 150-year-old man.

My Big City GP, Dr Aries, suspects anaemia and recommends a physiotherapist for my increasing lameness (!). He makes me take blood tests (needles!) and provide DIY poo samples. Aries and the Big City labs are 60 kilometres away. The tests are proving nothing. We do them again. We do others. Then more. 120 kilometres a time.

Finally, Dr Aries decides I should see a Big City Specialist. It's perfect timing, of course, since Christmas is nigh and specialists are thin on the ground, but a Dr Virgo agrees to see me for a 'consult'.

In a week or so. After Christmas.

He too is puzzled by the stubbornness of the scans and of my blood to confirm the location of the … something. 'We're going in full-bore,' he says. By which he means he's going full-bore into me! Colonoscopy (!) and endoscopy (!). Rectally (!) and orally (!) with big black hoses with cameras and scissors and all.

So, on January 21, 2006, my 55th birthday, I am, like a new fish in the prison, on Virgo's table dressed in fetching pale-green paper, ready to be raped. They put a gas mask over me. I count from 10 to –

I awake. It's all done. No pain. Feel good.

'We'll have the results in a couple of days,' say Virgo and Aries.

Oh, goody.

'Dr Virgo didn't find anything,' says a puzzled Aries. 'You're losing blood. But we don't know from where.' The equally puzzled Virgo presses on my tummy and prods and pokes. Nothing sore. Nothing hurts. I can feel his frustration. Jimmy Dancer's making fools of us all. 'Come back in three months,' says Virgo, 'unless something changes.' Like the status of my mortality, for instance?

'I think,' says Aries, 'it's time for a second opinion.'

An old school chum, Vincent Starr-Webb, is not a surgeon. King of a Private Hospital. Expensive Marx Bay, Queensland. Expensive house. Big pool. A few months back, Starr-Webb had invited me to stay with him for a few weeks, maybe sail on his expensive yacht, maybe slip me a freebie lap band operation for my Humpty Dumpty weight. No need for lap bands right now. I'm 20 kilos lighter than I was last month and heading down like the Biggest Loser you ever saw.

Starr-Webb loves me. We go back 45 years. He thinks me and my writing are the bee's knees. Once we were young and pretty. Now he's stayed above the fray by morphing into a middle-aged Sean Connery clone. I'm grey. I shuffle. I'm 200 years old. 'Starr-Webb, I need a second opinion.'

'Get here. Now.'

Starr-Webb studies the reports, examines the pictures. The most puzzling problem for him is, 'Where are the chest X-rays?' Huh? Chest? Nobody said nothing about chests. He's furious in a cool 007 way. He whisks me to his fiefdom, the hospital, and gets me X-rayed. And there it is. Left lung. About the size of Peru. Very aggressive. Hello, Jimmy.

Starr-Webb sets up all manner of public and private tests (freebies, natch), kindly explaining, 'If it's spread to the brain or the lymph nodes or anywhere else, forget it. If we don't think you're strong enough for an op, forget it. Surgery would be a waste of all our time.'

It dawns on me that good old Starr-Webb is explaining something I'd never known: you don't just have a cancer op, you audition for it first. And they say showbiz is brutal.

It hasn't spread. 'This is very strange. It's huge and aggressive but it's stayed in the lung,' says Dr Libra, a Starr-Webb mates-rater. He's a Brisbane surgeon. He's ready to operate within the fortnight. 'Definitely doable. Have it here or have it at home. But have it.'

Home? Did he say home? Sunsets-over-the-sea? The silky sands. The glassy waters. My Always Bay? So I, O Mighty Brainiac, decide I'll have it at home, thank you. I mean, why leave a steel circle of medical pros who've taken five days to arrange things for little old me like they do for the big ole rich them? Indeed, why not have it right there at home where so many laboured so long searching my bum for a lung?

Lead me, Zeus, and you too, Destiny, Wherever I am assigned by you; I'll follow and not hesitate. But even if I do not wish to, because I'm bad, I'll follow anyway.

— CLEANTHES, STOIC. 200 BC

. . .

AUTUMN: Home. Who'd have thought it? I have to audition *all over again* for the hometown op with a Dr Sagittarius. For four weeks, five? I waltz with Jimmy from district to city to charming boutique hospitals – from Wino Valley Memorials to King Bruce Publics to Saints Mary of the Suffering Lepers – from strange faces to stranger faces – from getting my skeleton nuked to Being Totally Enclosed Inside A Machine (!). The only constant is Dr Sagittarius's receptionist, who smooths paths, rejuggles things, cheers me up, advises sotto voce on when to pay a few hundred for a private test or consult to kick things along.

Finally, the Day of the Peru Lung Operation arrives and the good Lord settles on April Fools' Day. I arrive at Big City Public with robe, slippers, PJ's and books. And ... no beds left. Do I mind coming back in five days?

No probs.

All I clearly recall about the Pre-Op and Op is coming back in five days and then being in the ward with Dr Sagittarius telling me it had gone 'very well', even if we both knew Jimmy had booked a few more tentative dates for me. Post-Op emails, calls, even flowers from old friends and foes. A catheter in my penis (!) and a chick-magnet scar. Hell, I'm so strong and brave, they send me home after five days. There'll be four months of weekly chemo and six weeks of daily radiotherapy. I'm so strong and brave, I don't care! Lead on, Destiny!

Bring it on! I'm right behind you. I'm right here!

. . .

WINTER: Mid-June. Always Beach. Notes. Remember: *3am. The first post-op night in the cancer ward. Ah! The man in the next bed BARKS! When he coughs. I can almost taste his blood. Silence. From way down the hall a long moan. A woman, I think BARKS! Silence. Night nurses rush by, a bit panicky. Someone dead? If I'm going to go into panic mode, this would be the time. When the hell did I learn courage? Serenity? Grace under pressure? I roll over to sleep. If I don't roll back over in the morning, well ... I'm not going to know about it. BARK!*

Remember: *first chemo appointment. In one waiting-room, a distressed woman in her 50s. obviously in great pain, hubby at her side. An hour or so later. Different waiting-room. The woman's hurting a lot less. They take her away. She's got a brain tumour. 'Size of a cricket ball.' A nurse comes in. For some reason, the medicos have been taking a plaster-cast of the woman's face. They need hubby. She's panicked. And why not? Buried alive in a mask, buried alive in a coffin. Pick one.*

President Bush's new press secretary said in Washington recently that getting colon cancer was 'the best thing that ever happened to me'. I sort of know what he means. I've found myself noticing beauty more, especially in faces. Have women always been this lustrous? Men this rugged? Old folks so finely lined? Have kids always been so cute? Have birds and dogs always had such crazily individual features? Is that me in the mirror or did some 40-year-old spunk-rat switch heads with me?

Still ... *'best thing'*? Even as the secretary spoke, I heard steam rise from the souls of a few million cancerers and their carers. Tell that to my child. To my friend. To the one I love the most who's got this 'best thing' and isn't rich. Tell it to the old and feeble, the poor, the overburdened, the lost. Tell it to someone who has no one.

Remember: *You've had a lot of advantages during this dance. Education. Nudge-nudge hurry-up money. Friends. Car. Starr-Webb's Old Boy Network. Most important, you live near a big city where the services are, and not in a regional centre where, increasingly, they aren't.*

Which leads to the political question, 'Why the health system?' Are the ignorant mutts who infest federal and state legislatures really, truly going to keep getting away with their killing spree? Hospitals are being underfunded and allowed to close. The mutts say, 'Who cares?' Country people literally lose their farms travelling back and forth and having to 'live' in the city for days, weeks, months. Pensioners die. So what? Not our fault. Ministerial responsibility? What dat? It's the states' fault, it's Canberra's fault; it's Labor's fault, it's Liberal's, say the mutts. We, the people, could double the money going into health by insisting that it's too important to leave in two sets of lust-for-glory bureaucratic hands. We, the people, had better realise life is not a left/right, Lib/Lab thing, and while ever we think it is, the politicos will keep gulling us. Vote the mutts out. All of them. Every time. Vote Independent. Then vote them out. Every time.

And we'd better decide quickly if we want perfection or reality from doctors. There's a lot of preventable death on the way, and medicos will not stick around if they're going to lose their houses for every mistake in this farcically financed system. (That's why medicos order so many expensive interesting-but-not-terribly-useful tests. Cover your arse. Incoming lawyers!)

Remember: *Talking to a medico, I suggest that whatever the chemicals that kill cancer patients' appetites are, they should be bottled and marketed by pharmaceutical companies as diet drugs. She tells me they're working on it. She's not kidding. Good.*

My voice is higher and lighter. I like it. I sound like one of them colourful mafia hoods. And what's with my *knees*. They're *steel springs!* The knees of a 20-year-old! How the hell can cutting out a lung do that? My nasal hair is thinning very nicely. Am realising how much joy I get, and have always got, from making people laugh. I pick up my guitar and sing more often now. Blues and gospel. Just for the hell of it. My pickin' and singin' is awesome. Writing is so engrossing, so pleasurable, I can barely stand it.

Philip Roth: 'Old age isn't a battle; old age is a massacre.'

. . .

WHAT DO I 'DO' WITH CANCER?

11 JUNE 2006. LAST ENTRY: Make it plain that, despite the odd diagnostic blooper or two, never once did I feel anything but total commitment from medicos – by which I mean everyone from assistants to nurses to doctors. They wanted me fixed and they wanted it to be painless as poss. Never once did I feel anything but welcomed and protected in the gloomy chambers they run so humanely.

The theological question – 'Why cancer?' Is there really, truly a God who, along with sunsets, dreams this foul stuff up just to torment us? I say no. I say immortality is for suckers. I say we live in an essentially benign universe and are lucky to be here. The question is as silly as 'Why sunsets?'

My 'Pentangeli Papers' novels have been bought for TV. A telemovie. Maybe three. Goody. About time, too.

Woody Allen: 'I don't want to achieve immortality through my work; I want to achieve it by not dying.'

Breathing isn't as good as it has been. Wouldn't it be ironic if all this therapy's useless? If I learned Jimmy had gone waltzing into my brain or liver anyway? And that it really, truly is a matter of weeks? Won't I look silly if I crack up now? Mind is on fire. Brain racing and tongue always a few steps behind.

Remember: *I ask Starr-Webb what my odds are. He says, '100 per cent. In the end, the odds of your dying are exactly 100 per cent.'*

Good Lord, *now* he tells me.

. . . . . .

A Perfect Circle

PETER SYMONS

What does his father do when he's dying? He sings.

For my father

It is the middle of April and my father is dying. As I walk across the park that separates my house from the hospital, I hear my footsteps crunch on the ground. There is the first suggestion of frost on the grass. Winter is ahead of me and the days are becoming shorter.

I have done this, walking across the park to visit my father, every day for the past two months. Sixty days. I have thought about measuring it. Ascertaining precisely how many metres I have walked over this time. I like to measure. To know. I always have. I have learnt to know my father. How he breathes when he is in pain. I have learnt how his face contorts when he is hungry. I know when he is thirsty.

I stop my walking for a moment and look to the sky. There is a clarity to the sky at this time of year. It is as if the cold had refracted the light into a perfect blue that shimmers and touches everything. I take a deep breath. I have also learnt to love these early mornings. Ahead of me, perhaps two hundred steps away, is the hospital. I walk on. Perhaps tomorrow I will count how many steps it takes me.

. . .

My father lies, as he has done for the past two months, on his back on the hospital bed facing the ceiling. And I, as I have done for the past sixty days, approach his bed cautiously.

I reach the chair next to him and quietly put my bag on the floor. His eyes are closed, but he is breathing. I take his hand and watch his eyes open. It has been the two of us for twenty years. My mother died when I was six, and I am an only child. I don't recall my mother's death. I only remember my father's sadness.

My father turns his head towards me. His blue eyes a little clouded. Death has a presence, long before He takes over entirely. I can sense this, and I believe my father can as well. My father opens his mouth then swallows awkwardly. I stand up quickly and find the water jug on the drawers next to his bed. I pour water into a plastic cup, then gently tip a little into his mouth. My father manages to swallow and then pauses. When Death is near, a sip of water becomes a joyous luxury. I put the cup back and hold my father's hand again. We have a routine, more than that, a ritual. I arrive at 8am. I stay for twenty minutes, then I walk to my office in the city.

I look at my watch: 8.20. I bend down and kiss my father's forehead. He squeezes my hand. Sign language. He is saying, goodbye, I shall see you again. I pick up my bag and walk quickly out.

. . .

The next morning I begin my walk again. Day sixty-one. I am halfway across the park when I realise that I have forgotten to count my steps. Perhaps tomorrow. It is colder than yesterday and I keep my hands in my pockets. A slight breeze plays with the grass at my feet. I have not heard my father speak for forty-one days. I am beginning to forget what his voice sounds like. Suddenly, there is a hotness behind my eyes. I swallow hard. I have not cried during this whole time. I swallow again and stand still. I wonder, is it possible to stop time? I look to the sky. The same cold, clear blue. There are two trees in the distance ahead of me. If I stand still, stone-still, can I stop time? The breeze stops. The grass does not move. There is silence. No birdsong. I hold my breath. The earth is still.

But then two birds burst out of the trees and the breeze picks up. I breathe again and walk on.

. . .

At my father's side once more. I feel the rhythm of our ritual. I am holding his hand, he is facing me lying on his left side. His mouth opens and I reach for the cup next to me. But he is not thirsty. I hear a low noise; at first I think it is the sound of the traffic outside. But it is my father. More than words, a note. A low note, held. So soft. I lean. I lean closer to him. The note changes, a little higher. My ear is five centimetres from his mouth and the notes continue. Then I recognise it. *Ave Maria*. A picture of myself as a child forms in my mind. My father and me in church. He is singing the same song. *Ave Maria*. I can barely hear his singing, but my mind is bursting with memories. The church. I am singing too. Something else. There is some sort of emotion. A sadness locked to the pictures in my mind. I clasp my hands to my head. My mother's funeral. My father and I are singing. My father's tears. Twenty years fall upon me and draw a perfect circle between then and now. I move back so I can see my father. I begin to sing with him *Ave Maria*. Softly. So quietly only the two of us can hear. I find my father's hand and hold it tightly. As we finish the song, I close my eyes. When I open them again I can see my father smile, very slightly. I stroke his hair. I look at my watch. It is time to go.

. . .

Day sixty-two. Three beautiful days in a row. I turn into the ward where my father lies. Once again on his back. His face to the ceiling. But there is something missing. Something I already knew. I sit down next to his bed and reach for his hand. But I stop before I touch him. There is no breath. No movement. I place my hands on my lap and look at my father. Standing, I kiss him on the forehead, then turn to speak to the nurse who keeps watch from the desk behind me.

. . . . . .

At the Morgue

HELEN GARNER

'A dead body, stripped of clothes, makes perfect sense of itself in no language but its own.'

In everyone's mental image of a city there is a dark, chilled, secret place called the City Morgue. We know these exist because we've seen them at the movies. If you had asked me where Melbourne's mortuary was, I wouldn't have had a clue. I might have gestured vaguely towards the murkier end of Flinders Street – but like most Melburnians I had no idea that half a mile from the leafiest stretch of St Kilda Road, in there behind the National Gallery and the Ballet School and the Arts Centre with its silly spire and its theatres and orchestras and choirs, stands a wide, low, new, clean, bright, nautical-looking structure, with a cluster of slender steel chimneys and a crisp little landscaped garden: the Coronial Services Centre, which was opened in 1988 and houses the Victorian Institute of Forensic Pathology. This is where I found the mortuary.

If you die in an accident, or unexpectedly, or by violence, or in police or state custody, or by suicide, or in a fire, or if no doctor is prepared to sign a certificate stating that you have died of natural causes, your death is called a reportable death. Your body is taken to the mortuary, where you enter the jurisdiction of the coroner. He, on behalf of the people of Victoria, wants to know exactly why you died. And until the cause of your death has been established to his satisfaction, in most cases by means of an autopsy, your body will remain in his care. You have become what is known as a coroner's case – a coroner's body.

The first one I saw, from a raised and glassed-in viewing area, was lying naked on its back on a stainless-steel table in the infectious room of the mortuary. It was the body of a young man. Because he had been found with a syringe nearby, he'd already had a battery of tests. He was infected with hepatitis C, a virulent form of the disease for which there is no vaccination and which eighty percent of IV drug deaths are found to be carrying; thus, the lab technician was not only gowned up and gloved like a surgeon, but was wearing a hard clear perspex mask which covered his whole face and gave him the look of a welder. The other actor in this odourless mime-autopsy was also a man, a pathologist. He wore no mask but was otherwise dressed like the technician. Both of them moved around on the spotless tiles in big stiff white rubber boots.

Before I could get my bearing (and my notebook was already hanging by my side, forgotten) the technician stepped up to the corpse's head and sank a needle into its left eye. The first sample of fluid laid aside, he moved down to the dead man's hip, plunged another syringe into his abdomen just above his pubic hair and drew out a sample of his urine. Then he picked up a scalpel and walked around to the right side of the dead man's head.

I would be lying if I claimed to be able to give a blow-by-blow account of the first autopsy I witnessed. The shock of it made me forget the sequence. Time slid past me at breathless speed. The pathologist and the technician moved as swiftly and as lightly as dancers. My eyes were too slow: they kept getting left behind. If I concentrated on one thing, another procedure would suddenly be launched or completed elsewhere. So this is not official. It is not objective.

I saw that the scalp was slit and peeling forward over the face like a hairy cap, leaving the skull a shining, glossy white. The skull was opened by means of a little vibrating handsaw. The brain was lifted neatly out (so clean, perfect, intricately folded – so valuable-looking), but also, before I could contemplate it, the torso was slit from the base of the neck to the pubis in one firm, clean-running scalpel stroke, then someone seized a pair of long-handled, small-beaked shears and smoothly snipped away the arcs of ribs which protect the heart and lungs – and there it lay, open to view, the brilliantly, madly compressed landscape of the inner organs.

It can't be, but I thought that the two men paused here for a second, to give us time to admire.

Out come the organs now, neatly scalpelled away from their evolved positions. The technician, working blind in the hollow cave of the torso, lifts them out in glistening slippery handfuls. I recognise small and large intestines, liver, kidneys: but there is plenty more that I'm ignorant of, an undifferentiated collection of interior business. The technician lays it all out beautifully on the steel bench for the pathologist, who is separating, checking, feeling, slicing, sampling, peering, ascertaining. Each organ is put on the scales. Its weight is scribbled in blue marker onto a whiteboard on the wall. The contents of the dead man's thorax are heaved out: his lungs, his heart, his windpipe, even his tongue, the topmost muscle of this complex mass of equipment: to think he used once to talk – or sing! Now his neck looks hollow and flat.

His intestines, his organs, all his insides are examined and then placed between his legs on the steel stable. I can't believe all this has happened so fast. But the technician is scouring out the hollow shell of the skull, using the same rounded, firm, deliberate movements of wrist and hand that my grandmother would use to scrub out a small saucepan. At this moment I think irresistibly of that action of hers, and her whole kitchen comes rushing back into my memory, detailed and entire. I have to shove it out of the way so I can concentrate.

The technician balls up several pages of the Age and stuffs the cleaned skull with them. He slots into its original position the section of the skull he removed earlier, and draws the peeled-down scalp up off the face and over the curve of bone where it used to grow; he pulls it firmly back into place. He takes a large needle and a length of surgical thread, and stitches the scalp together again. He stuffs the hollowed neck with paper, forming and shaping skilfully and with care.

He places the body's inner parts into a large plastic bag and inserts the bag into the emptied abdominal cavity; then he takes his needle again, threads it, and begins the process of sewing up the long slit in the body's soft front. The stitch he uses is one I have never seen in ordinary sewing: it is unusually complex and very firm. He tugs each stitch to make sure it is secure. The line of stitches he is creating is as neat and strong as a zip.

At some stage, without my noticing, the pathologist has left the room.

During the sewing, most of the watchers in the viewing suite drift out of the room. Only two of us are left behind the glass, standing in silence, keeping (I suppose) a kind of vigil: it would be disrespectful, having witnessed this much, to walk away while he is still half undone. The stitching takes up more time (or so I calculate, in my semi-stupor) than all the rest of the process put together. The meticulous precision of the job is almost moving: the technician is turning an opened, scientifically plundered coroner's body back into a simple dead one, presentable enough to be handed back to the funeral directors and to his family, if he still has one – his family who are presumably, at this very moment, somewhere out there in the oblivious city, howling or dumbly cradling their grief.

It's almost over now. Outwardly, he is whole again. The technician turns on a tap and hoses the body down. With wet hair the young man looks more life-like and more vulnerable, like someone at the hairdresser. But the water flows over his half-open eyes which do not close. Yes, he is dead: I had almost forgotten.

His fingertips and nails are black. As the technician raises the body slightly to hose under it, its right arm flips out and protrudes off the edge of the table in a gesture that makes him look more human, less like a shop dummy, less obedient. The technician replaces it alongside the torso, and once more the young man is docilely dead. The technician dries the young man's face with a small green cloth. This closes his eyes again. His mouth moves under the force of the cloth just as a child's will, passively, while you wipe off the Vegemite or the mud; his lower lip flaps and then returns to a closed position.

The technician removes from under the young man's shoulders a curved block of wood which, yoga-style, has been broadening out his chest and keeping his chin out of the action throughout the autopsy. His head, released, drops back onto the steel surface. The table is tilted to let the water and a small quantity of blood and tissue run down the plug-hole near the corpse's feet. His genitals are long and flaccid. His hands are scrawny. He is very thin. As the technician pulls the trolley out of the dissection bay and swings it round towards the door, the sudden turning movement displaces the young man's hand so that it flips over his genitals, covering them as if in modesty or anxiety.

Now, because of the danger of hepatitis C infection, the

technician must manoeuvre the body feet first into a thick, white plastic bag. It's hard for someone working on his own. It's like trying to work a drunk into a sleeping-bag. It takes a lot of effort and muscle. At last he has the body and the head encased in plastic. He draws up the neck of the bag, grabs a bit in each hand, and ties it in a neat knot. He slaps a sticker onto the outside of the bag. It's big and I can see it from here. It reads: BIOLOGICAL HAZARD.

The technician opens the door of the infectious room and wheels the trolley out. The room is empty. I look at my watch. I have been standing here, completely absorbed, for forty minutes.

On my way home I would have liked to jabber to strangers about what I had seen in the mortuary, but at the same time I felt I should keep my mouth shut, probably forever. I stopped off at the Royal Women's Hospital to visit some close friends whose baby daughter had been born early that same morning. The labour had been long and hard, and they were all exhausted, but calm. The baby was still bruised-looking and rather purple. Her struggles to be born had left her head slightly lop-sided, an effect which the doctors said would soon correct itself. Somebody said, 'Her head is shaped like a teardrop.' We all laughed.

I didn't tell my friends where I had spent the morning. I stood beside the baby's cot and gazed down at her. Her eyes were closed. Her hands were clasped near her cheeks. Her mouth moved constantly, and small waves of what looked like expression kept passing over her wrinkled face. The baby and the corpse did not seem to be connected to each other in my mind. They inhabited separate compartments, and my thoughts skipped and slithered from one to the other and back again.

The people who work at the mortuary are not used to being interviewed. They know that the picture the general public has of them is a macabre cliché. But they are not the skulking ghouls of legend. Far from it: they are as ordinary as can be. And they are young. Except for the coroner himself, Hal Hallenstein, a sombre, chastening man in a dark suit, I am at all times the oldest living person in the room. The more time I spend with the manager, the scientist and the technicians, Rod, Jodie, Barry, Kevin and (although she is a Bachelor of Science) 'Little Alex', the more impressed I become.

Just as well. You need somebody trustworthy for a guide when you're taken into the big storage chamber called 'the fridge' and confronted with a long row of dead bodies, twelve or fifteen of them, laid out on steel trolleys.

I experience an atavistic urge to make a sign of reverence.

Only one of the bodies is covered: a very small baby, wrapped up, as firmly as if it were alive, in a pastel cotton blanket, and laid on a metal shelf at eye level.

A dead body, stripped of clothes, makes perfect sense of itself in no language but its own. It packs a tremendous wallop. In its utter stillness it seems preoccupied with some important matter that you are ignorant of. It has an authority, in its nakedness, which transcends whatever puny thoughts you, the stranger, may entertain about it. It has presence. And yet it is no longer a person.

But it takes me more than one visit to realise this. At first I keep pestering for each body's story. Oh, what happened to this poor man? Look at this lady – oh, poor thing – what have they done to her? To the technicians and the pathologists, these matters are of academic interest only. They are patient with me and, because I'm their guest, they oblige me by calling up the deaths or 'the circumstances', as they call them, on the computer. Fell off a truck, they say. Suspected heart failure. Looks like a suicide. MVA (motor vehicle accident).

But their tone is abstracted. They can't afford to dwell on the personal or the tragic. They get at least one suicide a day – 'we've got bags and bags of ligatures out there', somebody tells me. They have to perform autopsies on dead babies and murder victims. Their detachment is very highly developed and they have to maintain it. It is precious to them. It is their only defence.

So after a while I control myself and try to copy them. Some of their composure begins to rub off on me. It's amazing how quickly you can get used to the company of the dead. Of course, I am in the privileged position of an observer. Later, Barry, a brilliant dissector who worked and studied his way up from being a porter at Charing Cross Hospital in London to his current position as senior technician, remarks to me, 'You never get completely detached. I've been in this work for eight and a half years. Every now and then I say to myself, "Well, now I've seen everything" – and then next day a case will come in that'll shock even me. You never get used to the homicides – what people will do to each other.'

'It's not such a different job as other people think it is,' says Jodie, who at twenty-five is senior scientist in the mortuary. 'Often I think our lab's just the same as any other, except that our specimens are bigger.' She is sitting in the manager's office in her blue surgical gown and her socks, having left her huge white boots behind at the mortuary door. Like all the technicians who spoke to me, she has a very direct gaze, and an air of unusual maturity and calm. 'I was the first woman here,' she says. 'The guys taught me everything. The first day I was here I went home all worked up, I'd had such an interesting and exciting day. Day two, it caught up with me. It was the smell, maybe, or the blood. They were doing eight post-mortems at once and everyone was busy; they were all gloved and gowned up, and someone looked at me and said, 'Jodie, you're going pale.' I walked into the change room and passed out.

'But the techs were fantastic. Someone said, 'Come over here. I'll make you concentrate on one small area.' I did, and then I was all right. But it took me a while till I could step over that red bench into the lab without thinking, 'What am I doing here?'

She laughs, sitting there quietly with her hands folded in her lap. She is not what you would call tough: she's got a rather sweet, open face, with intelligent eyes; but she has the firmness of someone who's had to work out a few important things earlier than your average Australian twenty-five year old. She commands respect without having to try.

'Staying detached,' she says, 'is hardest with the kids that come in. The cot-death babies, or kids that die in accidents or fires. It's terrible. With every grown-up case you can manage to convince yourself that there's a reason, but with kids – they're innocent. They haven't done anything. One day I was working with Barry, who's got young kids. We opened up the little coffin, and when we saw the baby in there, so young, wrapped up and holding a furry toy, we looked at each other and we both had tears in our eyes.' She shrugs, and drops her glance to her lap. 'We quickly started work. You can't afford to feel those things. You'd go crazy.'

'With the SIDS babies we take extra time. We wash and powder them. And during post-mortems we're really careful not to damage them. You feel they've been through enough. We rebuild and reconstruct them really carefully. Funny – when you're holding a dead baby in your arms, you know it's dead, but you still have the instinct to support the head, and not to let it drop back.'

'You've got death at the back of your mind all the time,' says Barry. 'Like when you're backing out of the drive, you're extra conscious. The child that gets crushed by a car in the drive is always after a toy that was under the car. It's always a toy.'

'You realise how easily death can happen,' says Jodie. 'And there's a certain case for each of us – something you see that you relate to in a way you don't ... like. It might be a shoe on someone that's brought in, a shoe like ones you've got at home, or the sort that your brother wears. Only a small thing ... but it can trigger something in you. You have to keep a split between your natural feeling and what you do.'

Everything the technicians say stresses their mutual respect and their sense of being a team. I ask why they appear to be doing all the cleaning of the mortuary, as well as their scientific work. 'There's a lot of weird people in the world,' says Jodie. 'People you wouldn't want to trust around dead bodies. And other people refuse to come in here. Sometimes we can't get tradesmen to do maintenance work. They won't come in unless we can guarantee they won't see anything upsetting. Still, our floors are shinier than the ones in the rest of the building – did you notice? – shinier than the ones the contract cleaners do.'

To spend hours in the eight-bay lab, standing at the elbow of Barry as he works in silent absorption, or beside David, a pathologist and assistant director of the institute, is to realise that it's a place of study, of teaching and learning, of the gathering and organising of information. David is a natural teacher. He chatters to me as he works on a body, wanting me to notice the creamy-yellow, waxen globules of subcutaneous fat, or the weak, exhausted-looking muscle of a damaged heart, or the perfect regularity and beauty of the striations of windpipe cartilage. 'Exactly like reinforced garden hose – look!'

The radio is on softly in the far corner of the room, spinning out a long, dated guitar solo. Someone in the corridor whistles along to it. Somebody else, going to the shop, calls out for lunch orders. It's not so different from the outside world after all.

'After I'd been working here for a while,' says Rod, 'I found I'd lost my fear of death. I don't know what the soul is – that spark – and no one knows what happens to it at death. But it's certainly gone before people reach here.'

'You have to realise,' says Jodie, 'that what we deal with here isn't really death. We see what's left behind after death has happened – after death has been and gone.'

For days after my visits to the mortuary my mind was full of dark images. At first I kept thinking I could smell blood, on and off, all day. Once I tore open a paper bag of pizza slices which had got squashed on the way home, and the dark red and black of their mashed surfaces reminded me of wounds. My bike helmet knocked lightly against the handlebar as I took it off, and the sound it made was the hollow tock of a skull being fitted back together after the brain has been removed. In the tram my eyes would settle on the wrinkled neck of an old woman: she'll soon be gone.

There is nothing so utterly dead as a dead body. The spirit that once made it a person has fled. But until I went to the mortuary I never had even the faintest inkling of what a living body is – what vitality hovers in its breath, what a precious, mysterious and awesome spark it carries, and how insecurely lodged that spirit is within the body's fragile structure.

. . . . . .

NOTES ON CONTRIBUTORS

Robert Adamson is the publisher of Paper Bark Press and the author of 17 books of poetry, including *The Clean Dark*, winner of the 1990 Kenneth Slessor Prize, and an autobiography *Inside Out*, published in 2004. He lives on the Hawkesbury River with his partner.

Philip Canon lives in Melbourne with his young family. He has been published in *Meanjin* and has recently completed the second draft of his first novel.

Ian Callinan is a High Court Judge. He is the author of five novels: *The Lawyer and the Libertine*, *The Missing Masterpiece*, *The Coroner's Conscience*, *Appointment at Amalfi* and *After the Monsoon* and three plays, *Brazilian Blue*, *The Cellophane Ceiling* and *The Acquisition*, as well as numerous reviews and short stories.

Laurie Clancy was born in Melbourne and taught English Literature for many years at La Trobe University. He has published numerous essays and reviews and is the author of 11 books, including four novels and two collections of short stories. His most recent books are *The Customs and Culture of Australia* and a collection of short stories, *Loyalties*.

Bill Collopy works and writes in Melbourne. His stories have been published in anthologies, literary periodicals, newspapers and on-line magazines. His first novel, *House of Given*, was published in 2006.

Liam Davison lives in Melbourne and has published several novels including *Soundings*, *The White Woman* and *Betrayal* as well as two volumes of short stories.

Michel Faber, who was born in Holland, moved with his family to Australia as a child. His first novel *Under the Skin* (2000) was short-listed for the Whitbread First Novel Award. Other fiction includes *The Crimson Petal and the White* (2002). His latest collection of stories, *The Apple* (2006), continues the tale of some of the characters from *The Crimson Petal and the White*.

Beverley Farmer's books include three short story collections – *Milk*, *Home Time* and *Collected Stories* – and two novels: *The Seal Woman* and *The House in the Light*.

Helen Garner, who was born in Geelong, has worked as a journalist, reviewer and scriptwriter. She has published several novels, including *Monkey Grip*, a collection of short stories, *Postcards from Surfers*, and an anthology of essays, *True Stories: Selected Non-Fiction*. Her controversial book *The First Stone* was an instant bestseller.

Julie Gittus has had a short story included in the *Hidden Desires* anthology published by Ginninderra Press, and other stories broadcast on ABC radio. She lives in Maldon, Central Victoria. Her young adult fiction novel *Saltwater Moons* will be published in 2008.

Ken Haley is a Melbourne journalist who has worked in London, Bahrain, Hong Kong, Athens and Johannesburg. He is currently continuing his travels, in a wheelchair, to gain material for a sequel to his first book, *Emails from the Edge*.

Elizabeth Jolley, born in England's industrial Midlands, settled in Perth in 1959. Her published work includes four collections of stories, 15 novels, poetry and radio plays. She died in 2007.

Cate Kennedy's short stories have won several awards. She has written two books: *Sing and Don't Cry: A Mexican Journal* (2005) and a collection of short stories, *Dark Roots* (2007).

Margo Lanagan lives in Sydney. Her books include *The Best Thing*, *Touching Earth Lightly*, *Wildgame*, *The Tankermen*, *Walking Through Albert* and two short story collections: *White Time* and *Black Juice*.

Joan London has written three collections of stories: *Sister Ships*, which won the *Age* Book of the Year, 1986; *Letter to Constantine*, which won the Steele Rudd Award in 1994 and the West Australian

Premier's Award for Fiction; and *The New Dark Age*. Her first novel *Gilgamesh* won the *Age* Book of the Year for Fiction in 2002.

Anthony Lynch's fiction and poetry have been published in Australia, the UK and the US. His short stories have been broadcast on Radio National. He works at Deakin University and is editor of the literary annual *Space: New Writing* and publisher for Whitmore Press.

David Malouf has written two collections of short stories, *Dream Stuff* and *Every Move You Make* (2006), as well as several poetry anthologies. His novels include *Remembering Babylon*, which won the first Dublin International IMPAC Prize.

Paddy O'Reilly's publications include a novel *The Factory*; a short story collection *The End of the World*; and a novella *Deep Water* (published by The Five Mile Press in *Love and Desire*, ed. Cate Kennedy). She has also written for the screen.

Luke Slattery is a Sydney journalist, writer and honorary associate of Sydney University's School of Social and Philosophical Inquiry.

Steve J. Spears is the author of the classic Australian play *The Elocution of Benjamin Franklin*. He now works full-time as a novelist and essayist. His most recent work is a blackly comic crime novel, *Murder by Manuscript*.

Peter Symons is a writer and teacher who lives with his partner Trish and pet dog Frankie in Melbourne. He has been previously published in *Overland* and *Island* magazines.

Tim Winton's novels include *Cloudstreet*, *The Riders*, *Blueback* and *Dirt Music*. He has written four collections of short stories: *Scissors*, *Minimum of Two*, *Blood and Water* and *The Turning*, for which he received the Christina Stead Award, 2005.

Danielle Wood's first novel *The Alphabet of Light and Dark* won the Australian/Vogel Literary Prize in 2002 and the Dobbie Award for Australian women writers in 2004. Her second book, *Rosie Little's Cautionary Tales for Girls*, has been published in Italy and the USA. She lives in Hobart with her husband, daughter, dog, cat, chooks and sheep. She teaches writing at the University of Tasmania.

ACKNOWLEDGEMENTS

Barry Oakley and the publishers thank all the authors whose stories appear in this book. They are also grateful to the following organisations and publications for permission to reproduce their stories:

ABC Books for **Luke Slattery**'s 'Ithaca' from *Dating Aphrodite*, 2005.

Allen & Unwin for **Margo Lanagan**'s 'Rite of Spring' from *Black Juice*, 2004.

ArtStreams, October 2005, for **Bill Collopy**'s 'In Shadows'.

The *Bulletin*, December 2006–January 2007 for **Danielle Wood**'s 'Fear of Flying'.

Central Queensland University Press for **Ian Callinan**'s 'The Romance of Steam' from *Travellers' Tales: Best Stories Under the Sun, vol. 2*.

Chatto & Windus, London, for **David Malouf**'s 'Elsewhere' from *Every Move You Make*, 2007, and Rogers, Coleridge & White Ltd, London.

Ginninderra Press for **Laurie Clancy**'s 'In Barcelona' from *Loyalties*, 2007.

Good Weekend, 30 September 2006, for **Steve J. Spears**'s 'What Do I "Do" with Cancer?'

Island 98, Spring 2004, for **Peter Symons**'s 'A Perfect Circle'.

LiNQ, vol. 31, no. 1, 2004, for **Anthony Lynch**'s 'Night Growing Longer Now'.

Meanjin, vol. 65, no. 2, 2004, for **Philip Canon**'s 'The Worst Thing'.

Penguin Australia for **Elizabeth Jolley**'s 'The Fellow Passenger' from *Fellow Passengers*.

Picador for **Joan London**'s 'Travelling' from *The New Dark Age*, 2004; and **Tim Winton**'s 'Big World' from *The Turning*, 2004.

Scribe Publications for **Cate Kennedy**'s 'Dark Roots' from *Dark Roots*, 2006.

Text Publishing for **Robert Adamson**'s 'On the Trail of *Ptilorus magnificus*' from *Inside Out: An Autobiography*; **Michel Faber**'s 'Serious Swimmers' from *The Fahrenheit Twins*, 2005; and **Helen Garner**'s 'At the Morgue' from *True Stories*, 1996.

Transit Lounge for **Ken Haley**'s 'September 11, 2001', a chapter from *Emails from the Edge*.

UQP for **Liam Davison**'s 'Stone' from *Collected Stories: Liam Davison*, 2001; **Beverley Farmer**'s 'Matrimonial House' from *Collected Stories: Beverley Farmer*, 1996; and **Paddy O'Reilly**'s 'The Last Visit' from *The End of the World*, 2007.